THE ALMANAC

THE
ALMANAC

❋❋❋

NMN Wang

The Almanac

Published by nmnpublishing
Copyright © 2026 NMN Wang

ISBN: 979-8-9934776-0-2

Book cover and interior design by Coverkitchen.

To my friends, family, and partner.
Without all of you, I would not have the
solid ground to stand and feel confident
enough to put my work into the world.

And to Ms. Little, whose words still
ring in my ears when I ask myself if my
writing is worth someone else's time.

May every student have a teacher like you.

PROLOGUE

"It's *happening*. I'm telling you, dude, it's happening."

"Whatever, *dude*, it's not happening."

"What do you mean? We've both been in these calcs for months! How can you deny the numbers?"

"Twenty years at the Weather Service, you get used to being mostly useless. It's gonna take a lot more than some celebrity scientist to convince me and everyone else that we're worth all the talk the politicians and Hightower have been spouting. I'll believe it when I see it. I suggest you do the same, newbie."

Gerald pinched the bridge of his nose where his glasses had formed a permanent crease. They'd been at it for months now. It'd been decades since cycles of unpredictable freezing weather made their jobs a joke. Cycles that would wipe out crops, stretch fuel reserves to the limit, and had the Depths living on a knife's edge of desperation. People were hungry for any semblance of predictability and had all but given up on the prospect. Gerald had spent months in the calcs too, and even he had to admit there was hope and even pride welling up in his chest. This felt real.

But now that they finally had something concrete to offer, the infighting was endless.

"Listen, guys, can we relax for a second? We've been at these calcs for over a year, and the numbers are as sound as they're gonna get. Ten hours from now either the Freeze happens or we're all out of a job. I don't know about everyone else, but I don't plan to spend those last hours here arguing!"

The room fell silent. Low-level analysts tried to look busy. Senior managers tried to hide their expressions of concern or feign disinterest. The head of their division had gone home hours ago, leaving Gerald holding the bag. Typical.

A countdown clock glowed an angry red overhead, accentuating the stress they'd all been feeling for weeks. Hundreds of man hours, billions in research, all culminating in either permanent job security or a quick, merciful death to an agency long relegated to obsolescence since the Freeze started nearly a hundred years ago. All on the promises of Teresa Hightower and Richard Vandley. No big.

"All I'm saying is how could you not be *excited*? My family's been picking around these freezes for years. Stocking up, falling behind, not making enough, now we can finally be ahead for once!"

"Look kid, we've been on this ride before, and my family were farmers for generations too. The only difference now is when we're wrong, we won't be talking in these out-of-date cubicles ever again."

"Man, we've got the science now. Imagine, pickers like my family actually *planning* the next cycle's harvest instead of rushing to gather young sprouts in case a Freeze cycle shows up faster than the last. Industries being able to set production schedules to an actual *clock*. Recyclers being able to focus on what to salvage based on what was short this cycle and anticipating the next. Imagine! I'm telling you, since Vandley started the program—"

"Come *on*, kid! You really think that even if the countdown works its magic, it'll be peace throughout the Depths and equality for all? The industrial families will still own all our asses. If you want to delude yourself, then fine, but leave me outta your—"

Gerald barked at the two of them to stop. Their debate had crossed the line from spirited long ago that even he couldn't ignore the tension they were kicking up.

"All right, guys, enough, either we're here for the rest of our lives or we're in line with the recyclers for next season. Either way, drinks are on me if we can shut up for the next few hours for once. We're all feeling tense, and this discussion isn't getting us anywhere. Now, I'm headed to the breakroom, where countdown discussion will be strictly civil or not at all. If I hear any more arguing, all of you can wait for the inevitable *outside*."

That got their attention. Everyone rolled back sheepishly to their workstations and tried to look busy. Gerald got up from his desk and tried to remain composed as he shut himself in the breakroom. That was enough debate for tonight. He pulled out his phone to try to distract himself, but every channel had a different version of the countdown going. Every talk show, every pundit. There was no escape. He leaned back in his chair and called about some reservations at an old recycler level dive he hadn't been to in years.

He swiveled around and looked out his office window. Through a small slit, he was able to see what little light there was left in the day streaming between the tall buildings of the surface downtown area. Even if this was his last day on the job, at least he could get a little more of the surface vista before having to move back underground into the Depths. He'd always felt fortunate to be in one of the few government agencies that by necessity needed to be above ground, but tonight the clear skies and warm sun felt scalding the longer he looked. He closed his eyes and willed the sky to darken and the atmosphere to chill. He pictured pulling out his heavy coats and the heat of the Boilers rising through the Depths as the world was enveloped in a sudden arctic frost. Gerald let a sense of artificial confidence calm his mind before he pulled out his hidden alcohol stash. He'd been saving the unrecycled stuff for when the countdown hit zero, but why wait. He hoped this would be his last restless night.

3

* * *

"Do we know if it's happening?"

"*Nobody* knows if it's happening, Claire, that's the whole point of why we're here!"

"Y'all gotta calm down, yelling ain't getting us *nowhere*."

"That's easy for you to say Jacob, *your family* wasn't short last cycle—"

"Easy, EASY, everybody, if we could just—"

Jenna banged her gavel desperately as the Silo devolved into an uproar. It hardly made a dent in the noise as arguments shook the small barn that served as the bloc's meeting house. Jenna tried to control her fear as she watched the faces of the pickers she knew, farmers living in the same bloc she'd grown up in as a kid, contort with anxiety and uncertainty. Neighbors now at each other's throats. She remembered how they came together, Freeze after Freeze, to support one another. Camaraderie broken at the first sign of good news.

"QUIET DOWN."

The mic sent a harsh shrill through the Silo. A sea of angry, fearful faces turned to the podium where Jenna was standing. They'd made her head of the bloc just a few years ago, a largely ceremonial role until now. Until Vandley.

They'd been meeting weekly for the last three months without any relief. Someone had put up an oversized countdown timer in the hall several weeks ago as a celebratory gesture, but now Jenna could see that mocking glare even with her eyes closed. She couldn't imagine nine more seconds in here, much less nine more hours. She tried to summon a sense of authority that her position didn't have.

"I know y'all are scared. I am too. My bloc came up short last cycle, and my clothes still don't fit me right. But we have *a plan*—"

"No *plan* has stood up to the Freeze, we known that for generations now! Now this damned science comes in from a bunch of eggheads up at that *useless* weather service and what, we're sup-posed to listen to bunch of suits and ties that ain't picked a second in their life? *We're the ones starving here if we're short, not them!*"

Karen's outburst fed murmurs of agreement quickly turned into a furor as her argument grew in strength and speculation ran wild. Jenna gripped the sides of her temples. Months of planning, years of pooled picks, and for what? There hadn't been a divide this strong since that weather cult prediction of '97 that wiped the town's reserve of food and fuel in a single cycle.

"Listen, LISTEN." She could hear the desperation in her own voice, but it was too late. Her voice was quickly drowned out in a tidal wave of screaming and accusations.

"If y'all wanna sit here all night and lose a whole day's worth of picks to this damned clock, then *be my guest*. I'm *not* coming up short again."

"Then YOU don't come runnin' to the fuel reserve after you burn your fuel pickin' through crop that won't be viable NINE HOURS FROM NOW."

The arguing continued for another half hour before the en-ergy dissipated. Voices ebbed and flowed in waves as people fil-tered out of the Silo. Someone had unplugged the clock on their way out and cut the cord. Jenna didn't need it; she could feel her pulse beating in time with the timer burned into the back of her eyes. She hoped it was her last sleepless night.

✳ ✳ ✳

Finally, it's happening.

Elder Moison leaned back in his rickety chair and tried to con-trol his excitement. Monitors cast shadows around the small room and on the tired faces of multiple Polar Vortex members. The true believers had been working for weeks in shifts. The insignia of their group was barely visible amid the glow of computers: a black tornado set against a green background with an angry red eye accusing the world of an injustice they long felt. The heat of the room was usually oppressive given the proximity of the terminals, but Moison hardly felt it now. Not when the time was so near. *For once that glorious countdown finishes—*

His thoughts were interrupted by a tap on his shoulder.

"Hey Dad, you sleep at all last night? I sure didn't. Too excited."

Elder Moison met his daughter's gaze. A permanent, mischievous twinkle had seemed to settle into her eyes since she became a teenager. He had mixed feelings about how involved Anna had become in Polar Vortex, but her curiosity begged to be nurtured. Especially since her mother left. Anna was a force of nature, just like her father.

"I really wish you wouldn't barge in here without warning. You know it's important to keep a professional structure, Anna."

"Tell that to Joe. He's the one who let me in. He needs another refresher course."

"Ha, is that what he needs? Are you volunteering?"

Anna spun Elder Moison's chair around playfully before taking the breadth of the room in a single stride. She gestured dramatically to a countdown clock above her emitting an eerie red glow.

"Ain't that the idea? Anyway, why are we talking business on this glorious day? The second this baby hits zero, the *world's* gonna know what we've known for years! *Weather the Storm!*"

A chorus of "Weather the Storm" shook the room. She'd learned how to work a room quickly. Elder Moison felt a swell of pride at what he'd accomplished. What *they'd* accomplished. All he had done was try to expose the truth. These *Freezes*, as they called them. And all they got in return was mockery. Called crazies, lunatics, a *cult*. And for what? Trying to reveal the truth behind these unnatural cycles? Protests in front of the Weather Bureau. Petitions for government materials. In the early days, they at least had debates and discussions with scientists trying to refute their evidence. Now, nothing but snide comments and open disdain.

No matter. Once this countdown hit and the world Freezed over for the hundredth time, there would be no need for explanation. For if a man, this Vandley, could predict the weather that was once known to be unpredictable? Well...

Elder Moison rose from his chair and cleared his throat. A dozen sets of eyes turned in rapt attention.

"Everyone, listen here. They may watch from their decadent mansions on surface or from their desperate hovels in the Depths, but tonight is OUR night! You've followed me for years through the mockery, through the disdain. Tonight is the night all will see what we have known for years now! That the 'Freeze,' as they call it, is a testament to humanity's hubris! Together, we will *Weather the Storm!*"

Elder Moison felt a smile tug at his face as another round of cheers grew into a cacophony of chants. He saw Anna jumping between the other members as the floor buckled with their enthusiasm. Other members couldn't help but follow in her cheers.

Yes. Tonight was their night.

❋ ❋ ❋

"I got 10,000 creds on this thing happening. I hope your brainiacs at the weather service know what's at stake here. I haven't lost a bet to Chairman Curry, and I don't plan on starting now."

Senator O'Riley let out a light laugh as he walked away, drink in hand. The sound of polite laughter and conversation echoed through the foyer of Geraldson manor. A large chandelier hung above an entryway made almost entirely of white marble. Portraits lined a twin set of staircases leading up to an upper balcony, where Teresa could made out the Depths' elite hobnobbing as if tonight was just another reason to gather and celebrate rather than the historical event that it was. Waitstaff weaved expertly between guests, taking empty glasses and offering full ones without acknowledgement. She even recognized some of them from her working-class days, but they expertly avoided eye contact before she could acknowledge them. She'd come a long way. *They'd* come a long way.

Teresa had never liked coming to these things, but over the years it had been a begrudging responsibility. Getting the political willpower behind Richard's theory, let alone the funding for the Weather Service to pursue it. It required her to rub elbows with those who wouldn't have given her a second glance in her days working as a recycler in the parts of the Depths many tried not to see. If she'd known that being the head of the Weather Service would be so political, she'd have told Richard to find someone else. She'd always envisioned herself as his scientific collaborator rather than his most vocal supporter. But the work had to be done, for the Depths. She just hoped that tonight was the last.

"Teresa! Glad to see you again! It's so hard to lure you out of that dreadful bureaucrat's office lately, I don't know how you can spend any longer than necessary there!"

A high voice interrupted Teresa's thoughts. Michelle Geraldson; married two times, on the third fling, end of a long line of industrialists. Farm equipment? Those political flashcards her assistant prepared were handy. It was hard to shake how the industrialists all blended together. Even walking among them, she still saw what many others did: the powerful and unassailable.

"Michelle! How's production this year? I know that nerves are running high, even with the best catering in town. I do hope that it's been a boon to your industry." She gestured toward the gilded grandfather clock at the center of the back wall, its pendulum swinging lazily back and forth as the time drew near.

"Most certainly! I mean, as certain as we *can* be. I confess we've still built up quite the backlog of equipment in case your little geniuses forgot to carry the one or something, but we've seen plenty of pickers stocking up as well, so it hasn't changed our balance sheets much. At least this cycle. You can tell me, though..."

She drew closer to Teresa, her perfume growing oppressive.

"...you think this Vandley really has the Freeze worked out? You know I can keep a secret."

Teresa suppressed the urge to roll her eyes. Every industrialist from surface to Depths wanted the edge. It was their nature to use advancement in science as one for growing their station. It took almost a month to stop the disdain from showing on her face.

"I've been with him from the start, and the calculations are sound. I know it hasn't been easy for everyone here to get behind the Weather Service, given our record, but we've had the best minds across the Depth making sure that time will finally be on our side."

Michelle let out a squeal of delight. "Excellent! Well, you know you'll always have a place with us. I can only imagine that this is the first of many Freeze galas. Let me get you a drink. I'm sure you need it!"

Teresa watched as she sauntered away toward the crowd gathered around a vintage-era bar. She let out a sigh as she tried to find refuge in a quiet corner. Hopefully it would take a few minutes between conversation for Michelle to get back to her with a drink. She glanced toward her phone, her screen displaying the official Weather Service countdown. Unlike the revered clock, it recorded the time in an eerie red glow. Richard had insisted on it. To the point and impossible to misinterpret. A scientist to a fault. No replies from Richard yet, but that was hardly a surprise. This was his baby, after all, and everyone knew it, no matter how much publicity focused on her. She doubted either of them would be getting any rest tonight.

* * *

Richard Vandley rose from bed, rubbing the sleep from his eyes. He'd been sleeping for days now, but it felt like there was always catching up to do. He'd expressed his confidence endlessly to the media, but there was always more doubt, more questions. He couldn't blame them; they thrived on uncertainty, and he promised anything but. He'd finally been able to dodge them for the last few days, and with the countdown on every channel, he'd become a low priority.

Vandley moved ten feet from his bed to a nearby window, drawing the curtain slightly. Teresa had set him up in a fairly nice studio surface-side, especially compared with where they had started. He recalled talking through numbers with her in between their shifts as recyclers in the lowest parts of the Depth. Pounding caffeine and its Freeze cycle replacement when stores were scarce, trying to get the right eyes and ears to care. Crammed into multi-family studios where sleep was hard to come by, much less peace to think through complex calculations. He never cared about the conditions of the work. Just the work itself. Though he was grateful to Teresa, without her his theories would've died in the womb. Getting people to care enough to take a risk on your theories, that was a miracle he could never pull off. He pulled the curtain back and took a look outside.

No people on the street, no reporters. He could sense the anticipation in the air. Uncertainty was not a curse he understood. His attempts to dispel it had only been met with skepticism, and he was tired of it. Soon there would be no more doubt.

He checked the clock and went to his closet, pulling out his comforters. He had just enough time to put together something to eat before the temperature dropped and he could get back in bed. He assumed he'd be one of the few to sleep comfortably tonight. He walked through what he knew was going to happen. At precisely 2:34 a.m., the temperature would drop precipitously, an average of eleven degrees Celsius an hour until the noonday average was -5C, -30C if a storm was brewing. Recyclers would start their endless shifts soon, shoveling anything combustible into Boilers and turning over anything salvageable coming down on the Freight line. He'd still be there himself if it wasn't for Teresa.

Vandley instinctively drew his robe around him as the sun set. Based on the sun's position, he calculated there wasn't long now. He withdrew a small handkerchief from his robe and took a long breath in. He could taste the fumes hit the back of his throat as his mind wandered. A nasty habit he wouldn't have to keep up anymore now that the work was done. He smiled as the sky darkened and the air became heavy with frost.

1

Detective Chen gripped the edges of his heavy coat together in a futile attempt to shield himself from the wind. He had picked his apartment for its easy commute to the shuttle, but there wasn't much in the way of comfort. Despite it being near the Boilers that pumped hot air into the Depths, they were more worried about that heat making it up toward those on the surface than out toward the rest of them. They said there wasn't much they could do. After all, hot air rose, and redirecting it was a waste of precious resources. No one really believed that.

He'd been able to get thirty minutes of restless sleep before being called out again. It'd been five hours after the Freeze started. A decade after the predictions were supposed to change it all, but the work marched on. He was already on his way to the seventh crime scene of the night.

The shuttle rocked back and forth as he rode toward his destination. He was crammed in like a sardine, especially this time of year. The Freeze transition was more than just the changing weather. Chen glanced at the dirty faces around him. They were recyclers headed deeper into the Depths for jobs. As the season changed and the fields switched from production to preservation, the fight for field work transformed into competition over work recycling used materials. The end of harvest signaled a frantic need for seasonal labor. A whole growing season's crop needed to be preserved for the upcoming cycle in just a few weeks. A farm's equipment winterized before that first rapid drop in temperature. It seemed like a lifetime ago now.

His gaze wandered up the central shaft that pierced the length of the Depths. He watched as other shuttles wound around the circumference, full of denizens darting between neighboring communities tunneled haphazardly into the bedrock like spokes on a wheel. Freight trams rocketed downward down the center on rails, crammed with last cycle's outmoded tech for upcycling. As his shuttle wound downward, Chen could feel the unsteady rattling of the vehicle as it transitioned to the deepest parts of the city. The tracks at the lowest level had been built early as the city dug desperately to insulate itself against the early Freezes. They were also the least maintained, given the low socioeconomic status of the region. If it worked, then any problems were for next cycle.

He looked past the inky blackness that separated Depths from the surface. His family would be retiring the machinery for the cycle. His brother would probably be doing maintenance in Chen's absence. His father, however, was another story. Chen shook his contemplation aside as the shuttle pulled to a stop.

He nodded to Dr. Morgan Stills from Forensics as he walked to the scene. He was happy to be paired with her on assignment. She was dependable, intelligent with just the right caustic sarcasm. Residential lights were just beginning to blink into existence as the morning broke. The irregularity made it look like a speckled mistake on a perfectly dark canvas. An artifact of an ancient electrical grid hobbling along. The bags under Morgan's eyes were heavier than usual, reflecting his own.

"Happy Morgue Day, Chen."

"Happy Morgue Day, Morgan. How many you catch tonight?"

"Third one so far. We got a pot going. Jerome in Team B's up to five already, but he actually likes Morgue Day, if you can believe it. Every Freeze, these freaks think forensics suddenly doesn't work.

You think they'd know that after ten years of accurate predictions, we'd know how to work around it. And it's my sleep that has to suffer their ignorance."

"Yeah, well, if only geniuses murdered people, we'd all be screwed. The body this way?"

Morgan nodded and gestured toward a tarp near one of the large Boilers. It loomed overhead like an aluminum goliath, its low hum of burn punctuated by a bright flame barely visible through a bus size grill in the front. From far enough away, it looked like a metal fireplace that would heat a log cabin. If its occupants didn't mind the stench of fuel and garbage. Chen could follow the shimmering air to the top of the Boiler and through an intricate series of metal pipes disappearing upward toward the surface. This time of year, the richest on the surface would be getting the warmest air directed through a series of Boilers connected in series. Violent crime was a lot less appealing when you were warm and comfortable. Boiler workers huddled curiously around the tarp, their faces caked with dirt. Only the desperate worked the early Freeze days. The warming sequence often required shoveling material at a manic pace that broke as many people as it supported. Chen tried to avoid their desperate looks as he examined the scene.

The murder site wasn't subtle. Not an uncommon dumping ground, but the Boiler was a high-risk zone. A lot of foot traffic given the upkeep needed, especially as the Freeze started and the Boilers grumbled to life. They must have been confident or desperate. Based on the rate of burn, it looked like the workers here were pulled off the Boiler several hours ago, just shortly before the Freeze started. A public site like this was bound to be discovered quickly. Any killer from this neighborhood would know that. The cameras weren't likely to be online, though he forwarded a request to tech anyway. Best to work this by the book, though whether that meant he was getting his night back or not, it was too soon to tell. Chen pulled the tarp back in one smooth motion.

A wave of decay blew up from the uncovered body, sticking to every piece of Chen's clothing. It invaded his nose and stuck there, causing him to let out a hacking cough despite trying to keep a straight face. Morgan let out a light laugh and slapped him on the back.

"Jesus, Morgan, you could've warned me about the *smell*. What the hell is that *stench*?"

"What'd be the fun in that? It's actually a pretty good dump compared with the normal stuff we get this time of year. Top half's frozen, bottom half's overheated. Boiler gets the hottest in the first few Freeze days to pump up the Depths, concentrated in the first few hours. We'll have to talk to Nash about this one."

Chen rolled his eyes. Victor "Doc" Nash. That was a problem for later. He held his shirt over his nose and took a closer look at the body. Middle-aged, underdressed, rough shape at best. The hair and beard were unkempt. There was a slight difference in decay between the top and bottom halves, but it was easy to miss without Morgan clueing him in. He looked thin. Chen could spot slight bruising along the buttocks as he examined the body. Some kind of repetitive pressure injury, it seemed. It wasn't common for people around here to sit so much, it hurt them. The face was somewhat familiar—

"Hold up, is this *Richard Vandley*? Weather Service Vandley?"

"I'm surprised you can recognize him through the shag. Even with his last public photo, I could barely tell."

Chen put some gloves on and turned the head carefully. The skin was hardly more than a thin layer over a set of cheekbones sticking out at two sharp angles. The facial hair was soft, likely from a poor diet. Chen was able to barely gather the beard into one hand and cover the mustache with a free finger. A little more life in the eyes, and Chen could see the face staring back at him from countless schoolbooks describing the generational genius he'd written essays about since grade school. Yep, it was Vandley.

"Damn, I remember spending three months on this guy in school. Hasn't he been a recluse since the early countdowns?"

"Beats me. I just remember my dad going on and on about his *genius* and how important *school* was and how I could change the *world* one day if I applied myself. Last thing I wanted to look into more was Vandley at the end of the day."

"Sounds like he's ruined both our nights. May I?"

"Sure, go ahead. We got our pictures, and I got my paperwork. We'll need him on a slab to get any more detail. Just be careful not to move the body too much. Thin skin like this? I don't want to have to explain how a bunch of new scratches showed up after I left the scene."

Morgan got up and headed toward the morgue van along the side of the road, leaving Chen to take in the scene. He stood and took a step back to get a better look.

There wasn't much to take in. No scattered personal belongings, and there were marks where the killer had likely obscured their own footsteps on the way out. As Morgan said, they were likely looking at a dump site. The killer was seasoned. They had the headspace not only to dump the body but also to cover up afterward. There was hardly a face to see under a mass of scraggly facial hair. Whatever had kept him going seemed barely above maintenance calories. Looking closer, it was clear the smell wasn't just the accelerated decompensation from the Boiler. Vandley had been living rough for months at least, years more likely. Chen could make out the edges of a deep head wound that was likely the cause of death, along with signs of struggle around the shoulders and back, likely occurring during the murder, given the coloration of the bruising. Besides that, no signs of callouses on the hands, no scarring around the knees, or even broken fingernails, which would have been typical for anyone working the odd jobs to survive in this neighborhood. The recyclers hadn't gotten to the body yet, otherwise not even his minimal clothing would be left. There were very few personal belongings poking through his threadbare clothing. A thin jacket flapped open, showing a small-size shirt that sat on him like a parachute with a matching set of comically oversized shorts. Even the most destitute would have bundled up with refuse before stepping out dressed like this. It'd be suicide otherwise. It didn't take long to go through what little was in his pockets: keys to an apartment near the shuttles, mangled phone, an empty wallet, all carefully assembled in evidence bags around the body. A perk of working with a professional like Morgan. Hopefully the tech department could piece together recent contacts. Chen traced the trail the killers took to the street, where it ended abruptly. If he had to guess, this was the job of multiple perpetrators. It'd be the only way to dump the body and clean up without being spotted by the transients living in the area.

Chen gripped the edges of his nose in worry. A famous scientist dumped by professionals by the look of it. Luckily, a case this high-stakes would be pushed up the chain to Upper Crimes and it'd be their problem soon. Lower Crimes had enough scenes to worry about tonight, and Vandley was bound to tie up resources they didn't have. He left the body and joined Morgan near the morgue van as she slammed the back doors shut.

"Well, I'm guessing this guy just jumped the line."

"Ding-ding. Chief wants us back to debrief in the next few hours. Barely enough time to thaw this guy out, much less do a rush autopsy. You all set, Chen? I wanna get going so we can start on the body with Doc. He's the only one with the experience to work Vandley on such a short timeline."

"Yeah, not much else to do without the full examination, and I doubt we'll be primary on this anyway. I'm gonna take the long way back on the shuttle, try to get some shuteye. I can stop by the coffee shop on the way. Morgue day special?"

"Morgue day special. Make mine a double. I'll see you back at the station."

Chen zipped his coat up to the chin and headed back to his shuttle stop. The station wasn't too far from the scene, and he knew a good place to pick up some coffees on the way back. If he was lucky, he'd still have time before they switched coffee grounds for upcycled chicory. It'll be a much longer night without the real stuff.

* * *

Chen walked into the Lower Crimes, nodded to the deputy at the desk, and badged in. The floor was abuzz with activity in contrast to the angular, beige appearance of the place. It'd looked like it was dated when he first started five years ago, and time had numbed him to its appearance. Less funding every year, more bodies, and now an actual high-profile case. Well, until the cowboys up top swooped in to take it, and the good publicity, from them. He nodded politely at the patrolmen he passed, trying to keep his balance with a drink tray in both hands.

Chen caught a look at the board. Two maps were laid out side by side, a displacement map showing the entire Depths from surface to its farthest depression and a topographic one of the area closest to the station. The Depths were put on full display, the central shaft like the root of some planted vegetable with smaller tendrils reaching out into the void, representing its various neighborhoods. The city looked as if a family of inebriated moles had burrowed the tallest caverns near the top and lost their enthusiasm the deeper they went. The lowest neighborhoods extended out less than a few hundred meters, with low ceilings to match. Small dash marks circled the central pillar, representing the shuttle winding its way down. A thick black line ran through the center of the shuttle's track, representing the large freighters that moved decrepit materials down broken to the recyclers in the Depths and brought the refurbished back up to surface. Red splotches each represented a Boiler, becoming less populated the higher the map went. Pins marked dozens of scenes with nearly illegible details written by half a dozen teams. Chen had only seen pins multiply in the five years here.

He headed up to Chief Victoria's office. Its large windows overlooked the bullpen. From a distance, he saw several people gathered around her desk. Chen could hear tense conversation as he opened the door and looked for a familiar face. Word had gotten out about Vandley's case, and everyone was doing a poor job hiding their concern. Chief Victoria looked stressed as she shuffled through papers for the meeting. Chen sidled in and sat down next to Morgan, handing her one of his few real coffees. The room was fairly empty considering how high-profile this case was. Chief Victoria stood up and cleared her throat to gather everyone's attention.

"Thank you for coming, everyone. As all of you know, we caught a big one today. Richard Vandley, best known as the mind behind the weather prediction model, was found dead in the Boiler District. He hasn't been seen since the Weather Service's first prediction a decade ago, but his name still carries weight, especially with the public. A murder like this is bound to draw attention and make our jobs that much harder. I'll keep the wolves at bay as we start this investigation, but I won't be able to hold them off for long."

A rush of confused whispers ran through the office. Chief Victoria took a moment to regain control of the room before acknowledging a raised hand.

"Chief, all due respect, don't these kinds of cases get passed up the chain? Why hasn't Upper Crimes got their hands on this already?"

"Usually, yes, but it seems that some of the more colorful comments he made before becoming a recluse ruffled a lot of feathers, particularly the ones about the Weather Service. He's become a nuisance that the Uppers would rather forget. It's clear we're on our own for this one. Doc, if you don't mind walking us through the forensics?"

A lanky man rose from his seat behind Chen. Doc Nash, the head medical examiner, was a man of few words and not one to circumvent rules. The idea of a VIP victim skipping the examination line likely rubbed him the wrong way. To be fair, not much rubbed him the right way either. Chen handed him one of his dwindling bean coffees. Doc did not acknowledge the gesture.

"I've been asked to push Vandley's forensics to the top of our already impressive stack. Given the timeframe I've been asked to work with, I'll be brief. He was found this morning near a Boiler in the first early hours of the Freeze. While it complicates the forensics somewhat, we have determined that our victim was likely killed by a single blow to the head at least several hours before it was reported to us. There was a substance we couldn't identify in the killing blow, but I'll be having Doctor Stills work her sources for that. Given the lack of blood at the crime scene, he was likely moved from a different location. Despite his poor appearance, his physical health remains average, even with clear evidence of ongoing Fuel abuse. His substance abuse was already detailed in public media but seemed to have intensified, likely over the last few years at least. There were no signs of poison and minimal signs of struggle indicated by bruising on the body. Given his physical state, it was unlikely he could put up a fight against even an average attacker. You'll find my full report uploaded if you have any questions."

Doc ignored the raised hands and quickly took his seat near the back.

"Thank you, Doctor Nash." Chief Victoria retook her place at the front of the room. "We've already started redirecting calls from the media, and we're projecting it's going to get orders of magnitude worse. We're not going to be able to keep this under wraps for long before public scrutiny becomes our worst enemy. Even with the ire he drew from up top, he still means a lot to the Depths, and it's sure to bring every armchair detective out in force. Therefore, I'm starting a small team on this. Everyone in this room is under a strict code of silence. Loose lips sink ships, people. Any news about this case should go directly through me, and any leaks will be severely reprimanded. No one else knows about this case until we're ready to let them in. Detective Alec Chen, Dr. Morgan Stills from the morgue, Piotr Asimov from Tech, Detective Ellen Clark, stay after class. Everyone else, dismissed."

The rest of the office cleared out, leaving the four of them looking to one another. Chen chuckled to himself. Chief had been trying to bring some semblance of organization to Lower Crimes since her transfer from up top, but it hadn't stuck quite yet. Give it a few more years, and even she would embrace the chaos. He got up with the others to the four chairs at the front of the room. Morgan spoke first.

"Chief, with all due respect, why aren't we handing this one off? I know Upper Crimes is disinterested, but if we froze out every case we thought was dull, we'd all be back to where we came from."

"Your concern is noted, Morgan. I've reached out to my contacts on High, and they've made clear that there is no political will to find Vandley justice. Apparently, the comments he made in public about the Weather Service were tame in comparison to what he said in private. And you know them; it's all politics up there."

Piotr spoke next. "Wow, they must be pissed not to want this win. How bad could his comments have been? I mean, he practically created the world we live in now. Without him I'd still be back in the Junction making barely functioning computers out of surface scrap."

"I won't go into details here, but suffice to say that he burnt every piece of goodwill left before disappearing. Hightower, the head of the Weather Service, wouldn't even touch this with a ten-foot pole. Either way, it's clear we're on our own. I know we've been stretched for a while, but this is our way forward. We solve this one and the public pressure alone will get us funded for the next decade. The four of you give us the best exposure on this, especially with the people we'll be interviewing. Since you four came up in the career transition program, it gives us the best chance to ask questions among those in the Depths, rather than just another bunch of cops. Whatever resources the four of you need, you'll have a direct line to me, and I'll make it happen. Within reason."

Chief Victoria was right. Piotr was formerly a Junction recycler. Morgan came up from a farming family, much like Chen, and Ellen was Depths through and through. Without Vandley's accurate predictions, the career transition program would never had the funding to come to fruition and give them, and many like them, a chance to pursue something other than a career built around survival. They represented the chance Vandley gave all the citizens of the Depths, rather than just another set of career cops. If a witness was to talk, they'd talk to them.

"And what resources *are* those, precisely?" Piotr quipped. Chen found that everyone leaned in toward Chief Vic's desk at the question.

"Again, your concern is noted, Piotr. Whatever few contacts I have left will get us most of what we need. Whether that's interviews of those on High, Vandley's previous research notes, or whatever friends he still has left, consider it done. I still have a few strings left to pull. Any other questions?"

Morgan spoke up. "Yes, Chief. Why us? I mean we're not the only members of the career program, and there are clearly more people aware of the case itself. Why not bring them in rather than swear them to silence?"

"While it's true that over the last few years we've been able to benefit from the career change program, you four are some of the first to go through it. I'd rather not have any green members on the team who aren't aware how delicate a case with on High's attention can get. Vandley made a lot of noise among the most powerful of the on High families, in particular the old industrial names that hold a lot of sway. We all know how touchy they can be about their reputation and how they've come down on people in the past for even insinuating impropriety, much less interviewing them about a murder of someone they all disliked publicly. No, the smaller a footprint we keep, the quicker we can run this investigation without looking over everyone's work. Besides, I'm aware of my reputation in the precinct as a transfer from on High, and I think being a boogeyman from the surface is enough to buy the silence we need to get this done."

"Do you remember what he said to get such powerful people so sensitive?"

"I won't go into details here, but my contact on High assures me that it went much farther than the public statements he made. During his last public interviews, he insinuated that the industrial families held too much sway over the progress of scientific advancement, while in private he practically accused them of it at every function he could still get into. His closest ally, Teresa Hightower, tried to protect him from the fallout, but the optics were too ugly to ignore. She eventually left him to fend for himself. He disappeared from public life shortly after that and suffered the grisly fate we're untangling now. I presume finding out more about his reclusive years would be a good place to start. Any other questions?"

The four of them glanced at each other, shifting uncomfortably. Chen handed off the last of his coffees, reserving a chicory one for himself. He understood the need for discretion, but he couldn't shake the fear he always got when being asked to work off-book. He couldn't say no if Chief Vic was the one asking, but he'd have to keep his wits about them. The others traded looks before Chen finally spoke up.

"Doesn't look like it, Chief."

"Good. You four can have the conference room as an operations suite. Overtime is granted within reason. Let's solve ourselves into job security, people. Dismissed."

Chief Victoria rose from her desk and gestured toward the door. Chen followed the rest of them down the stairs and into the conference room, an elevated name for what was the biggest closet in the department. Boxes were stacked to the ceiling with forgotten cold cases and broken furniture. The beige wallpaper was discolored from cigarette smoke and years of neglect. A hum radiated from the fluorescent light above. They each took a different broken seat around a wobbling table hardly big enough to fit the four of them. The tension in the air was broken by Ellen.

"Well, we are stupendously fucked. Ever since we came up from the program, we've gotten the shit cases, and now *this*? We earned our place here, unlike these career cops, and our reward is to be thrown to the sharks. What, now I represent every recycler on their way up in the world?"

"Ellen, you know it's not like that. It makes a real difference to kids in my old farming bloc seeing us here. Besides, Chief's right. We're gonna be knocking on a lot of doors, and it helps them to see our face instead of some lifetime cop," Chen replied.

"Besides, I wouldn't exactly call your face friendly," Piotr joked.

Ellen made a sour face and flipped the bird to Piotr before he continued speaking.

"I doubt it makes a real difference for all the upcyclers who can peer through the walls of my frigid tech dungeon anyway. I don't like it either, but it sounds like if we don't do this, the department's screwed, starting with us. We'll be the first ones they throw under the bus if this goes down. I doubt there'll be any more goodwill in the budget for a bunch of washed-up pickers and upcyclers like us. Might as well claim as much overtime as we can."

"I agree with Piotr." Morgan jumped in. "Besides, this job's been nothing but boredom. Most of the cases end up in here rather than the solved pile. Sometimes I even daydream I'm back in the field."

Ellen scrunched her nose in disapproval. "Christ. Well if we're gonna get fucked, I'd rather get kissed afterward at least. We solve this and we got the juice for any detail we want after. I'll be point and start with information-gathering, see what kind of comments he made to get him so screwed with on High that they'd rather see his killers walk free. Chen, you start the canvass. I hear you got keys to Vandley's place, and I recall you living near the shuttles too. Morgan, soon as you get more on the autopsy let me know, especially whatever mysterious shit Doc was alluding to in the conference. Piotr, keep working on that phone. I'll keep Victoria appraised. Daily check-ins, people, don't make me chase you down."

Chen leaned back in his chair. Classic Ellen; she always enjoyed taking charge. Ever since they had started together, she was more like a freight train than a team player. That was why he always gave her chicory coffee. Decaf Ellen was already enough.

"I'll head over there as soon as I get a little shuteye. I could use the overtime."

"Let's plan to meet at Tech or Forensics, whoever gets the update first. Let's get out there and find ourselves some job security."

Ellen was the first out of the door, followed quickly by Piotr and Morgan. Chen took a sip of chicory and left the station. He could feel the looks of those who knew his assignment. A mix of pity and curiosity followed him out the door as he turned the corner and headed to the nearest shuttle stop. He drew his coat closed and looked at his watch. Just enough time to stop by his own place to get a change of clothes and wash his face. Maybe an hour to close his eyes if he was lucky. He took out his phone and browsed Doc's full report as the train left the station and began to circle the central shaft farther down into the Depths.

```
Vandley, Richard
Age: 67
Gender: M
Occupation: UNKNOWN
Next of Kin: UNKNOWN
Method of Discovery: Anonymous call
Cause of Death: Blunt force trauma to the
right temple, fragments of an unknown
crystalline substance found in the wound,
```

forwarded to tech for identification.
Time of Death: Estimated
in the last 10 hours.
Please see comments below.
Description of Body: Elder male in state
of good health prior to death. Lower than
average BMI. Dryness around the nose
and mouth point to potential long-term
substance use, likely the one commonly
known as "Fuel." Body is in a state of
mixed rigor due to proximity to a Boiler,
which makes time of death more difficult
to ascertain. The body appears to have
been cleaned prior, leaving little
physical evidence.
Bloodwork: Initial examination shows no
signs of poisoning other than chronic
substance abuse as indicated.
Internal assessment: Chronic liver and
brain disturbance, when combined with
external findings, indicate long-term
Fuel abuse, likely up until recently. Old
injuries to connective tissue aligned with
the subject's previous work as a recycler.
Well healed and maintained.

Signed,

Victor Nash
Attending Medical Examiner

Chen let out a laugh. Even Vandley wasn't immune to the spikes
in Fuel use. Each year it'd been easier to produce excess energy,
and each year it was funneled straight into people's noses. Before

the countdown, it was unimaginable to use something as precious as fuel, the lifeblood of farming machines and Boilers, and refine it into a recreational drug. Vandley had fallen victim to his own boogeyman.

Chen looked outside as the buildings grew more dense and disorganized. He'd been here for years and still wasn't used to the lack of sunlight. Even at the Depths' highest point there was still a solid sheet of dirt and rock between civilization and the sun, punctuated only by surface-reaching service tunnels. It acted as the perfect insulation for the underground but at the price of the only natural warmth left in the world. On the long train rides home, he sometimes dreamed of the sun when he had worked the fields on surface, gleaming so bright some days, it felt like there was no horizon. When he was offered the opportunity to move on from his picker work, he jumped at the chance. The mobility program only became possible with predictability, and it offered him the same. Income, professional mobility, moving beyond your station. All brought to you by yours truly, Vandley and the Weather Service. He laughed at the thought.

Layers of mismatched houses passed by winding clockwise with the shuttle toward a deep, inky blackness punctuated sporadically by modest residential lights. He remembered the first time he boarded the shuttle and saw the maw of the Depths shaft stretch down and out in front of him. Chen had come to the Depths before to get parts for their machines back home, but never longer than a day. He had felt a shimmer of excitement then. The darkness seemed to extend a hand, echoing the promises the program did. Tonight, it looked like it always did: infinite and eating up every hope and dream that made up this place.

Almost home.

2

Chen looked at his reflection. He had just enough time to wash his face and moisturize the dry skin around his nose and mouth. Had to keep up appearances. Chen walked through his small studio space. Takeout boxes were piled high in the trash. The small desk he'd gifted himself when he first moved to the Depths sat crooked in the corner with a lopsided stool. A secondhand couch he had rescued from the sidewalk sat against the opposite wall. He'd cleaned it thoroughly at first, but accumulated neglect caused it to regress back to how he first found it. A small TV sat on a cardboard box, the only new thing he owned. Chen had gotten it after he first moved as a small present to himself for leaving the family farm and had been unable to afford anything new since. It was paycheck to paycheck, something he made sure his family back home never knew. The point of the program was for mobility and financial security. So that he didn't have to stretch each piece of machinery way past warranty to make it from season to season. So far, all that meant was moving almost a mile toward the center of the Earth.

A passing shuttle shook the walls of the apartment and out of his thoughts. It'd taken him years to get used to the noise, but he still had trouble at the start of each cycle as transit needs increased. Chen tried to ignore an argument he could hear through his ceiling as he left the apartment. He'd only been able to afford this place recently, but it felt much the same as his previous dwelling. Everything had a habit of blending together without sunlight.

Chen buttoned up his frayed coat and locked the door. It was mostly the convenience that kept him in this hive-like network of bachelor hovels. All the better since Vandley lived not too far from him. Chen's complex was right at the edge of the central tunnel and befitting the price. Everyone had said he'd get used to the noise in time, but it was the unpredictable vibrations of the shuttle tracks that jolted him awake most nights. Still, better than paying the prices farther in his district's tunnel.

Chen took Vandley's keys out of his pockets. The key fob was from a place called "Deep Dive." He remembered the place. He had toured it when he first arrived as a patrolman, but not even he was desperate enough to spring for a place there. What brought someone as famous as Vandley there, he couldn't guess. He thought about calling ahead but figured it was better to keep it a surprise.

He hopped onto a train stop a couple blocks from his house. He had to jostle just to stand in the rush of recyclers. The shuttle rocked as it passed through district after district. When he had first arrived, he enjoyed looking out the window as the shuttle made its descent, as if he was peeking into all the lifestyles each different neighborhood offered. He quickly learned that much like what the mobility program hawked, choice was just an illusion afforded by the countdown. An otherworldly glow from a fiery sea of Boilers punctuated the few stops to Chen's destination. The pipes twisted up, carrying hot air to the fortunate above while radiating passive heat to the people that kept it running. They were the only constant source of light this far down.

He got out at a stop several blocks from his destination. The closer you were to the surface, the more developed the adjacent areas were to the central shaft, and thus you could expect more transportation services: lateral shuttles, bus systems, even cab services as far down as the Junction. Where Vandley and Chen lived, you had to get used to walking up to half a mile from the stop to get where you were going. The streets were uneven and crowded with those unable to find work for the season or simply too sick. Quite a fall from grace for the scientist of their generation.

Chen walked up to the main office of the Deep Dive, a small space the size of a parking booth. He saw a skinny figure slumped over the counter, their rhythmic breathing barely visible from a distance. The nameplate read *Lewis*. Chen startled him awake by dropping his badge onto the counter.

"Lewis, is it? What can you tell me about the gentleman who lived here?" Chen dropped Vandley's keys on the table.

Lewis rubbed the drowsiness from his eyes. Dry skin was visible around his mouth and nose. He pulled a binder from the shelf behind him and slowly flipped the pages, making a point of leaning in to read to the chicken scratch handwriting.

"Oh, 203? Some suits already marched their way through there. You with them?"

"Other guys? What other guys?"

"What, you cops don't talk to each other now?" Lewis chuckled. "These lifer-looking badges walked in here, all business, asking to get into that apartment. More giving me a heads-up than asking for permission. Real grim types. Dressed in black head to toe. I barely saw them leave, must've been like...a while ago, I dunno."

Chen could feel his jaw tighten. All-black uniforms didn't sound like any department he knew of. He was just lucky that Lewis was conscious enough to recall that detail. He looked at least multiple rag sniffs in.

"You get their names?"

"Dude, do I look like I wanna get picked up? Cops are down here every couple of days. I'm not here to be a squeaky wheel, you know?"

Fuck. Chen scrunched his eyes in frustration. The kid's brain had probably been fried by Fuel. He doubted any more useful information would be coming out of him. "Okay, kid, when did they leave? They take anything with them?"

Lewis frowned in concentration. "Dunno, few hours ago? I think they took some boxes with them, but they were real secret agent about it. Like I said, business. They were out so stealthily, I barely even saw them leave, and I wasn't about to give those types the fifth degree."

"They head toward the shuttle? Had a car waiting or anything?"

"Nah, dude. Didn't see them head toward the shuttle or anything. I think they got into some jalopy; looks like anything you'd see in the street around these parts. Recycled to shit, you know?"

"All right, Lewis, you keep our conversation under wraps and let me know if they come back, okay?"

Chen slid his card across the desk. Most people in this neighborhood could seldom access car parts, let alone enough to put together a working vehicle to carry several passengers and their haul. Whoever they were, it seemed worth the effort to avoid scrutiny on the shuttle. They were connected. Connected to what, Chen would have to find out.

"Right, *right*, you got it, Officer." Lewis offered a half-hearted salute with a playful laugh. His voice rasped with a dryness Chen knew well. Kid probably just started on the stuff, didn't know enough yet to use lozenges to cover up. Or he just didn't care.

Chen turned to leave, returning an exaggerated salute. As he exited the office, he looked around the dilapidated complex. Doors of each apartment faced the street, arranged much like a motel. The building was made of recycled metal that had likely already been rusted on reuse. Now they served as windowless tin cans that would rust through in a year or two, finally past any point of recycling. He headed toward 203. The metal steps creaked under his weight. Chen could see doors open cautiously in response to the noise. Desperate faces young and old leaned from their stoops to look at him before retreating into their homes with a slam. He couldn't shake the feeling of being watched by more than just the occupants. Secret agent types? He hoped that was just Fueler talk.

The door to 203 opened without resistance. Chen surveyed the room from outside. No obvious traps from what he could tell. The apartment was small enough that he could take in the whole apartment just from the stoop. The place was turned upside down. Little was left that wasn't on the floor. A single dresser had its drawers overturned, what little was in the kitchen cabinets was on the linoleum, and a small twin mattress on the floor was completely cut open. Chen put his finger on his service weapon as he swept the room. Luckily, there wasn't much to sweep. Whoever had been there before him was efficient. Little wasted movement in tossing the place.

Even for the slums, Vandley's apartment was threadbare. One single table with a chair, enough dishware for one, and no real clothes to speak of. And papers. Papers littered nearly every surface, each filled with numbers, equations, way above Chen's head. Given that this was likely just part of what was left, Vandley must've had enough to fill several binders. If there was a pattern here, he wouldn't be able to see it. Hopefully, Morgan would understand some of it. With any luck, the attackers were just as ignorant as Chen and had accidentally left something of use.

The kitchen appeared ancient and unused. Takeout boxes littered the counters and floors. Pests swarmed as Chen carefully stepped around the mess. Even at his busiest, he couldn't live this way.

He was rifling through some papers around the floor for anything remotely useful when something caught his eye. There were clear streaks of blood along the corner of the desk extending out into the far corner. The stink of Fuel hung in the air, with handkerchiefs scattered in variable states of decay. The stench of genius.

Chen moved over to the desk and took a seat. There was unlikely to be any notes of consequence left, but he shifted through the leftovers regardless. There was a wear pattern where Vandley had sat for hours, maybe days at a time. Deep, smooth grooves decorated the floor where the chair had been pushed in and out over the course of months. Possibly years. The desk was made of cheap wood, likely recycled beyond the legal point. A dark red stain colored the corner closest to his right hand. Likely where the killing blow was struck. He went through what papers were left on the desk. Nothing stood out until he went to get up and felt a small envelope taped to the bottom of the chair. It blended well with the color of the wood. Inside was a collection of food receipts, each comment line populated with a short message: *For the Work. Weather the Storm.*

Weather the Storm? He hadn't heard that since he came up as a patrolman. Polar Vortex, or "that weather cult," was little more than a joke in the Depths. He'd broken up some protests or the occasional hardcore cell in his early days, but they weren't ever something to be taken seriously, even by the top brass. Their members inevitably ended up on street corners either as a raving lunatic or tourist stop for some family visiting from a smaller city looking to experience the Depths for the first time. To find their slogan here?

He looked around the rest of the apartment but found no other signs of Polar Vortex paraphernalia. Usually, these true weather believers were *hardcore* believers. In his experience, each cell was festooned with banners, shirts, and even buttons commemorating their major disruptive activities from decades ago. But with Vandley, nothing but the receipts.

Chen tracked the blood streaks starting from the desk corner. There was a pool of blood on the floor a short distance away, likely where Vandley had experienced his final moments. As he bent down to track the trajectory, a glint caught Chen's eye underneath the desk. Intermingled with the blood were specks of crystal reflecting the light from his phone. He took out a pair of gloves and carefully bagged them. This one was probably too sensitive for the rank and file to collect.

Chen took one last look around the apartment. He couldn't shake the feeling that he was two steps behind and losing ground every second. He felt his phone ping in his pocket:

Morgan's on something big. Chen, meet her at the university in the morning. She'll be waiting for you at the entrance. I want daily reports first thing in the morning.

Ellen

He didn't need to see Ellen to hear her tone. Chen could tell she was stressed. Chief Victoria wouldn't hand something over of this magnitude without expecting results, doubly so after the resources she had promised them. Now with these spooks who beat them to the punch, time was not on their side.

Could Polar Vortex have beaten him to Vandley's apartment? And if so, why? A cult based on pseudoscience was an unlikely partner to the greatest scientific mind of the time.

Still, it was a lead. If anyone knew about Polar Vortex activity, it would be Lieutenant Everett, head of Night Watch. He had a stubborn dedication to his detail and had refused promotion several times over. He insisted that no one knew the streets of the Depths at night better than him and no one could do the work justice. Their mutual love for staying by the book kept Chen in his good graces, and he hoped that courtesy remained. Chen checked his watch. If he rushed, he could catch Everett in the early hours of the morning when there were less distractions and pick his brain. Maybe catch a few hours of shuteye between the shuttle ride there and the barracks before his appointment with Morgan.

Chen stuffed his phone into his pocket. He could feel the exhaustion taking hold. He was reaching his twenty-seventh hour on shift and the fourteenth hour of overtime. The thought of comparing notes with Everett, then Morgan, was far from appealing, but speed trumped sleep when Chief Vic was involved. He knocked on some doors around the complex but was greeted by more dry lips, desiccated nostrils, and slammed doors. As he crossed the gate, he took one last look around the darkening streets of the Deep Dive.

He couldn't shake the feeling of being watched from every dark corner. Best to put it out of mind for now. He needed to focus on the only lead he had to offer Ellen and Chief Vic.

⁕ ⁕ ⁕

"Chen? What are you still doing up? Have you been working since they let you out of that meeting with the chief earlier today?"

Ben smiled back at him from the desk with a mix of curiosity and concern. He was a newly graduated patrolman from the same program that had brought Chen from his bloc to Lower Crimes. Like Chen, he had started on the night beat under Lieutenant Everett, almost as enthusiastic as Chen was years ago. He looked around. Same dank concrete square box, same mystery stains along the ceiling. The graveyard shift in both name and appearance.

"Ben, you know that's on a strictly need-to-know basis."

"It sure feels like a need to me, Chen. Come on, it's gotta be big if Chief Vic called all of you program freshmen in."

"Cut it with the 'freshmen' talk, Ben. You know it won't be long before another class comes up in the program and you'll be right behind me."

"As if. There's no class greater than mine. So, are you here to loop another of your brethren in or you here on business?"

"You wish. I'm here to see your lieutenant. He still posted up in his office?"

"Yep, just like he always has. I'll buzz him to let you know you're coming. Word to the wise, it's been a long night."

"Thanks for the heads-up, Ben. I'll catch up with you later."

Chen walked down the concrete steps in the corner of the room and through a dark hallway. An old, wooden door stood ajar, casting a thin light. A brass nameplate read *Lieutenant Everett* on the front. Open-door policy as always. As Chen pushed the door aside, Everett glanced up at him from his computer. The walls were adorned simply with a few accommodations and awards from the past police chiefs. A small photo hung above his desk at the far end of the room picturing a much younger Everett shaking hands at his promotional ceremony, easily two decades ago. A much older Everett gestured from underneath the photograph to a plastic chair in front of him. He looked old but like an ageless sentinel.

"*Detective* Chen. What brings one of my former patrolmen to my basement domain tonight? They finally wear you down upstairs in Major Crimes?"

Chen couldn't help but smile and take a seat. It wobbled, much like it had years before when Everett was still teaching him the importance of working cases by the book. How doing so kept you safe from scrutiny and, most importantly, how you were saving your own ass from crossing the line.

"Not yet, Lieutenant, but not from lack of trying. Is that why you're still in the dungeon?"

"Dungeon? You mean my kingdom? I know what it's like to work in someone else's domain, and I learned a long time ago it ain't for me. I know every patrolman sees Major Crimes as the big leagues. Hell, plenty coming up in the program now interrogate me about how you got promoted that far. But sounds like you learned the same lesson I did. To play their game, you gotta follow their rules. Or lack thereof."

Chen tried to think of a counterpoint, but Everett always had a way of making a point that was hard to argue. This thing with Chief Vic and Vandley...

"All right, Chen, what brings you down to the dungeon? I'm sure it's not for one of my lectures. Or do you need a refresher?"

"Not quite. I wanted some info on your beat. Polar Vortex to be exact."

"Polar Vortex? This got to do with what Chief Vic pulled you in on?"

Chen could feel himself visibly cringe at the mention of Chief Vic. Everett was as sharp as ever and noticed his discomfort.

"You know what, don't tell me. That's the kinda shit that keeps me down here. The farther I am from their games, the better. What do you need to know?"

"Thanks, Everett. I can't read anyone in on this unless previously authorized. I need to know what the current activities of Polar Cortex are. I remember the cult's activities were the purview of the night watch, and I'm hoping that hasn't changed."

Everett slid out his chair and leaned to one side to access a desk drawer. After a minute or two, he brought out a manila folder labeled *Polar Vortex* and placed it on the desk.

"Not much to tell these days. They'd been on the decline since even before you started with us. Even when I was still in uniform, it was hardly more than breaking up some nutjob protest here and there."

"Yea, I remember reeling in a few rabble rousers or guarding a protest or two outside the Weather Service, but nothing notable."

"Not much has changed since then. I'll send a detail to a pre-arranged protest every month or so. We haven't had to pick any one of them up for a long while. Honestly, if you weren't here asking me about them, I'd say we're in a well-deserved break. Violent crimes have even hit a five-year low in the deepest parts of the Depths. This new class could grow soft at this rate."

Chen reached out to grab the folder and started shifting through it. It was as thin as Everett implied. Flipping through, Polar Vortex activity was much as he remembered. Protests, sit ins, some "educational" lectures a professor lookalike scammed into giving at a half reputable university. Faces of all ages angry with civil disobedience held signs reading things like "Give Us the Truth!" and "You Can't Freeze Us All Out." The earlier protests were even held at the homes of the supposed conspirators, the members of the major industrial families. Chen was surprised they didn't crack down harder under those circumstances, but even the powers that be knew; sending in the troops was giving them the legitimacy they craved. To the general public, Polar Vortex had started as a curiosity and quickly became a joke.

He'd almost passed through the end until he got to a man's portrait. It was taken at booking. His features were stark, with thin cheekbones hovering over a grim frown. His dark eyes seemed to interrogate Chen as if questioning the motives of anyone looking on. The nameplate read *Clifton Moison*. Chen took detached the photograph from the file and held it up for Everett to see.

"Who's this? I don't remember every being briefed on a 'Moison' when I was on patrol."

"That was before your time. 'Clifton Moison,' a.k.a. 'Elder' Moison, was the founder of Polar Vortex. These kinds of groups had always existed since the Freezes started happening, but few had the staying power that Polar Vortex does. He made Polar Vortex more than just a bunch of doomsday preppers and nuts hanging out and practicing mock drills in some compound. He was a force. Moison took a bunch of loners and gave them meaning. A vision to follow. So even when he started insisting members call him 'Elder' and developing all the hallmarks of cult leader behavior, some genuinely smart people threw their lot in with him. Students, recyclers, professors, even some pickers like your folks gathered under the Polar Vortex banner to right the perceived wrongs of this world. At least in the beginning."

"Where is he now?"

"Gone, that's all we know. He wasn't one to stay in the spotlight, but he didn't avoid it either. He used to attend the bigger protests, leading chants or giving lectures to open-minded students, but it's been bupkis since Vandley's first countdown. Moison's name and face are still attached to many of the materials they send out; pamphlets, QR codes, and the like. The brass thinks that the countdown undermined the whole operation. Once people didn't need to adjust around the insanity of unknown cycles, the appetite behind it all dried up and so did the need for groups like his. It turned Polar Vortex from a joke into an embarrassment."

Chen sat back and turned the photo around in his hands. The theory made sense. Chen remembered his first few years on patrol and the demonstrations he was tasked with policing. The older patrolmen he was paired with would whine about the need for security at all. A curious passerby or tourist might even stay and listen to the speeches, take a pamphlet, and get on their way. By the time Chen got there, it was often just to check permits and sit in their patrol car, trying not to fall asleep. Counterprotests were nonexistent. After all, what more proof did you need than over a decade of Freezes going off without a hitch to the beat of Vandley's drum?

"What do you think, Everett? The brass got this all zipped up?"

"Honestly, I haven't thought much about it. You know me, I live in the moment. Night watch is about putting out the fires, not trying to find the next one. It's simple, and that's one of the perks of watching over rugrats like you. The sooner newbies learn that keeping investigations straight and by the book keeps us all accountable, the better."

Chen had forgotten how refreshing and frustrating Everett's point of view could be. It was the complex investigations like the murder of Vandley that convinced him to move on, not only from night watch, but from the farm itself. But he couldn't help but feel that Everett was right. Investigations like the Vandley case kept Lower Crimes opaque, much to everyone's detriment. Except to the top brass. At least the information was good. Chen got up and waved the photo in his hand.

"Mind if I keep this? Could come in handy."

"Sure. Ain't got a use for it these days. If you ask me, Polar Vortex is either dead or dying."

"Well, knowing you, you won't let a little thing like low crime rates get in the way of whipping the newbies into shape. Especially Ben. Keep an eye on that one, he's a little too familiar at his age."

"Ha, you got that right. Reminds me of another trainee I knew, came in here fresh from the farm, bright-eyed, buttons on his uniform so polished it'd blind you."

"Yeah, well, lucky for him the dress code gets a lot less strict the more bullshit you gotta deal with. Thanks, Everett, a little perspective always helps."

"How are your folks anyway? I remember that same trainee answering a lot of tense phone calls during and after work hours."

Chen felt something catch in his throat. A few years after the countdown, he'd jumped at the chance to join the mobility program, but it left him on bad terms with his old farming bloc and his family.

"Could be better. A lot less of those phone calls that drove my senior officer crazy, at least."

"I hope not for lack of trying. I only made it this far because I've got something to go home to. If there's a chance of having that for yourself, you should take it."

"I'll keep that in mind. Got any room in the barracks tonight? I've got an early start tomorrow, and I'd lose all my sleep time to taking the shuttle home."

"Sure. They've cut back on patrol some this year, so one of the corner rooms should be available. I'll let them know to steer clear until shift change. Noise is about as bad as you remember it."

"Thanks, Everett. Goodnight."

Chen shook Lieutenant Everett's hand and tucked the picture of Moison into his jacket pocket. If Everett had read the situation right, which he often did, it was hard to imagine such a pivotal figure leaving the limelight, much less the group he had created. He headed out of the office, down the hall, and dipped into one of the rooms with the door hanging precariously on its hinges. Chen carefully placed the door into the frame and pushed a chair into the corner farthest from the hinge. The door shifted into place, just like riding a bike.

The room looked much the same as it had back in his day. A green cot sat pushed up against the far corner. A desk and chair were against the opposite wall. He flicked the light switch pointlessly on, then off. Chen took off his layers and hung them on the chair, then lay on the cot, counting the familiar stains on the ceiling he could make out against the soft ambient light spilling in from the crack under the door. Shift change was coming up, and the basement was getting livelier, though the noise was nothing compared with the shuttle he lived next to.

Chen thought about what Everett had said about having something to go back to. Everett had helped him more than he realized, especially that first year. He'd been rushed through the normal cadet training in nearly half the time since the program had been born between recruitment cycles. Then, long on self-doubt and short on sleep, he was put on Everett's detail along with every other dubious recruit either to flame out or see the bad habits burned away. But he knew better than just to push. Especially on those milestone days when other cadets' families arrived, brimming with pride as Chen sat in his seat, waiting for the festivities to end. Everett would ask but sit silently when Chen chose not to answer.

His brother would be helping the clean up about now. The heavy machinery would be in the shed, waiting for repair. His father would be with the other family leaders in the elders' barn, tallying this cycle's fuel and crop stores. Probably a little light as it always was. A few surprise mouths always showed up that needed feeding. The physical pandemonium of harvest would've given way to anxious calculations by now. Would they have enough to survive after giving the Depths their share?

Chen sent a message over to his brother, polite and short. He'd probably be asleep. He wasn't nearly as good as Chen at fixing the machines, but he had a better sense of when to quit and rest.

Chen's mind swirled with questions. Was the Polar Vortex lead viable? What did Morgan have for him to see tomorrow morning

that deserved immediate attention? He reached for the handkerchief in his pocket and took a deep breath. Chen could feel his
mind slow as the darkness in the room engulfed the rest of his
vision.

3

Chen had been on the shuttle for hours now. He was able to get a few hours of sleep before starting the long ride to Geraldson University, but his dreams were relentless and vivid. His brother hadn't messaged back yet, but given the time of year it wasn't a surprise. Many on his old bloc would be pulling twelve-hour days winterizing with barely time to eat, much less socialize. Once they got through the preservation and transportation phase, the prep for next cycle would begin.

Since starting at Lower Crimes, Chen had little reason to make trips to the surface. He'd forgotten how long the ride took. It felt like a trip through history. As the shuttle wound upward, the neighborhoods became more organized and often had a clearer sense of purpose. The construction was usually newer as early desperate years gave way to desire for luxury. The tunnels reached deeper and were often planned. Chen could feel a wave of heat as they stopped at the Junction, where they upcycled much of the technology the Depths used.

Many affluent riders disembarked at the Exchange, where much of the commerce took place. It was strategically placed between the recyclers below and the wealthier denizens above and exuded an air of efficient business. The streets were straight and clean, signs for shops were clearly stated, and regular patrols from the surface moved in pairs to instill a sense of safety necessary to keep business moving. Chen knew from his training that it was one of the largest neighborhoods underground. Each sector had its own dedicated zone, which necessitated an impressive amount of space. Almost a quarter of the ride up were stops at the Exchange.

Stops of business then gave way to the affluent. Efficiently designed streets morphed into winding, residential neighborhoods that tried to bring the surface underground. Homes for the few took the space of many. The inconsistent heat of the Boilers disappeared into a uniform room-temperature warmth. There were no Boilers, no filth. The maze of pipes that crisscrossed much of the Depths fed into hundreds of hidden grates for the denizens of the High Gardens. Well-dressed shuttle riders flashed their resident cards to guards at each exit and progressed to a place of comfortable waste second only to surface dwellers. Chen tried not to gawk, but it was hard not to imagine a life of casual waste. Here you could spend fuel heating a bathroom simply for comfort or toss your electronics because they weren't the latest model.

Finally, before the surface there was the Guts. This was where much of the surface material was loaded onto the central freight rail. Much of what was loaded was considered either beyond repair or too specialized to go straight for commerce at the Exchange. Workers dragged their breaking bodies off the shuttle and into dedicated trains that took them to their work assignments, where they would spend hours loading what the surface considered refuse either to the skilled upcyclers in the Junction or the most desperate recyclers deep in the Depths. It was the only "neighborhood" with its own train system and thus had its own maintenance area running parallel to much of the surface. A complex network of columns stood between this and the rock that supported the surface. The original architects couldn't fathom how far their original vision would come, not that there was much of one. Early on, design followed function. The dig down was prioritized, and the Boilers reflected that, a heating system that was easy to expand and cheap to fuel. What was once an easy way of keeping the work going had now morphed into something that was a luxury for some and necessary for others, generations building on that first desperate gasp for survival.

Chen winced as sunlight crested the horizon. The weather academics got the privilege of surface time year-round. He could hear the roar of heaters in the shuttle come to life. No amount of shielding could protect against surface frost, though with five times the fuel expenditure, it could be overcome.

The shuttle emerged into a dense urban area. Buildings of various sizes flanked the track as it progressed farther to the outskirts of the surface neighborhoods. Homes and apartment complexes up to ten stories tall were packed tightly to serve as wind breaks, but even with solar panels providing power, it took ten times the fuel to live safely here than anywhere in the Depths. Most smaller homes had been fabricated in the early Freeze cycles as the wealthy clustered together to survive, and this age showed in their eroded exteriors. As the shuttle left the central hub, the buildings grew taller as Freeze-resistant techniques were developed. Then came the research district.

He squinted as Geraldson University came into view. The light bounced off multiple glass surfaces, overwhelming his vision. The building itself was largely glass with a central tower rising into the sky, piercing the rising sun. Two behemoth boilers flanked either side. It was the only way to keep such a tremendous glass building habitable on surface. It let the eggheads conduct their research in relative style without the thick coats impeding their movements. They always said the glass was for better observation of natural phenomena, but Chen always believed it was just a big flex.

The shuttle pulled directly into the station at the base of the tower. He flashed his surface dispensation to the security desk at the entrance and was waved through. A cavernous foyer extended dozens of floors up. He could see scientists hustling on the walkways above between offices and labs. A plaque thanking the

Geraldson family for its contribution to the recent redesign was embedded in the floor in front of him. Chen's footsteps echoed as he followed signs for the Vandley research center. A voiceover in the elevator expounded upon the history of the university. Sponsored by one of the original industrial families, one of the first to "Conquer the Freeze," at the forefront of weather research, all the same drivel.

He took the elevator to the top floor of the tower to a sprawling glass office. Chen could feel the blast of Boiler air no matter where he went but without the deafening roar that pervaded the Depths. All the warmth, a tenth of the noise. Chen's thoughts were interrupted when he spotted Morgan. She waved from behind the large, wooden welcome desk and motioned him in.

"Hey, hey, Chen. You ever been to my alma mater before?"

"Can't say I have, Morgan. Never figured you for a place this posh. And I've never had a reason to go somewhere so luxurious."

"Yea, well, lucky, I guess. Went from best in my bloc to a scholarship kid and now needing special dispensation and a visitor's badge just to get a little light. Just one big circle. Anyway, let's head back. I've known Wayne since we were taking prerequisites together. Little word of warning, he's excitable. Almost like a dog. I've found it best just to run with it once he gets that little glint in his eye. You'll know it when you see it. Come on, it's this way."

Morgan motioned down a long hallway. Large lab spaces occupied either side. Natural light streamed into every crevice. Chen felt like he needed sunscreen just walking through the halls. Men and women in lab coats moved about, drawing hieroglyphics on whiteboards and shuttling metallic cylinders back and forth. They followed the long, sunbathed corridor until it opened into a large glass sphere Chen had spotted on the shuttle as he came in. A central gangway ringed around the circumference of the space with radial catwalks projecting toward the center. A large tower pierced the center of the sphere, reaching from the north to south poles of the entire room. It hummed with activity, barely audible through a glass shield. Chen could hear wind funneling through the central computer tower. The one benefit of the Freeze for these brainiacs was natural cooling for their power-hungry tech. Morgan waved at a figure near a control panel in the center, who smiled and returned the gesture with twice the enthusiasm.

"Morgan! How long's it been? Ten years? Fifteen? It's good to see you again! I was surprised when you reached out, but it's been more than worth it with what you sent. It's fun stuff."

"Wayne, are you still skipping meals? You're getting skinnier every time I see you! If the material I sent you was just another excuse to get in the weeds, I won't let you get away with that. This is my partner, Chen. I hope you don't mind if he tags along?"

Wayne was a lanky man, tall, and moved awkwardly as he rubbed the back of his neck. He extended a thin hand out to Chen as they came closer and then withdrew it into a playful surrender gesture.

"You caught me, officers! Even with Vandley's predictive model, there is still a trove of data that needs to be gathered. Not to mention my own research. Then you add in the crystalline material you sent along and, well...eating's always the first to go, as Morgan knows. It's good to meet you, Chen." Chen shook his hand. It was delicate and free of calluses.

"Thank you for taking the time. What is it you do in this glass castle, Wayne?"

"Well, I'm the steward of everything Vandley! Every time that countdown takes over your screens and minds, that's the result of the work we do here." Wayne took a moment to gesture around the sphere. "Vandley's model takes quite a lot of data to make happen. Humidity, wind speed, temperature, precipitation. I have yet to fully understand how he transformed that data into a countdown on a screen, but I certainly can gather it! I hope to someday recreate the logic behind it all, but for now I can improve upon it. Every cycle we add a little more time to the countdown so the dash can be a little less mad for everyone in the Depths and beyond."

"Wayne's been a weather nut since long before I met him. As talented as he is, the Vandley model still depends on intense data-gathering, even while we're in a cycle. That's why I hate to ask this of you considering..." Morgan gestured around the sphere, "... all you have going on, but we're stuck without someone with your know-how. Given Vandley's specialty, I figured the best place to start was here, since you're carrying on his torch. I know how exciting a scientific mystery is to you, but don't make me regret it. I don't want to have to come back here to force-feed you."

"Yes, yes, Doc, all these years and you still haven't changed. If you haven't heard, Chen, Morgan's been my mother away from home. As long as she's been around, she made sure my health came first. I remember one time I was working on this grant that would make or break my dissertation. Gave myself an ulcer from just slamming coffee for a week with hardly any real food. She locked my papers away and wouldn't give me the key until I ate a sandwich."

"You're leaving the part out where you kept up your end of the bargain by making that sandwich last the whole week after while doubling down on your caffeine intake."

"Semantics, Morgan, semantics. Anyway, Chen, I know you're not here for war stories. I got the sample you sent over. If both of you could follow me."

Wayne gestured toward one of many consoles adjacent to the one he was working. A small set of glinting crystals were visible in a dish below a microscope. Wayne's workstation was littered with empty coffee cups and thin, microwaveable food wrappers. Looked like whatever Morgan sent had caught Wayne's attention.

"I was able to run some preliminary tests on the fragments you sent me. Physically, it's pretty durable stuff. It must have taken a lot of force to form fragments this small. Luckily, with Geraldson's resources, I can make much ado with nothing."

Morgan and Chen stole a sideways glance at each other. Wayne was too enamored with his presentation to notice.

CHAPTER 3

"I managed to vaporize a small piece, and that's where the real magic happened." Wayne's face lit up with a playful smile. "The original structure itself is old. Decades old, even. Without the extensive database here, I wouldn't have known where to start. Even had to have research assistants bring up microfilm from the basement to chase it down. Here, I'll show you."

Wayne pulled up a 3D image. Dozens of lines extended out of a central molecular structure leading to text boxes. Chen saw a mix of computer-generated texts in addition to pictures of old film Wayne had collated to the relevant points. It was clear even to Chen this took up an unreasonable amount of time Wayne probably didn't have.

"Here you'll see what I was able to work out. The examination progress leads to inherent degradation, so the simulations are less than perfect. Some guesswork can't be avoided, but I'm reasonably certain the structure I've created is a near facsimile. The backbone of the structure is a stable motif, but it's the outer branches that lends the substance its activity. There isn't enough left to fully run the simulations, but if we look closer, here there are some references you'll find interesting."

Morgan leaned in closer as the image enhanced. Chen took a seat and leaned back in his chair. He knew from experience it was best to let two eggheads crack against one another before seeing what spilled out. Questions and interference just threw them off their groove, or worse, made them frustrated.

"Here on this arrangement, there are a few notes that I had to dig out through microfilm. It has some very old references from the early years of Geraldson University. Turns out most of these references are from before our time. You see, before we'd been able to predict the Freezes, the Weather Service was reaching for anything. They approved projects for genetically modified crops, desperate methods to create fuel from recycled materials and the like. I even found some entertaining proposals amounting to little more than employing psychics. Through one of those ideas, they'd established the backbone of what we use today to try to gather Freeze data. The Weather Service deployed a series of weather balloons at every level of the atmosphere, but they still couldn't tell the temperature of the next day, much less the onset of a Freeze. That is, until Vandley. Fortunately, the data from the balloons themselves led to Vandley's seminal work."

Chen watched as Morgan looked from resource to resource. He hadn't seen her this excited since they started in Lower Crimes together, when everything still had some shine to it.

"This is some pretty old stuff, Wayne. Why did you have to go so far back?"

"Good question, Morgan. I was asking myself the same thing. You may not know this, Chen, but scientists are often packrats. Not only do you need a data trail to prove your methods work, but you also never know when prior research is going to come in handy. In this case, the only comparable stuff was a defunct terraforming project."

"Terraforming?" Chen leaned forward, flipping his notebook open. He made a mental note of how excited Wayne had become. It was all he could do to stay out of the way as Wayne threw his arms around with reckless abandon, explaining concepts far above his understanding.

"Yes, you might have seen something similar in old films. The idea was essentially to create conditions more habitable than nature allows. It was a desperate last gasp before the powers that be decided that something was better than nothing and dug the great big hole we now know as the Depths."

Morgan scrunched her face in thought. "So, is what we're working with this old? How could some reference to this dead project be relevant today?"

"That's the rub, this material can be dated to the last few decades at the oldest. However, the relation is only tertiary. The base structure holds some resemblance, but it seems to have changed quite a bit, well after the original proposal of terraforming was ever proposed. This stuff is clearly still useful to someone."

"What use would that be? It sounds like the project died in the crib and without any real application."

Wayne's face lit up again. "Now that's a very good question! One I don't know the answer to quite yet, but I'll keep you in stride. If someone is still making the stuff, they'd need access to a lab, staff, and funding. I need more time to access some of the older microfilm to be certain, but odds are a trail for something this advanced is hard to hide. It's mostly archival work from here, so only a matter of time before I better understand the purpose of this little beauty."

Chen let Morgan and Wayne talk for a few minutes while he took notes. First Polar Vortex and now this? He was beginning to feel that this murder case had roots much deeper than any of them suspected.

Chen stood up. "Thank you for everything you've done, Wayne, but I'm sure you have other pressing issues to work on—"

"Don't bother discouraging him, Chen. I know the look in his eyes. He's a dog with a bone on this one. You try to yank the leash, you're more likely to lose a finger than get him to sit. We owe you one, Wayne."

"I take payment in package fresh-bean grounds, Morgan, you know this."

"Deal. Half now, half on delivery. But only if you go down to the cafeteria today and eat a real piece of solid food." She extended a friendly hand to Wayne, who playfully rolled his eyes as he shook her hand.

"You wanna stick around, Morgan? There are some fascinating projects coming down the pipeline I think you'd be interested in. Ones with forensic applications. We've been freezing bodies at various timelines—"

"Thanks for the offer, Wayne, but if you knew anything about Ellen, then you'd know we can't stay. Don't make me come back up here. I'll know if you're not taking care of yourself."

"Yea, yea, don't be a stranger, Morgan. And you either, Chen! We've been working to try to outmode the Boiler system since we've had the luxury of Freeze calculations for years now. If you ignore the lack of political will, the alternative methods of heating the Depths and above are incredibly gratifying to explore. Water-based, personal heating units, the possibilities are—"

"Thank you, Wayne, for the offer. I'll take you up on it sometime. You've been more help than you realize." Chen nodded politely as he turned to leave. He made a mental note to bring bean coffees next time he came. Morgan followed him along the gangway, through the lab space, and down the elevator toward the shuttle stop. The steady hum of Boiler air followed them.

Morgan turned to him at the station as scientists hustled to make their train at the end of the workday. "It's times like this I really miss working up here, even if I was back to picking. The sun on my skin, wind unsullied by that burning fuel smell. You don't miss it at all?"

"Parts of it. I miss never having to get a special dispensation for just getting some sunshine. I remember working around these kinds of places more than looking in. Now I can see why. Terraforming? What kinda sci-fi shit is that?"

"Yea, we're way off the bloc on this one. But I trust Wayne. And seeing that twinkle in his eye, we're in good hands. He won't be able to let this go until he's satisfied. What it means for the case, though, I don't know. It feels more like a film than anything else."

"Definitely. Would you mind typing this one up? I only understood every other word, and I'm not sure I would do it justice."

"Of course. I'll meet you back at base? It looks like Piotr has some updates for us."

Chen looked at his phone. There was a message from Ellen.

Piotr found a live one. Meet back at Chief's in the morning. Full updates by end of day.

Terse and to the point. He'd worked with Ellen on other cases in the past, and she was always single-minded in closing cases, much like Everett if he actually cared about public perception. At least with her spearheading things, their ragtag group was certain to make some headway.

"I'll see you there. You got the coffees this time?"

Morgan offered a curt nod. Chen boarded the shuttle and felt the blast of the train Boiler hit him as he found an empty seat among the commuters. He felt his ears stuff up from the transition to the much louder shuttle Boiler system. Terraforming? And what good would it even do in an age of extreme predictability brought by Vandley himself? Thoughts flowed through his head as he leaned against the window. He could feel the sun's rays receding on his face as he entered the darkness of the Depths.

He liked Wayne. He reminded Chen of an earlier time when he was just starting in Low Crimes and imagined that his days would be spent closing case after case. Chen remembered a feeling of usefulness then, much different than his days repairing machinery on the bloc, only for it to break down in fits and starts because they stretched a part too far or pushed an industrial picker a cycle more than it was warrantied for. It was an inescapable cycle where a job well done was presented with another job to do. No accolades, no remembrance. Just survival. The cycle his brother was pushed into now. He hadn't heard back yet, but that wasn't surprising. His brother made up for lack of skill with sheer determination, so jobs lasted a lot longer without Chen around.

Chen looked down and saw the maw of the Depths laid out before him, swallowing his thoughts. He reached for his handkerchief but thought better of it. He'd need a natural sleep for a meeting with the rest of the team.

4

"Fucking *terraforming*? What the *fuck* does that have to do with anything?"

Ellen gestured toward the ceiling in exasperation. It was rare to see her this animated, especially in the chief's office. She was accepting the recent updates poorly, to say the least, and it put the rest of the team on edge.

Chief Victoria sat calmly at her desk, hands folded in front of her. After all these years, Chen could see through her calm exterior. She was concerned.

"Ellen, I understand your confusion, but let's stay focused here. It may make some sense once we grasp the bigger picture. Morgan, good job working your contact at Geraldson. Let's make sure to stay on him for any developments. Chen, how's the Polar Vortex angle? I understand you worked closely with Lieutenant Everett on Night Watch back in the day. I thought they'd been low priority for a long time now?"

"You're not far off. I spoke with Lieutenant Everett a couple nights ago, and he confirmed that Polar Vortex has been quiet for a while now. He thinks that the former leader, Moison, has either stepped back or left entirely. Without him, Lieutenant Everett thinks they lost all momentum. A protest here, a sit-in there, but nothing as visible as back in their heyday."

"I'd feel pretty good about that in normal circumstances. I'll put some feelers out, see if anyone on High has anything to offer. For now, Chen, focus on more cogent leads and keep us in the loop. I'll send out anything I learn about Polar Vortex. They haven't been relevant to us or the public for years now, and I'm not looking to stir a pot unnecessarily. Piotr, what do you have for us?"

Piotr leaned forward and placed Vandley's phone on the desk. The screen was irreparably destroyed, but a connected monitor showed a display of recent calls. At a glance, Chen saw calls and texts from a litany of numbers. Likely burners. The call history tracked back a couple of weeks before his body was discovered. Something Vandley would be unlikely to do unless directed. A cluster of calls appeared more recently, coming from the same contact prior to his death.

"Our man was not a social butterfly. While the call history was clearly wiped on a regular basis, there was little to recover, even on a short timescale. These calls you see here are from burners that were likely disposed of shortly after use. In other words, mostly dead ends. That is until a sudden increase in calls about two weeks before he bought it, increasing to daily up to the week of his murder. All from the same number. Whoever it was tried to mask it, but did a shit job—"

Ellen leaned in impatiently. "Yeah, yeah, we're on the edge of our seats, Piotr. Who the fuck is it?"

Piotr let out a wide grin. "Patience, grasshopper. These messages came from Teresa Hightower."

Chief Vic turned to face Piotr. "The head of the Weather Service? How can you be sure someone wasn't just using her office phone? We have to be certain before we shake trees that grow this high."

Piotr's voice rose in excitement. "She had too much faith in the system. When a government employee uses the encryption service, they input a request code to stop any Tom, Dick, and Harry from making free anonymous calls just by being on campus. Usually, that moment of request is scrubbed from the system after their code is matched with a voice imprint. However, it seems the frequency of these calls strained the system, and whoever's job it was to anonymize her late-night chats got sloppy. I was lucky enough to unmask enough calls to trace it back."

An air of tension filled the room as Piotr leaned back in satisfaction. Chen and Morgan exchanged nervous glances. Ellen turned toward them to offer a face of incredulity. Chief Victoria leaned forward on her hands slowly, trying her best to keep a stony face, though he guessed she was feeling the way Ellen looked. This was bad.

"I hate to say it, but this is the best lead we've got. Given what we know about Hightower and Vandley's past, these calls are more than coincidence. We need to exercise caution now more than ever. I was already stretching credibility and funding to make this investigation happen, but if this ever gets out, we're dead in the water. We need to close this fast. Or at least have something to show for it sooner rather than later. I don't need to tell you all what's on the line here."

"Chief, all due respect, are we really taking it up this far? On High was already pretty clear in their disdain for the guy. What happens if we start digging around one of their own? We're a little out of our depth here. They're much more equipped to question Hightower than any of us are."

"Chen, I understand your concern, but this case is more than just us. Many like you have been able to move out of their bloc, out of the Pits even because of Vandley. He saw things other people didn't. The last idea he had changed the world as we know it. If this is something worth killing over, it won't end with just him. The calls themselves prove that. Whatever he was into is important to somebody. They wouldn't lose a resource like that and continue like nothing happened. They're out there, and I mean to find root them out. Understood?"

Chen knew she had a point. The people who sponsored Vandley, and the ones who killed him, wanted more than the man. Otherwise, ransacking the apartment had no purpose. They wanted whatever his last idea was.

There were murmurs of agreement as Chief Victoria surveyed the room. Chen hadn't seen her this resolute since she was transferred to Lower Crimes a few years back. This was big.

"Good. I can get you an audience with Hightower, but we need to keep a small footprint. Piotr, update Chen on whatever messages you were able to salvage. Chen, I'll message you when I can make the meeting happen. I'll focus on what little there is on Polar Vortex, and the rest of you focus on your assignments. Morgan, you stay on Wayne. Piotr, continue working the phone. Ellen, keep everyone on pace, and I'll have you run down the leads my contacts dig up. Any questions?"

Morgan cleared her throat. "What about Wayne? If this is as delicate as you say, he should know what he's getting himself into."

"Good call. He's on surface, so Ellen, I want you to babysit him from afar until I contact you with new leads. I'll clear your dispensation up top. We'll be sure to intervene if there's any sign of danger. Any other concerns?"

Morgan visibly relaxed in her chair as Chief Victoria continued. "You all have your assignments. Any sign of turbulence, you stop and message Ellen or me directly. Remember to *tread lightly*. Dismissed."

Piotr motioned Chen to follow him as they all gathered their belongings. They moved quickly through the department and down into the tech unit. They wound through tight corridors, taking turns at a breakneck pace. Chen rubbed his hands together. It was one of the few parts of the precinct that remained cold throughout the Freeze so the equipment would stay at the right temperature. Piotr moved with nervous, squirrely energy. Piotr looked around the corner before speaking.

"I don't fucking like this, Chen. It was already shady to begin with, and now this? What are we doing here? You're going to question someone that high up and I'm going to dig through their shit? No way this isn't going to blow back on us, even if we do solve this thing. I'm no one's sacrificial lamb. They can all get fucked for all I care."

Chen took a seat near Piotr's workbench and let out a heavy sigh. Piotr paced manically in the small tech lab, dodging jerry-rigged machines wedged on too little counterspace. He tried not to match Piotr's energy, but he was feeling it inside too. They were in uncharted territory, and they could both sense it.

"I won't blow smoke, Piotr. We're definitely off bloc on this one. I don't think I've ever seen Vic or Ellen this tightly wound. I get their point, but if we keep going farther, we'll get strung up even if we crack this thing."

Piotr nodded rapidly. "*Exactly*. No amount of public good's gonna wash the stink of how we did all this. On High's gonna want someone to take the fall. *Especially* if one of them was in on all this. And Hightower? She's risking even more than we are talking to Vandley! She's gotta be crazy or stupid to risk her whole career, and we've got to be even fucking crazier to dig into something like that."

Piotr was right. Chen's conversation with Everett told him what he already knew. Whatever they were doing, it was rotten. It was hard to imagine what end could justify these means. For now, he had to play along and wait for an opportunity to exit this investigation or close it fast enough that they didn't break too much first.

"You're not wrong, Piotr. Right now, all I know is that we've got orders, and I can't blow a meeting off set by Vic herself. I need everything you have on these messages, so we can close this case fast. Hopefully that'll give us enough time to get clear of whatever blowback there'll be. I have a feeling we're knee-deep in it, but if we're fast enough we can stop ourselves from drowning."

"I hope you're right, Chen. I've got some of Vandley's last messages here, but more importantly, I've set up a separate channel without Ellen or Vic through our devices. Shit rolls downhill, and it doesn't get lower than the three of us. Vic's gonna save herself, and Ellen will be on the last shuttle off this ride along with her."

"You sure it's safe?"

Piotr rubbed the dry skin from his nose and nodded. "Yeah, I'm sure. I've already talked to Morgan about it, and she's in. I've looped you in and sent some of Vandley's last messages to you. We'll be a shadow in a shadow, I promise you. Keep us up to date; I'm about ready to jump outta my skin."

Piotr reached out and patted Chen's shoulder, not as reassuringly as he hoped.

"All right, I'll take the long shuttle home and look through everything you sent. I'll update you both as soon as I have something real with my conversation with Hightower. Morgan's got a strong sense, and if she's in, I'm probably in the right place."

"Keep me in the loop."

Chen nodded and turned to leave. He walked slowly through the station, looking toward Vic's office on his way out. Ellen was sitting across from her, both looking tense as they digested the updates. He could feel the skeptical looks from the bullpen. Ellen and Vic gave the investigation credibility, but the optics were too suspicious for that to be enough. Chen couldn't blame them. From their perspective, he was getting special treatment while they were stuck doing the scut work. He'd trade any overtime now to switch places with them. As Chen walked to his stop, he pulled his device out to review Vandley's last received messages:

You don't know...doing, you've always been stubborn but can't... what's at stake.

Please, just LISTEN to me.

That can't be the only...

You don't know everything, what you're saying, the price, it's too high, and we'd all be paying it.

Just let me come over, we'll talk it out...

PLEASE...

Chen felt the desperation from Hightower's messages as the shuttle twisted and turned. He selected the scenic route and hoped it would be reflective. Instead, his thoughts just grew louder with each rocking motion until the Boilers were a distant hum. Sounded like Hightower was desperate, and Chen needed to know why. His thoughts turned back to when the rift between Vandley and the Weather Service started. It'd been ugly. The news covered it non-stop. Vandley took every chance he could to denounce the methods of the very government agency that had funded his countdown in the first place. It wasn't long before his rantings got old and people moved on with the system he had worked to create. His ravings were soon pushed to the back of the public mind as new stories overtook it until he was nothing but a name discussed in hushed conversations or old gossip. Vandley's messages didn't have that tone to them now. Hightower seemed to be the one in the corner, shouting about the sky falling to an unfeeling public. She was desperate.

Chen knew the feeling.

5

Chen awoke from a fitful sleep. His phone buzzed incessantly in his ear. It'd been getting harder to sleep these last few days without Fuel assistance. He'd kicked the habit after making the transition to detective meant fewer late nights, but this was an exception. Anything that made chief nervous made him nervous. He could hardly operate without sleep, even if it was a fitful one. After this case, he wouldn't need it anymore. He checked his phone to a message from Chief Vic:

Meeting set with Hightower today at 1pm in her office. Message immediately with any updates.

Chen reluctantly rubbed the tiredness from his eyes and put moisturizer around his mouth and nostrils. He checked the forecast; it was going to be a particularly cold one. He had to dig through several recycled layers of clothing to find his single up-cycled coat for such an occasion. The weather service was a long ride, and their compound had only gotten more expansive since Vandley's prediction model. It seemed all the on-High families wanted a piece of the cutting-edge research, especially the Geraldsons. The money they put in was obscene. Before Chen made the transition to Low Crimes, he could see in real time as they pumped more and more resources into the Weather Service. It was mirrored by a decline in their machined production line. Chen had to jerry-rig a lot more repairs in the days before he left the bloc. Now it was up to his brother.

Chen pushed through recycler crowd to find the shuttle map. He'd have to transfer to the internal Weather Service system and show his special dispensation to continue farther. It'd been a while since he had to transfer off the Depths system. It often took weeks, even with good cause, to get the dispensation Chen held in his hands. The families on High didn't like surface and Depths mixing. The official reason was to avoid contamination of the agricultural soil with the chemicals of the Depths. Unofficially, Chen believed the oligarchs didn't enjoy mixing with the help.

He exited into a massive surface station that separated the Depths network from the government's internal shuttles. The transfer station was much better maintained. Security guards patrolled the platforms in pairs, wearing well maintained uniforms with nonlethal weapons at their sides. It was a stark contrast to the Depths, where you were more likely to see a mugging than security. The stench of Boiler air was replaced by a fresh surface fragrance that wafted through the surroundings. Gas recyclers mixed Boiler heat with the outside breeze. It made it so the saturation of fuel that penetrated the Depths didn't offend the nostrils of those above. Highly inefficient, but worth it if Fuel wasn't a limiting factor. Chen joined the crowd for special dispensations. A mix of uniforms reading SANITATION, CULINARY, ASSISTANT, and the like. The line moved slowly toward a single security agent still rubbing sleep from their eyes. A parallel line for government employees and researchers moved at a brisk pace through automated turnstiles. Chen dutifully waited his turn and showed his special dispensation to the attendant, who hardly bothered to look up at his face before waving him through. The shuttle Boiler offered a pleasant hum as it ran the express line to the heart of the Weather Service.

Chen emerged into a dizzying complex of glasswork. A map in front of him showed the entire campus, acres and acres of surface dedicated to research, forecasting, and support staff. There were covered walkways from building to building to allow for safe travel during the Freeze, themselves needing their own dedicated Boiler network. Employees and visitors walked past him with purpose, most dressed in new or upcycled clothing that would likely set him back a month's salary. The shuttle dropped him off at the central administrative building on the northern edge of the campus. It loomed impressively in front of him, easily standing fifty levels tall. Light gleamed off multiple glass surfaces. It had been updated significantly since the first countdown began as an excessive pledge of confidence in the department and the assurances of predictability provided to the surface and Depths. The comfortable internal temperature encouraged him to take his time walking through the lobby. It was an expansive open concept that likely took enough fuel to harvest a whole bloc to heat. His attention was drawn to the center, where the service desk directed him to the glass elevator near the back. There were dozens of floors above him with crisscrossing transparent bridges. He could hear passing scientists converse excitedly as they went about their day. The Boiler system hardly made a hum.

Chen rode a glass elevator toward the top of the structure and exited into a large waiting room. The décor was muted, though it still made use of open and hard to heat spaces. Forgettable beige hues dominated the room. Brand-new sofas and chairs lined the walls. Illuminated pictures of the previous directors hung in stern judgment of Chen as his eyes followed portrait after portrait until his gaze rested behind the desk. Hightower's portrait sat in a place of honor behind a young woman who looked at him impatiently.

"Detective Chen, here to meet with Teresa Hightower." He flashed his special dispensation and badge.

"Just one moment, I'll buzz her."

Chen watched as she pressed a buzzer and held a headset to her ear. He could hear a tense exchange as the receptionist hung up and motioned him forward.

"Please step through these double doors and walk to the end of the hall. She is expecting you."

Chen made his way down a long hallway. Offices flanked him with scientists giving presentations, bureaucrats on phone calls, and assistants making frantic notes. The red lights of multiple surveillance cameras blinked steadily along the hall. They seemed to follow his movements as he passed under them. He could feel the on-High police force watching his every move. They were closer to a private security force than a public service. He approached a set of elegantly designed wooden doors and rang the bell to the side. The doors opened noiselessly as he approached a woman in her mid-fifties sitting at an impressive glass bureau. The office had wall-to-wall windows that let unfiltered light shine in. It was enough to make Chen wish he had brought sunscreen. She probably got more sun sitting in this office than he would in a month. Hightower herself sat on a small chair, her legs visibly shifting behind the glass desktop. She tried to look as confident as her portrait did in the outside lobby, but with this long on the job Chen could tell when someone was trying too hard. Her body language and inconsistent eye contact screamed anxiety. Not something he'd expect when someone on High was paid a visit from someone down Low, even if Chen was the law. She was probably used to being unassailable.

Hightower gestured toward a seat in front of her. A large mural covered the wall directly behind her, decorated with the seal of the Weather Service, a large gray cloud with a defiant man in the center, protected by a round, golden barrier reminiscent of the sun. An embossed name plate on her desk read:

Teresa M. Hightower

Head of the Weather Bureau

"Welcome, Detective, I understand you're here on behalf of Chief Victoria about an ongoing investigation. How may I be of use?"

Chen took a seat across from Hightower. The chair underneath gave to his weight comfortably as he tried to take a relaxed position. "Yes, thank you for taking the time to meet with me. I'm sorry to say I'm under strict orders to keep the details of our investigation under wraps, though I will share details where I can. Have you had contact with Richard Vandley recently?"

Hightower shifted uncomfortably in her seat. "I can't say I have. He has been largely estranged from the weather service since his comments decades ago. Any contact would not reflect well on my position. I'd be surprised if he even gave me any thought. He always valued data over sentiment."

She was uncomfortable. Lying wasn't her strong suit. Too much pressure and she'd probably shut down to further questioning.

"I understand the implications, but we do have receipts of multiple messages between the two of you. You can appreciate why this meeting was arranged given the situation. We understand the need for discretion. Anything that besmirches the Weather Service would shut our investigation down immediately, so we'll work with you the best we can."

Hightower's face turned ashen white. If she was innocent, she was not doing herself any favors. Chen leaned forward and placed his arms crossed on the desk. A little more pressure.

"I...I see. In that case I appreciate...the care taken in our meeting. May I ask, is Richard okay? Why are you asking these questions?"

Chen weighed his options carefully. A little truth might go a long way, and she was likely to suspect what'd happened to Vandley given the nature of their recent conversations.

"I'm afraid not, ma'am. He was found dead not too long ago. The circumstances are puzzling even without the political fallout. Given his high profile, we must pursue every avenue of investigation. Given your recent messages together and how asocial Vandley was, we believe he reached out to you for a reason. Or if you reached out to him, we'd like to know what prompted such a risk on your part."

Hightower glanced down. She seemed to tense up before looking at Chen and continuing to speak. He could feel her nervous energy radiating outward.

"I'm...so sorry to hear that. I'd been afraid for his well-being ever since I had to distance myself from him, but his mind is not easily swayed. I hadn't heard from him in years, though I thought about reaching out many times over the years. Am I to understand that I'm a suspect?"

"We can't rule anything out as a matter of protocol. From what we recovered, it seems you were the last in contact with him shortly before his death. What was the nature of your relationship recently?"

"He always was fiercely independent. I hadn't spoken to him in years, but he'd reached out to me months ago regarding some of his newer theories. Even with my know-how, they were a bit beyond me. I could tell he'd been working feverishly by the tone of his voice. I hadn't heard that from him since the early days of his predictive model. He'd always had the habit of diving so much into his work that he'd often forget to eat or sleep. Before we were fully sponsored by the Weather Service, I often made sure he didn't starve in addition to being his research partner."

"I see. Do you think he would be capable of working alone?"

"Not the Richard I knew. Without me, he probably couldn't sustain enough calories to keep his mind going. When we needed funding, I acted as the face of the project that backers could relate to while he continued to toil in relative anonymity. That is until the press finally uncovered the mind behind the model. Everyone thought we were the two great minds of our generation. Truth is I was more his keeper and translator to the public. He never did mind our division of labor. Richard always said that it was the human element that held back research. How science was easily perverted for profit and gain."

Hightower had slowly turned toward the window with a distant look on her face before coming back to reality. "I'm sorry, does that answer your question, Detective?"

Chen nodded with a friendly smile. He could see Hightower relax slightly. He had her in the right place, reminiscing more than answering questions.

"When we found him, there were clear signs of Fuel abuse. Do you think it had anything to do with his death?"

"I doubt it. He wasn't like other users you'd find on the street. Richard felt alive on it. Clear. He believed that it let him ignore the other parts of his mind that weren't purely scientific. He'd use Fuel most often when he was deep in thought about some new idea. When I first met him, I tried to get him to kick the stuff, but if anything, it made him more on edge."

Chen rubbed his nose and sniffed unconsciously before recollecting his thoughts. "In my line of work, trying to forget with Fuel is a common sentiment. Trying to forget the hours, the cycles, even life in general. Was there something Vandley trying to forget?"

"Things like sentiment, hope, and ambition. He thought they poisoned the well of objective science. That sentiment meant creating a dream first before acknowledging reality. He believed that trying to change reality was a fool's errand, a hopeless endeavor. That science was something to be observed and understood rather than changed for our convenience. That made it a hard sell for the public. It's hard, being close to someone like him, but I admired the mind behind the cold facts. There was always a right answer; it just needed to be found. The Fuel really seemed to liberate him from the cacophony of other people's expectations and ideas."

"Why do you think he reached out after all this time?"

"It's hard to say. He left the service after becoming disillusioned with the very model he created. After the stability it brought, no one was interested in listening to his theories about iterating his success. Everyone viewed his achievement as this pinnacle of modern weather application. There was no appetite for improvement or change. I think he grew...frustrated with what his creation had brought. He described it as an age of 'disinterest.'"

"Disinterest?"

"That's what he called it. I think what he meant was an apathy toward progress. The public seemed to think that the advent of the countdown put the Freeze in its place. That by quantifying it, we had conquered it."

"He didn't seem to agree? It was his brainchild, after all."

"Not for a second. It was hardly a week before he started to think about next steps. About how the countdown could be a stepping stone toward a greater understanding of our world. But the will was gone. Without public interest, the families withdrew their funding for new Weather Service research. Overnight, I watched as Richard went from a celebrity genius to a man raving his theories at an indifferent world. His rants quickly became hostile to the Service, to the families, and to the public at large. That's when I had to make a choice."

"To distance yourself?"

"Precisely. We didn't talk for years after that. At first, I was relieved to hear from him again, but he just wanted to talk about more of his theories. I wasn't sure what to make of it. I always had some trouble following his logic, but this time it was on another level. I could hardly make heads nor tails of his proposals. I think that my confusion frustrated him, and I could tell my concern was only pushing him further away."

Chen leaned forward and brought his device out. "I can understand how frustrating that would be. The last messages we have here, though, frankly seem more desperate than confused. Now, I've had to intervene on many a friend's behalf, but this? It seems more serious than that."

Hightower took the device and began to read. Her eyes widened with each passing line. Chen could tell she had prepared for an interview far less intrusive than this. Chen couldn't blame her. Even High Crimes put on the kid gloves when they interviewed a government official this senior, suspect or not. She set the device down and took a steady breath.

"I...I *was* desperate. I hadn't seen him that fired up since he first proposed the model. Vandley was capable of anything in that kind of mindset, and I wasn't sure what'd he do. In the past, I often helped him stay rooted to reality. Without me, it's hard to imagine what he was capable of."

"What were you afraid of?"

"I'm not sure. That was always the problem with Richard. Once he latched on to a thought or idea, he couldn't be discouraged, especially with Fuel involved. I was afraid that he'd get himself into trouble again, like he did with his comments years ago about the Weather Service. Richard had fame on his side then, but if he did something similar today, I don't think there would be a lot of tolerance for it. I just wanted to keep him away from trouble."

"Do you have any idea what theories he was working on? He didn't seem like a man to throw things at the wall until it stuck, especially if he reached out to you about it."

"I...I didn't. I could tell it involved dissatisfaction around the countdown, much like his feelings many years ago before he became a recluse. I never really could understand him well, and I could tell he'd been using Fuel again. When he got like that, he was nearly impossible to follow."

"Did you see him that night?"

Hightower cleared her throat. "No...I didn't see him as much as I hoped to. He was shutting me out. I could tell he wasn't taking proper care of himself."

"Where were you that night?"

"Home. I was home. I didn't know where he was, and I couldn't go through the Depths searching for him. I was stretching my reputation as it was even talking to him. If anyone found out about this, everything we've built through his model would be for naught. So please, if this could stay between us and the investigation, you'd be doing me a great service."

"Of course. Was anyone with you?"

"No...I was home alone. I'd been working late in the office that day and left well after eight. I spent the rest of the night by myself. We have plenty of security cameras to attest to that."

Chen didn't doubt that, but he made a note to have Chief Vic pull some favors for the security tapes. Probable cause wasn't enough up here, and they'd probably have to pull dozens of hours to avoid singling out Hightower in their request.

"Thank you, ma'am. One last thing. In his apartment we found some evidence suggesting a link with Polar Vortex. What do you make of that?"

Hightower visibly tensed. Her eyes widened in anger, and she did nothing to hide it. He'd hit a nerve on that one.

"Of–of course not! They're little more than a cult of personality set up around unsupported supposition! It flies in the face of everything Vandley worked on. The amount of time I had to spend denouncing their rhetoric. I mean it drove both of us *insane*. I would have no idea why they would even cross his mind. He was a man of facts. I doubt they would see anything eye-to-eye. If they had their way, we'd be cowering in the Depths, afraid of every cold breeze that blew across the surface. They're a joke of their own making. I mean, when's the last time they held one of their 'protests'? Years? Laughable."

Chen took a moment and watched as Hightower started to relax. Indignation radiated from her face as she started to calm down. There seemed to be genuine hatred there mixed with that same nervous energy she'd displayed since they started the interview. She had a point. Even Everett saw Polar Vortex as out of date, much less the public. Polar Vortex was a public embarrassment most would rather forget.

That outburst was probably the end of anything productive he could accomplish today.

"I see. We did find it peculiar given his history. Why would these references be littered throughout his personal belongings?

It seems odd given your assertions about how you both felt about them."

"I can assure you, Detective, I have no idea. Do you believe they're involved in his death?"

"We can't be certain of anything yet."

Chen took some notes and continued to watch as Hightower's breath started to normalize. He could imagine any employee of the Weather Service having such strong negative feelings toward Polar Vortex, especially the face of the agency. He doubted Hightower would be able to attest to much else given her position, not today and especially not here. Not even the highest ranking on surface could expect so much privacy. He flipped his notebook closed. He'd shaken the trees enough for today. Chen could tell her energy was waning along with the evening sun.

"Thank you, Ms. Hightower. You've been very helpful. Rest assured we will continue to handle this with the utmost care and discretion. Please reach out to us with any relevant information you remember. I'll do my best to keep you apprised of any developments that occur."

"Thank you, Detective, and please let Chief Victoria know I appreciate the caution she has exercised. I will avail myself of anything the investigation needs. I'd hate to remain a suspect for much longer."

She pushed a button on the intercom, and the doors behind Chen slowly opened. Chen shook her hand and left his business card on her desk. She looked at it like it was radioactive. He rose slowly and headed toward the exit. As he crossed the threshold, Hightower asked, "How did he seem when you found him?"

Chen stopped on his way out. She was concerned. "He lived in the way you remember. Single-minded."

Hightower relaxed and leaned back in her chair. "Well, thank you for your candor. Please let Chief Victoria know that I'm happy to set up another meeting anytime Lower Crimes needs me. Just reach out to my assistant and she'll clear my calendar."

Chen gave a curt nod and headed for the door. He messaged the team to have some patrolman check with government surveillance about Hightower's alibi. As he approached the shuttle, his mind swirled with possibilities. Anyone in Hightower's position would be defensive, especially with contact with Vandley, but how deep did her fear run? Chief did say that on High was all politics, but could it be just that? And how did Polar Vortex fit in with all this?

Chen sent a quick update to Vic and Ellen as the shuttle dove through the surface, Boilers shutting off abruptly. The chill seemed to enter his body faster than usual, and he pulled his coat tight around him. The new secure line Piotr had set up remained quiet for now. He gripped the handkerchief in his pocket tightly as he neared home.

Vandley weighed on his mind. Certainty was a rare trait through the Depths, and he had given that gift to them all. Men like Vandley didn't rest on their laurels; Hightower had said as much. In the end, it seemed restlessness was his fatal flaw. It was hard to believe a rarity would end up like that, alone in the Depths, strained from the only friend he knew. Seemed genius only took you so far.

6

Chen awoke to his phone ringing. Rare for anyone to call these days. The caller ID shocked him awake. *Nate*. He always preferred calling rather than texting. Some outmoded thought of professionalism more akin to bureaucrats than farmers.

Nate?

Hey bro, did I wake you? I'm sorry I haven't responded to your message yet. I'm coming down today for parts and wanted to see if you had some time to catch up.

It's good, I should've been up earlier anyway. Let me check in with the team. I should be able to sneak off for a couple hours without being missed.

Hey, no pressure, don't get in trouble on my account. I only got an hour to spare before Dad notices I'm taking my time. How close are you to recycler level? We still get parts from the same place.

I live close. How far are you?

I'm still a couple hours out. The ride's more of a pain than I remember.

Alright, I'll meet you there.

Chen could feel nervousness rise in his chest. It'd been over a year since he thought about reaching out to his brother, longer between meetings. Nate had been largely neutral in Chen deciding to leave, but there was a sense of abandonment he couldn't shake. Based on Nate's expression when he snuck out that last night, he probably felt the same.

Chen checked the time. Chief Vic hadn't reached out yet after Chen updated her about the interview with Hightower. Hightower's alibi was airtight so far, but the techs needed more time. He probably had a couple hours before they decided what to do with information this delicate. Chen rushed through brushing his teeth, moisturizing his nose and mouth, and layering up before heading out the door.

Most blocs got their parts from the same place, a dingy shambles of a marketplace commonly referred to as Last Look. It was where parts got their last chance for use. It was the busiest at the start of each Freeze as new parts made their way down by the freight track and the Depths' talented recyclers tried to scrape together functional parts from what the surface considered junk. Before their father discovered Chen's aptitude for repair, it had been a haven. A place where he could exercise his creativity in what others considered dregs. That didn't last long.

Chen rode the shuttle route by muscle memory, watching as the industrial zones passed: Boilers being fueled, the grinding of the shuttle and freight trams against their deteriorating tracks. Half a dozen stops from the end of the line, Chen exited with a dozen other passengers, empty packs slung over their shoulders. Chen moved with the crowd off the train stop and down thin alleyways flanked by shanties made of rusted, reclaimed metal. There were a few precious lights shining through the windows. Fuel was second only to food in this part of the Depths, and one of the last uses was for light. Sunken faces watched them with disinterest. Young kids circled them, hands extended, asking for donations. Chen patted his pockets. They knew better than to lift from an experienced-looking traveler, but it was best to be safe.

Half an hour later, Chen arrived at the outskirts of Last Call, a half square mile of covered shacks spread out haphazardly before him. Recyclers of various ages hawked their wares to anyone who would listen. Strings of lights provided just enough clarity to stop people from bumping into one another while they haggled for bottom-bin materials. A few months later, the good parts would dry up and anything left would be destined for scrappers to take to the lowest point of the Depths. For now, Chen patrolled the border of Last Call until he reached the industrial section. He could see Nate's tuft of unkempt hair bobbing a foot above the crowd. Chen shadowed him for a few minutes until grabbing Nate by the shoulders.

"JESUS, Alec, what the *fuck*. That isn't *funny anymore*."

Nate had jumped a foot in the air, the look of indignation trying, in vain, to hide a smile. Chen punched Nate on the arm and felt a grin creep on his face. It was good to see him.

"Speak for yourself, little bro. You're as jumpy as ever."

"You *know* I don't come down here. That was always your job. I mean, how do you *live* here? It's dark, cramped, and even with all the Boilers it's *cold*."

"You get used to it. For those with the nerve, that is."

"Yeah, yeah, yeah, you're a regular hardboiled flatfoot. If you're done, I've got my list and Dad's got a timetable. We're going this way."

Chen followed as Nate made his way toward a set of stalls along the outside border. Machines in states of disrepair were piled high behind each lean-to: engines, tractors missing wheels, recalled products. Recyclers stood in front of tables littered with parts. The more established vendors had an employee turning over products and explaining the functionality. The newer or desperate ones arranged their rusted inventory as neatly as they could. Chen followed Nate to a stall near the front where a crowd was already forming.

"Glad to see Trent's still in business."

"Yea, he's reliable as always, though his son had to start picking up the slack. Got his leg crushed jostling a pile of parts fresh off Freight."

Chen leaned around to look toward the stall. He could see the bent over form of Trent at the stall, his left leg extended in a ragged metal cast nearly rusted through. His hair looked much more salt than Chen recalled, and his dark skin had grown more wrinkles in the last several years than Chen had noticed in the past decade. A thin teenager in a sparse shirt and shorts ran between Trent and the pile of mechanisms behind them. Probably his son. Injuries like Trent's were more about living with them than healing down here.

"Shit, that's bad. Did he go see Vickers?"

"Yeah, got him hooked up with that cast and everything. Seen others live longer with worse. Dad greenlit the bloc to haggle with him less, help out where we can."

"That's good. What's on the list this cycle?"

"Gotta pick up a few carburetors, some crankshafts, some newer fasteners would be nice, something without a lot of rust in it yet."

"Ya'll must've had a good cycle up there."

"Yep, we got some play in the budget this cycle, so most of the families are coordinating wish lists and the like. I'm honestly surprised we lasted this long without needing to swap out. Whatever witchcraft you did before leaving lasted us up until now. We wore that shit out this growing season, but nothing up and broke yet. We're gonna meet the Depths quota, but just barely still. Even with the countdown and new seed lineages, we were harvesting until that last second ticked on."

Chen felt an old pride well up. He always was the best on the bloc when it came to repairs. Not only getting them to work again, but getting it to stick. Sounded like they needed every extra second of durable machinery they could get. Nothing new given the extreme pace they ran the harvesters at.

"It's good you're getting the fasteners. Better fasteners lessen the vibrational stress on the other parts. Key to longevity."

The line shifted forward in disorderly fashion like a wave encroaching the beach. Chen could hear concerned murmurs from other pickers as they anxiously looked toward the shrinking pile of parts. Trent's boy continued dashing between the crush of re-quests, taking notes and payment and deftly finding product in the maze behind the desk. Their business was generational, as old as the Depths itself, much like Chen's family farm. Steady work was hard to turn down, even in the most certain times.

"Good to know. How are you faring down here? You still on nights?"

"Not for a while. Made detective a few years back. No more night shifts help a lot."

"How can you tell the difference down here? I thought it was a bustle of activity with so many people, but you guys can hardly keep the lights on from what I can tell."

"Yeah, it's a lot to get used to. Made the night shifts easier at first, not being able to tell the difference, but making detective has made it more tolerable. Interesting cases, better overtime."

"Ho-ho. Big-shot detective just like in...what's that show we used to watch? Death..."

"*Death in the Depths*! I haven't thought about that in years. That's what got the thought of coming down here in my head. The way Detective Rockaway solved cases, always got his man. Dad would've flipped if he knew putting that show on got me to join the program."

Nate let out a hearty laugh, big enough that the people in front turned to look at him and the kids around stopped and started laughing a little themselves.

"No *way*, you're such a *cliché*. Down here cause of some old program. You're right, Dad would *freak* if he knew something he did led to all this."

Silence fell between them as they tried to push forward in the crowd. They were close to the front, but moreover, the topic of their father left a gap between them. Fights between Chen and their father; Nate trying to keep the peace. Tense calls in the first few weeks of cadet training when Nate would try to ask Chen to see reason where their father never would. How Chen would hang up at the thought.

"How has Dad been?"

Nate tried to play off his anxiety as impatience for the line by looking around the people in front. "He's all right. We had a good cycle, mostly due to a new initiative led by him and the Sanchez family. The cycle after you left shook him. Started prioritizing spending on good parts to improve harvest efficiency. It was a hard sell to the bloc at large, but with the Sanchez family he was able to vote it through, and it finally paid off this cycle. It was a big relief for everyone."

Nate didn't say it, but they both knew that without Chen, repairs in the bloc didn't last as long. Since Chen was a teenager, he'd had a gift for stretching the life of what many thought was irreparable. And since then, Dad had offered his services to any machine on the bloc that needed it. 'For the good of the bloc.'

"That's good of the Sanchezes to back him up like that."

"Yeah, it was. I'm not sure how Dad would've done without them. And to answer your question, yes, he's been asking about you."

"He has? Hardly seems like him."

"Jesus, I swear it's like talking to the same person. If you guys weren't so similar, you'd get along great."

Chen lagged behind a step as Nate stepped forward with the crowd. He was chafing at the comparison. Nate didn't turn around before speaking.

"I can feel you brooding back there. Don't they teach you professionalism in cadet class?"

Nate made a path to the folding desk where Trent was laid up. He looked up at them both and offered a wide smile.

"Well, if it ain't the Chen boys. What brings both of you down here? Ya'll must've had a killer harvest this year to spare both of you."

"You're not far off. Alec's been down here for a while now."

Trent turned awkwardly in his chair, taking care not to destabilize his metal cast, and made eye contact with Chen. He looked puzzled.

"Ain't that right? You been down here all this time and didn't stop by? What're you doing down here anyhow?"

Nate pulled Chen into a one-armed hug. Despite his best efforts, Chen felt a smile come on.

"He's a big-shot detective now! Hardly any time to make it in the sunshine, much less slum it down here with you."

"You don't say? Well, congratulations! You don't see many farm boys branching out, especially from families as old as yours. Good on you."

"Thanks, Trent. It's been a good change of pace from fixing things up on the homestead. Though I do miss getting that surface shine without needing to jump through hoops for it."

"I imagine it's harder for you than those of us born down here. I don't think I've ever had dispensation to get on the surface. Besides old documentaries, I don't really know what I'm missing, I guess. Anyway, enough jawing at you both. What can I do for some of my best customers?"

Nate stepped forward and passed a list of parts to Trent. After taking a moment to read through, he called his son over and whispered instructions into his ear. His son tucked a few bags under his arm and disappeared behind several piles with youthful energy.

"It's good of your boy to help out. I was wondering when we'd see Trent Jr. running the place."

"Yep, you aren't the only one to ask, Nate. Honestly, I been delaying the inevitable for too long. I started younger than him, but he always had a knack for headier stuff; so I been holding down the fort, until this shit happened."

Trent gestured toward his cast with a look of frustration. His eyes followed Trent Jr. as he delved between parts, filling bags expertly.

"Thought he had a chance at that program you went up in, Alec."

"I wouldn't be surprised; he seems quick enough for it."

"Yeah, everyone says so. But with me laid up like this, we can't really afford time without him. I mean, sure, the countdown helps, but these cycles seem to be getting shorter. Used to be that damn clock would cut us some slack for six, maybe eight months. Nowadays, they seem to be coming shorter, but faster. People need the parts, but demand's outpacing supply by a wide margin."

Nate's face scrunched up in agreement.

"You said it. Even that genius Vandley only got us so far."

"I'm glad you got your chance, Alec. It's not often someone gets outta the family business, especially a good one. It sounds like your bloc's getting on just fine without you."

"Thanks, Trent. If your boy wants to know more about the program, let me know. Still know a few people there."

"I appreciate that. Speaking of, where'd that boy go..."

On cue, Trent's son sidled up with four bags full of tinkling parts. As Nate had mentioned, most were refurbished and free of rust, a luxury for most. Nate passed Trent a wad of cash that Trent counted expertly before nodding to his son. Nate reached his arms out and took the bags while Trent's son passed Chen a delivery slip.

"The bigger stuff will be up with the next Freight delivery. You got some big-ticket items on there, so I'd get there bright and early. Jefferson on the night shift is still trustworthy; he'll get you in before the government folks show up on day shift to rouse the locals away."

"Appreciate it, Trent. I'll be by again whenever this cycle ends. And take Alec up on his offer, otherwise his head might get big enough to float him back up to us."

"You take care, boys. And don't be a stranger, Alec. Would do us good to see someone making the most outta that mobility program."

Chen nodded and tried to look toward Trent's son, but he had already disappeared between some stacks, fulfilling another customer's order. It reminded him of when he had first started in the program. Hungry.

Chen followed Nate back through the crowd and to the outskirts of Last Call. He felt his courage to ask about home fading. Nate met his gaze.

"The answer is yes, Dad does ask about you from time to time."

Chen let out a light laugh. Nate always was the emotionally intelligent one in the family.

"I find that hard to believe."

"Alec, come *on*. Dad's nearly sixty years old. I get why it's hard for him to change, but what's your excuse?"

Chen felt himself flush with indignation. He distanced himself from Nate to calm his nerves before turning around and setting his face with a passive expression. Nate continued before he could get a word in.

"Why are we here, Alec? You haven't reached out in years, now you're interested in making a parts run with me? Come *on*."

"Nate, I don't know what's got you so upset—"

"*You*, Alec! You and Dad both. You're both so damn *stubborn*. I'm tired of being the intermediary. Both of you want to know how the other's doing, but your damn egos won't let you just ask! I honestly don't know how Mom made it as far as she did."

Nate had become more animated. He paced back and forth until he made eye contact with Chen and let out a stressed breath. His shoulders slumped as he dropped the bags to the ground and found a curb to sit on. Chen hadn't seen his brother like this in years, ever since he told their father of his plan to join the mobility program. Worst of all, Nate had a point. Chen let his face relax as he took a seat next to his brother.

"How is Dad?"

"He's okay now. This last cycle was the real proof of concept. We've got a fuel surplus for the first time in years, and the bloc can afford the repairs we've been missing out on since you left. We're the lucky ones. He's been wondering about how you're doing down here. If it's warm, if there's enough food to go around. Little questions that I don't know the answer to. I think it's hard for him to imagine someone giving up as close to a guaranteed thing you'll get around here for all of this."

Nate gestured at the Depths around them, twisting his face in exasperation. Chen couldn't help but agree. After the surface shine the last few days, it was hard coming back.

"Alec, what do you see down here?"

The question caught Chen off-guard. He had to think for longer than he expected. Chen could tell Nate knew but chose not to remark on his indecision.

"I saw the Depths as freedom. The mobility program was a way to get there. I wanted to have a choice, Nate. I never felt like I had that with Dad. I know my leaving was hard for you too, and I'm sorry for that. It just seemed like something I needed to do."

Nate took a moment to digest Chen's words. He was always the more sentimental one, more prone to think of the family or the bloc first than himself.

"I still don't understand why this is so important to you, Alec. But I don't have to."

They sat there for a while, the sounds of the market echoing in the background. Chen hadn't given any thought to why he came in years. His conviction had carried him that first year, but since then he hadn't had the chance to reevaluate. Or he knew he wasn't ready to.

"Thanks, Nate. It's good to hear that from you."

"You know Dad feels the same way. He's just too proud to say it. Since this past cycle went well, he's gotten a lot more sentimental. Or maybe it's just old age."

Nate rose from the curb and began collecting his bags, handing some to Chen. They walked for several blocks to the shuttle, stopping at the entrance so Nate could arrange his things. Nate had a pass that was express service to surface, one Chen had a long time ago.

"Don't let Dad stop you from visiting, Alec. You can brood in the kitchen together. Just like old times."

"Ha, thanks, Nate. And thanks for the update. It's good to know the bloc found a way around repairs for once."

"Don't get too sentimental on me; there's only room for one of that in the family."

Nate scanned his badge and boarded the shuttle with a rush of other pickers and their salvage. The shuttle jerked under the weight, gathering the momentum until the sound of wheels grinding against rail dissipated. Ellen had messaged the investigation team several times already, then Chen individually as her messages went unheeded. Chief Vic herself sent him a thinly veiled demand to report to the station in the next hour. They had more leads to chase down and precious little time to do it. He'd just be able to make it on the next shuttle.

Nate had a habit of asking the right questions. Chen hadn't thought about why he first came to the Depths in so long. He'd wanted to escape the mundane work on the bloc, the thought of tomorrow being a repeat of today. How the needs of the bloc came before his own ambitions. How being part of something bigger meant choices made for the collective outweighed your own.

Chen tried to shake the thoughts out of his head as he boarded the shuttle with a wave of recyclers. He felt himself blend into a crowd of people that made the Depths run. Taking materials from one place and squeezing every piece of usefulness out of it. Stopping the desperation from turning into violence and disrupting the system. Punishing the ones that stepped out of line and reestablishing the equilibrium.

If Chief Vic was right, there would be time for these questions after the case was over.

Chen awoke to the noise of his phone buzzing. His sleep was fitful, full of stressful dreams. They'd spent much of the night chasing down leads that led nowhere, and it was taking a toll on his body. It was less of a problem when he had been a patrolman and used sleep aids regularly, but restarting Fuel was hard on the mind. Harder without it, he reasoned. He turned over, trying to banish the cobwebs from his mind as he read the latest messages from Morgan: *Our mutual colleague has developments in the gratifying world of Freeze calculations.*

Chen sat up in alarm. Morgan did not send cryptic messages, let alone do so needlessly. If she felt the impulse, then it must be urgent. He quickly gathered up his belongings and headed toward the nearest shuttle stop, trying to avoid the main streets. He felt eyes everywhere. It would be several hours before his mind was his own again. The ride to Geraldson passed in a blur. Chen tried to gather his more logical thoughts as the darkness of the Depths gave way to the surface. He flashed his badge absentmindedly at the transfer station. Security nearly tackled him after he accidentally forgot to show his special dispensation. By the time he arrived at the station, several hours had passed and his thoughts were halfway cognizant. Morgan waved him over, looking more exhausted than ever. Chen took several deep breaths, trying to replace the stale, inhalant laden air in his lungs with fresh, warmed surface gas.

"Chen, thank you for coming. I'm sorry for the cloak and dagger. This isn't exactly my wheelhouse here." She handed him a coffee, the smell of beans wafting up. Thank God, he'd need all the help he could get this morning. Especially if she felt the need to exclude Vic on this. Whatever it was, it was making Morgan nervous.

Chen took the coffee gratefully. "I get it, Morgan, nothing about Vandley has made sense yet. Why are we here? And how far are we off bloc on this one?"

"Honestly, I don't know yet. I'm probably just being paranoid, but I wanted to keep exposure on this low until I'm sure we don't need to. We're far enough off bloc as it is."

"I got you. So, what are we really here for?"

"It's Wayne. He's been up day and night chasing our lead, and he sent out an SOS last night. I'd never seen him so worked up before. His message was erratic. I could hardly understand what he was saying. All I know is that he's nervous. He wants to talk in his office ASAP. He wanted me to come alone, but I'm not sure that's a good idea right now. Ever since we started this case, nothing has felt kosher about what we're doing, especially misleading Wayne like this. Maybe if we were honest about what we were looking for in the first place, he'd have been more careful about what he was doing."

"Agreed. I've had the same feeling since we started. What do you think is going on?"

"Honestly, I'm not sure. It takes a lot for Wayne to look up from his screen, and this? I was already nervous, but to involve a friend as old as Wayne...it's insane."

"I'm glad you called. I know Ellen is supposed to be watching out for Wayne, but she's got her own leads to pick up, and if something spooked Wayne, she either got scared off herself or they were good enough to avoid tipping her off. I'm not a fan of either option."

"Definitely. You know that habit of yours isn't really helping."

Chen rubbed his nose instinctively. "I know you're worried. I have it under control. When this case is over, I'll be good, I promise. You think I'd disappoint my personal physician? Let's make sure your man's okay, then we can worry about me."

Morgan took a deep breath. "Okay, but you come to me if you need, you hear? I got you through it once, and we can do it again."

"Yeah. Now, where we heading?"

"Wayne wanted us to meet in his office, up near the top floor, near the lab where we initially met him. He said to be careful. He's not one to get paranoid without reason."

They headed up the glass elevator together, passing through floors of offices and labs. He tried to resist looking around every corner. Chen shifted restlessly as the elevator slowed and approached the fifty-fourth floor. Chen and Morgan exited the elevator and passed the same desk he had noticed initially. The activity he saw last time had been replaced by quiet tension. He instinctively slowed his pace to better take in the surroundings.

"His office is down this way to the left, near the end of the hall. We should probably hurry."

As they made their way down the hall, Chen noticed a man in a form-fitting black uniform exiting the office Morgan had pointed toward. Chen held his hand out to slow Morgan down and turned his head, pointing at an adjacent hallway close by. He signaled her to move down the length of the hallway quietly.

"What's going on, Chen?"

Chen held a finger to his lips and turned to peer down the hall. Several minutes passed as multiple figures moved in and out of the office, piling boxes and papers near the end of the hall. Chen couldn't see any distinguishing marks, but he knew from experience to assume the worst. Their movements were coordinated and efficient. This was a trained unit.

After about another fifteen minutes, Wayne was led by the arms by two agents at either side. Despite the exhaustion, fear was clear in his eyes. As they passed closer, Chen was able to get a better look at their uniform, black head to toe with a distinctive crest on the shoulder. A red background with a thundercloud in the center, electric tendrils extending violently outward. This was much worse than he had thought.

Chen motioned Morgan to move farther down the side entry as the trio passed them by. He could feel a jump in tension as recognition dawned on her face. Chen waited until he heard the elevator ding and several minutes passed without any footsteps peppering the hall. They were safe, for now.

Morgan was the first to break the silence. "What the *fuck* is going on, Chen? That was my *friend*. Who is taking him? Where are they going? And where is *Ellen*? She was supposed to keep him *safe*. This is the farthest thing from safe!"

Chen tried his best to stay calm, but his thoughts swirled around without end. He took a few deep breaths to try to regulate his heart rate. He needed to be calm for Morgan; he could tell that without a steady hand, she'd fall apart. There was time for panic later.

"I don't know what's going on, but what I do know is that those guys are bad news. They're the Shock Unit, a division on High sends for sensitive cases. They're closer to private security than a real police force. I wouldn't be surprised if Ellen bugged out the second she saw these Fuel jocks show up. They'd have picked her up first and asked questions never. She's probably gone to ground, and that's our best bet."

Chen took a moment to let Morgan catch her breath. He sugarcoated it the best he could, but that didn't mean it was palatable going down. He put his hand on her shoulder until she stopped hyperventilating. They needed to stay as quiet as possible.

"I'm sorry, Morgan, but if they're involved then the judicial process is already an afterthought. The best thing we can do right now is to avoid being picked up too. We can't help Wayne if we're taken."

Chen could see her clench and relax her hands in cycles as her knuckles grew stark white. Her chest rose and fell with increasing rate and force. Her voice could barely be heard through her gritted teeth: "What have we done, Chen?"

"I don't know, but we have to get out of here. I promise we'll talk about a plan later, but we can't stay here."

Chen watched as Morgan brought her breath under control. He could see her eyes mist over. She wiped them with her hand and met Chen's gaze, conviction smoldering in her eyes.

"No. We are not leaving without anything, Chen. Those boxes got my friend arrested or worse. It can't be for nothing. It just can't. Now, you can either help me or you can step aside. I'm finding out what's in those papers."

"Morgan, please, we don't have time for this. You don't know these guys like I do. Every second we spend goes to us becoming another ghost story."

"Then you better leave, Chen. Sounds like you don't have the time to lecture me."

Chen gripped his nose between his fingers in frustration. "All right. I don't know what I'm looking for, so I'll keep watch. You go ahead and get what you can from those boxes. Thirty seconds and we are out of here."

Morgan nodded in agreement and made her way toward the piles of boxes and papers. Chen's eyes darted between Morgan and the elevator behind him. Every time he looked away, he could hear the mechanism of the lift operating, only to turn back and see the elevator doors undisturbed. He felt his heart quicken in his chest as Morgan tossed through box after box, shoving a few papers in her jacket pocket. Every noise she made filled his ears to bursting. Morgan seemed to move in slow motion. What was taking her so long?

Finally, she turned to signal Chen to a rear exit stairway sign at the end of the hall. She seemed strangely calm. Chen could feel his heart burst out of his chest. His fogged sleep quickly gave way to vigilant stress. The unfounded Fuel-driven paranoia blended roughly into harsh reality. He followed, feeling the heaviness of the carpet underneath him as he felt the weight of more eyes than ever before.

They took the long stairway in silence as it wound down and down. There were no distractions as they passed each floor. Chen felt the urge to rush but was quickly dissuaded by the quiet resignation of Morgan's echoing footsteps. Her shoulders slumped in resignation as reality set in.

He remembered those early days on the force. They'd started in the mobility program together. She'd always had fewer hangups than him. She stayed the same late hours, worked the graveyard cases with unnatural dedication. Chen didn't have the same stamina, and she was the first to spot it when Chen started abusing Fuel. Morgan had been there for him, probably helped him keep the job. So he quieted each impulse to run, following diligently behind her. The heaviness left their steps as they arrived on the ground floor, the setting sun following them, casting long, dark shadows. Hours seemed to pass in a guilty purgatory.

Morgan turned to sit on the last step. "Okay, we should be good here. No one ever takes the stairs, and no cameras either."

She sat down on the bottom step and let her shoulders hang low. Her legs extended out, almost uncomfortably straight.

"Wayne and I used to sneak coffees and talk about our harebrained theories here all the time. He'd tell me about some new idea he'd gotten working on a professor's project. Most of them were ridiculous. I'd talk to him about what I planned to do after graduation. His ideas were so pie in the sky. A dreamer's ideas. It gave him supernatural energy. I made sure his body didn't fall apart, but he helped my mind run with ideas of its own. I just knew that wherever he went, the Depths would be lucky to have one of their own on High championing the cause. I can't believe that he…"

She reached to take out some papers from her jacket pocket. Her knuckles were white from gripping so hard. She turned it over several times in her hands before handing it to Chen. It was damp with her sweat.

"This was at the top of the pile. It was probably what Wayne was looking into most recently on our behalf. It'll take me a minute to digest it all, but here was the title sheet on top. I'm not sure what it all means, but if it's important enough to call in these 'Shock Units,' as you call them, then we have to look into it. For his sake."

Chen took a snapshot with his phone. Large, block text emboldened the middle of the page: *Project Persephone*. He caught a glimpse of the rest. Every other word was redacted with black marker. Whatever this was, Morgan was right. If it was important enough to pick Wayne up just for looking, then it was the best lead they had. How this connected to Vandley, that was still an open question.

"Chen, what the fuck is going on? Is this just a case? I see dozens of dead bodies a day, but this has got me freaked like nothing else."

He took a seat next to Morgan and put his hands on his knees. He was spent.

"I wish I fucking knew, Morgan. None of this feels right. We've been off bloc for too long. I'm doubting we even were on bloc in the first place."

"Off bloc? We lost the whole damn surface, Chen. What are we going to do? What's gonna happen to Wayne? We can't let him get caught up for a favor to us; it's not right."

"I know, Morgan. Things have gone way farther than they should've. If the Shock Unit's involved, this is political. Someone on High with a lot of pull made this happen, and we need to find out why. We need to bring Chief Vic on this."

"Yeah, fucking bang-up job she's done so far. Everything we've discovered seems to put us in more danger."

Morgan glanced toward the setting sun, the light causing her to squint as it slowly hid behind the horizon. The buzz of the Boiler intensified as the natural warmth faded from the room. They both got up without a word and headed toward the shuttle stop.

As the darkness of the Depths enveloped them, Chen leaned over on the window, trying to stay awake and alert. His breathing fogged the glass, obscuring his vision of the neighborhoods they passed. Morgan's eyes continued to dart about, but she quickly lost steam as the shuttle wound around the central tunnel. He always had trouble connecting to the Depths as a surface trans-plant, but this was different. Everything around him felt alien. He reached out to brush his breath from the glass, but it just left un-sightly streaks that blocked his field of view. He could hardly see the stops as they passed, much less anyone that could be looking in. As they got halfway to the station, both their phones buzzed with messages. One from Ellen:

We have a lead. Piotr traced a call to a tower in the Pit. Meet me there in 1 hour.

Another from Piotr on the secure line shortly after:

I'll meet you at the Pit in 30min. Be ready.

Chen and Morgan exchanged tense glances. They switched to a separate shuttle crowded with recyclers going home after a long shift. Chen had not visited that deep in Depths since his early days in Low Crimes. The most desperate recyclers ended there each cycle. Often it was full of materials deemed unsalvageable, though that didn't mean much to the truly needy. The shuttle had a wretched stench of Boiler fuel, old food scraps, and rusted metal. Chen sent a quick message to Vic for a meeting in a few hours and tried to lean near the window among the crowd. There was no reply. Chen stood straight, unable to relax as the shuttle grew bumpier and bumpier with each passing minute. Off bloc indeed.

8

They disembarked the train nearly forty-five minutes later with the tired masses. The ride had taken them longer than expected, but Chen thought it paid to be careful rather than punctual. It'd been years since Chen had been in the Pits, and from the look on Morgan's face it was probably her first time. The darkness alone here was suffocating, let alone the fumes of Fuel and industry in the air. Here was where materials came from all over the surface and Depths for recycling, often more aspirational than functional. Things with the faintest hope for reuse came by the ton day after day, and many more with no hope at all. The result was that the Pits was the largest informal trash heap in the Depths. The hopelessness was reflected on the faces around them, dirty and resigned. As they exited the shuttle station, more fresh recyclers impatiently took their places. There wasn't a hint of surface, no matter how high you look. Heat emanated sporadically from where the Boilers were being fed.

Morgan tried poorly to disguise her unease as they wound their way through crowded shanties. The buildings around them were precariously made. Extensions were built without license or consideration. Building levels were unplanned and constructed of raw, unapproved materials. Suspicious eyes regarded them with jealousy. Even Chen's modest clothing looked brand-new compared with what he saw. Morgan clutched her jacket tight and tried to avoid eye contact. Chen did the same. The sound of machinery was deafening.

"It's not much longer, Morgan, The smell is...unique to the area. They use a lot of strong chemicals to strip disposed materials, hoping to find some use for them."

Morgan scrunched her face. "Oh, you mean nowhere else smells like shit? Jesus, Chen how did you ever do a detail down here? The bodies I got were bad enough; I didn't realize what the source actually smelled like."

"Believe it or not, the Fuel helps. Destroys your sense of smell quickly while keeping you awake for the long shifts. People down here usually find it utilitarian. Until it isn't."

Morgan took a second to mull this over. "You too?"

"I haven't had to smell anything like this in a long time. I was lucky. I didn't need it long enough, so my sense of smell came back, though I suspect not all the way. Food hasn't tasted the same in years, and I've got a stuffy nose that I just can't shake. The people down here that use it habitually probably haven't tasted anything in years. We're coming up on the place now. It's that slum farther down, next to that recycling plant."

Chen pointed down several blocks to an irregularly designed housing complex. Several concrete towers jutted into the black sky at random intervals. Many of the smaller towers were unnaturally extended with shanties of recycled metal rooms balanced on support beams made of wood, metal, and densely packed cardboard. It looked as if it could fall at any second. A few of the windows blinked slowly with light. Fuel was rare here and often used in spurts when you couldn't feel your way around the dark. The houses were close enough to the Boilers that heat wasn't as much a necessity, but power for anything beyond the basics was nearly impossible to come by. It seemed almost worse than Chen remembered. At least back in his days on patrol he'd see some people with basic recycled devices or lights in their homes. It was hard to believe there was a place more desperate than he could recall. They headed toward a dark corner of the complex where Piotr waved them over nervously, crouched in a corner. He looked incredibly conspicuous, hunching like you would in an old spy movie.

"Where the *fuck* you guys been? I've been waiting here forever! We don't have much time before Ellen gets here, and we got a metric fuck-ton to talk about."

Morgan replied in a tense whisper. "With the *shit* that's happened today, you should be surprised I'm here at all and not in some pine box. Now what the *hell* is so important that we're talking before Ellen gets here?"

Piotr sighed in frustration. "Listen, we're all *fucked*. Earlier this morning I saw those damn Shock pricks taking Chief Vic out of her office in cuffs. She didn't even say a goddamn word as they took her to who the fuck knows where. They marched around like they owned the goddamn place, taking boxes, giving orders, refusing to say fucking *anything*. They had a wild fucking look in their eyes, man, so I just got the fuck outta there. And now Ellen wants us to meet in this shithole? You tell me I'm overreacting, Morgan."

Morgan's face twisted into open anguish. "*What?* The Shock Unit was there too? What the fuck is going on? First my friend Wayne and now Chief Vic? On High didn't even want this case in the first place, and now they're blowing this case up from the inside?"

"You mean this isn't the first time you guys have seen these Fuel jockeys? They're fucking all over the place, man. I've been looking over my shoulder the whole trip down here. I'm twitching every time the goddamn wind blows on my face. How long have they been on our asses?"

Chen tried to clear his mind as his thoughts came in fits and starts. It sounded like they had made a precision assault, coordinated to take out the investigation team. It was a miracle that they got away at all. But Piotr was right, why shut down the investigation now? And why take up Chief Vic when she was the one keeping in contact with on High to keep the case going?

"Guys, *guys,* I know we're all scared, but we gotta compare notes here. Piotr, did you see Ellen get picked up? Where has she been? How do we know if it was actually Ellen that messaged us?"

Piotr took a deep, ragged breath. "I don't fucking know. She's a monolith. I haven't seen her all day, but if she doesn't show up in the next few minutes, then we're well and truly up shit creek. They picked up a lot of people man, a lot of people..."

Chen assessed their surroundings. They were in a central plaza, in a small alcove off the main entrance to the goliath structure. A metal fence in disrepair couldn't keep a rat out, much less unwanted guests. They were enclosed on all three sides with a concerning number of windows looking down on them. He looked up into the endless towers. Besides a rare flickering light, he saw no other signs of activity, but in darkness this total it was impossible to be sure. His misplaced paranoia had now become very real. If this was a trap, there wasn't much they could do about it now.

As he scanned the street, he saw Ellen approaching, striding toward them with purpose. As she got closer, she met each of their gazes with confidence.

Piotr noticed her, and as she neared, he whispered, "Ellen, we deserve some *fucking answers.* I saw what happened to Chief Vic, and if I stayed, I'm certain I'd be with those High freaks too. What are we doing here?"

Ellen nodded in affirmation. "Well, it's fucking good to see you too, Piotr. All of you. It's bad. I was lucky enough to be monitoring Wayne as he got picked up. Otherwise, I wouldn't have the pleasure of being jawed off by you, Piotr. Let me tell you what we're here for. We're here to solve this fucking case."

Ellen smirked as her words hung in the air. Morgan, Piotr, and Chen looked at each other in confusion.

Morgan interjected. "The *case*? Why the fuck do I care about the case? My friend is being taken god knows where for god knows what, just for *helping* us! He was just trying to *help* us, Ellen! And now..." Morgan put her head in her hands. Her body shook as she tried to keep her sobs in check.

Piotr's voice rose beyond a whisper. "I'm not taking another fucking step until we get some answers! What the fuck does this case have anything to do with this? This isn't what I signed up for, Ellen."

Chen could feel his pulse quickening. "Look, Ellen, all due respect, this clearly is more than just a case. If I thought we could get on the radar of the Shock Unit just for working a case, I would've called up my bloc in a second and been back in the fucking fields. Now what are we *doing* here?"

Ellen furrowed her brow in frustration. "I hear you fucking guys, all right? We've been off bloc since the start. Vic gave us a shade of credibility, but we're beyond anything I could've predicted now. This case is our only way forward without being placed in a room without even a Boiler to light our way. You follow me for the next ten minutes, and if you're out, you're out. But you leave now, I wouldn't exactly bet on your chances of seeing the Depths again, much less the surface. So, I'd really think about following me if I were you."

Chen, Morgan, and Piotr glanced at each other. A tense silence filled the air for what felt like hours. Morgan broke the silence first:

"Ten minutes, Ellen. If I don't think this gets Wayne out of this, I'm out."

Ellen nodded and motioned toward the entrance of the building. A dilapidated sign hung above the building: *Pit Fall*. The double doors were unlocked and hung at unnatural angles. The foyer had clearly been abandoned for a long while. There was hardly any refuse that hadn't already been picked over by the most desperate of recyclers. Only scraps beyond repair remained. Ellen gestured at stairs at the end of a dark, unlit hallway. Every now and then a dark figure drifted between empty rooms, avoiding eye contact with them. The smell of Fuel made the air thick and difficult to breathe. There was no obvious security Chen could see. They turned to take the stairs five floors up, the steps made of uneven concrete. Their footsteps reverberated unnaturally through the empty halls and rooms, setting Chen on edge. The stench only thickened as they made their way farther up.

The four of them exited at the top floor. A steady stream of light was visible under the doors of the room in the hall. The hallway was well lit on both sides in stark comparison to the levels they passed on the way up. Two figures were placed near the stairwells on either side. On first glance they appeared as disheveled as anyone else on the street, but Chen noticed them making furtive eye contact as they stepped onto the landing. It was brief but purposeful. Ellen gestured toward a large door in the center of the hall. As they walked, Chen noticed the floor underneath was much better kept than he'd expected. This place had been cared for, at least minimally so. She rapped on the door, and a voice responded.

"Are you here to return the coat you borrowed?"

"Yes, but I may need it again to weather the storm."

9

The door opened with a wave of heat. A thin face greeted them with a grim expression. Their surprise was not mirrored as they entered. It appeared like any single-room apartment save for the dozens of people crammed into it. Small desks with screens were arranged along the walls. Exhausted people manned each computer, taking periodic breaks to breathe from drenched handkerchiefs. The stench of Fuel hung in the air, almost enough to ignite. The room was well cared for. No used food containers, dirty laundry; it would put even Chen's apartment to shame. There was a large mural covering the far wall bearing the mark of Polar Vortex: a turbulent black hurricane on a green background with a red eye gazing back. They'd been there a while, and they were well organized. As they entered, no one looked up at the strangers. Well-disciplined, too. If Chen had to guess, they'd been there a year, maybe more.

The thin man saluted at Ellen and led them through a broken wall to a connected room. In any other situation it would've seemed comical. A ridiculous cult with a pseudo militaristic style. Used to be a dime a dozen. Used to be. Chen could see a series of shattered walls through to a window facing the bleak outdoors. They'd clearly taken over the whole floor and expanded methodically. Very little light penetrated the space, though it'd be difficult to tell the difference given the eerie glow from the screens illuminating every corner. Polar Vortex posters, graffiti, and pictures littered the few unbroken walls that used to be rundown apartments. It was a series of greatest hits; protestors at marches, "professors" that conned their way into lectures, and a centrally localized photo of the man himself, Elder Moison.

Ellen motioned over to a set of chairs next to a line of desks. They exchanged looks of anger and exhaustion. Questions swirled in Chen's mind, too many to vocalize for now. Chen, Morgan, and Piotr took seats next to some busy-looking people in threadbare clothes. They looked up briefly with bloodshot eyes and quickly turned back to their work. Ellen remained standing as she turned to them. She was smiling like she was about to reveal an inside joke.

"Welcome to our new base of operations."

A heavy silence hung in the air as Piotr leaned forward. "What the *fuck* is going on here? I've never seen this much tech in all my life, and I've upcycled this kind of shit for years. What are you nutjobs doing with it? And what the fuck are we doing here?"

Morgan jolted up straight with impatience. "*Base*? Base for what? Ellen, you better give me a straight fucking answer here, or I am out that fucking door. I don't care if I have to find Wayne myself."

Chen let his mind run. The investigation. The Shock Unit. Chief Vic. They'd been able to traverse from the university to deep in the Depths. Sure, surveillance only got spottier the deeper you got, but up on surface? That was their home turf. And the *favors*. They'd taken for granted that Chief Vic was plugged into on High, but now? She wasn't in anyone's good graces if she got picked up the same as Wayne. And now *Ellen*. Clearly in charge here. Maybe more than they realized. It just didn't make... Chen cupped his forehead in his hands as the realization dawned on him.

"If we leave, we're fucked, aren't we, Ellen? We have to stay."

Ellen turned with a condescending smile. "Gold star for you, Chen."

Piotr and Morgan turned to Chen. He couldn't tell if they were more upset or exasperated. He couldn't blame them.

"What the fuck do you *mean* we can't leave? I'll walk out that goddamn room right now without a good explanation, and I dare any of these whack jobs to stop me. I don't care if all of you stay," Piotr lashed out.

Morgan's face mimicked Piotr's. "Yeah, Chen, what the fuck are you on? You're really gonna stay here and find out what these people have planned? And you, Ellen? We all came up together, what the fuck is all this about? We deserve an explanation!"

Morgan and Piotr were seconds from jumping out of their seats. Chen tried to stay seated and calm, but his own anxiety was running rampant. He clenched his fists and tried to take one breath at a time before responding. "Think about who these Shock jockeys picked up. Wayne, Vic, they nearly got you, Piotr, if you weren't so jumpy. Then the three of us ride the shuttle undisturbed all the way here? How is that possible? Even in the Depths, surveillance is good enough to pick us up, especially you, Piotr; you were in the line of fire."

Chen watched as Piotr and Morgan sat down, processing the information. Ellen watched him in amusement, like a proud teacher. Chen took a moment before continuing.

"All this started once we made some real headway in the Vandley case. They clearly wanted to shut this down quietly by giving it down Low, where his murder is a dime a dozen. Now they have to shut it down loud, and that means *us*. They should've known our faces from the get-go, especially if they raided Low Crimes for the chief. How the fuck did we all get here? Think about it. We didn't get here all on our own." Chen took a moment to look at Piotr and Morgan, giving them each a moment as their faces twisted in realization.

Ellen began a slow, mocking clap. "Chen, you're smarter than I gave you credit for. Those 'Shock jocks,' as you so lovingly called them, know no bounds. You go out there without the protection we so graciously offered you all, you won't last a single recycling shift before you're crammed in a concrete box to be forgotten. And trust me, we will forget about you."

Chen could feel his face twist in anger as he replied, "Fuck you, Ellen, and why the fuck are we even here? I know your type. You zealot freaks hold no loyalty but to yourselves and the cause. Why even bother shielding us from on High? All those 'connections' Chief Vic had? What do you even need us for? I thought seeing some cops get put away would give you nuts a rare reason to celebrate."

Chen could tell that one hit home as Ellen's mouth tightened in annoyance. These guys always hated being deemed a cult. It was an easy button to push. Hopefully, pushing her would reveal more than the ire they were bound to face. He didn't want to admit that he felt as betrayed as Morgan did. All these years, all the nights. Nothing to whoever Ellen really was.

"Well, Chen, like I said on the way in, I just want you all to do your *job*. We have the resources to give you three protection and access. The three of you have been working on our case from the start, and that's what I want you to do. That's what *we* want you to do." Ellen shot a sideways glance at Morgan, whose eyes could have burned a hole to the surface.

"The *investigation*? What does any of this have to do with a goddamn police investigation? You were never one of us in the first place, that much is clear."

"You're a little slower on the uptake than I expected, Morgan. Police investigation? You really think the Low police could devote a team to a single investigation? Much less one those on High would rather see dead in the water?"

"But Chief Vic's connections..."

"*I am* the connections! You think any on High *connections* would risk their position for a case nobody wants solved? It's been our money, our resources, *my way* all along!"

Piotr and Morgan both looked at Chen. If they were looking for comfort, they weren't going to get any. He felt resigned as his mind followed the logic of the last few days. It wasn't good.

Piotr sat back, "Those encrypted messages..."

"Yes! Everything! The meeting with Hightower, special dispensations to surface, all of it has been us. All those 'mistakes' that gave us the leads you needed to continue? *Us*."

Chen interjected, "Last time I checked, you freaks didn't have two creds to rub together, now you're funding whole investigations alone? Calling in favors on High for meetings? Not to mention—"

"One more *freaks* out of you and this conversation ends. For all of you, *are we clear*?"

All three of them flinched. Even for the Ellen they knew, the rage was uncharacteristic.

"Good. Now given your regressive...attitudes, you'll be on a strictly need-to-know basis. The comments Vandley made years ago put him on our radar early. His disdain for the very model he created attracted the leaders of Polar Vortex. Seems he came to the conclusion we knew all along. The Freeze is not natural. Despite how hard we've worked over the years to educate the public, they've yet to come to this basic fact. Vandley, though? He would've been impossible to ignore."

Chen could feel the connections forming. The receipts, Vandley's inability to operate alone, the discipline he'd seen on the way in. The focus. Vandley used his last moments just to slip him that envelope full of receipts. Even with all his faculties, he couldn't see a way out of their grasp.

"We've been his support for years now. You could call his lack of an audience and our mutual interests a perfect storm. And that's where all of you come in."

The confusion was clear on Morgan's face. "Vandley with Polar Vortex? How do you expect us to believe that?"

"I can't pretend to know the science, but he clearly saw something we've seen for decades now. We knew he was our best chance to prove it without a shadow of a doubt, so we started the work. For years we've supplied him with food, Fuel, and anonymity, just waiting for him to reveal the truth. All while the Depths thought of us as a joke. His death was almost the end to years of coordinated effort. We couldn't let that happen. Luckily, I knew of a few highly expendable intrepid investigators who are just oh so clever."

They glanced at each other. The last week had been the longest of their lives. The thought of extending that? Chen could feel the exhaustion creeping in.

"The Great Work must continue, even without Vandley. We know we're close, and Vandley's death only proves that. So close to the truth that everyone has chosen to ignore for the sake of *science*, private interest, and convenience. Now our goals have aligned. You want your freedom and your friend Wayne. We want the truth. What I want you to do remains the same, except now you really know the stakes."

Ellen extended her arm out in a fake team gesture. She seemed almost entertained. And why shouldn't she be? Chen couldn't see a way out of this without Polar Vortex, at least for now. Based on the exhausted looks on Piotr and Morgan, they had just gotten to the same conclusion.

Morgan whispered, "I'm sorry, Wayne, I didn't know what I was getting you into..."

"Point is, we're in this together as long as you're of use to us. I don't care whether you love science, believe in Vandley, or worship the almighty credit. You three won't survive the night without us. Think of it as an investment into all of our futures. The Depths deserves the truth. Now, I'm sure you three have a lot to talk about. Take the room. I'll be back in fifteen once you've all come to your senses."

Ellen pointed to several people in the corners of the room who wrangled the expressionless techies out. She followed right behind. They waited until the sounds of footsteps receded to look at one another. Chen pulled his seat out to face both Piotr and Morgan, their faces grim with anticipation.

"I don't like this, Chen. How can we trust these people? We've been doing their dirty work for weeks, and now they want us to keep risking our necks? They haven't told us the truth for a second, and now we're supposed to just believe everything they say? You heard Ellen, we're done for the second we do their dirty work. Fuck them." Piotr clasped his hands nervously, his knuckles whitening with tension.

"I agree with Piotr. What kind of deal is this? And look at how she talked about Vic, her *friend*. If she even has friends. A tool? What does that make us? She worked with us for years and she just turns off that switch like it was nothing!" Morgan's voice strained with stress. Her eyes darted toward where Ellen and the rest had disappeared. Piotr got up and started pacing the room with manic energy.

Chen took a moment to think. It'd been years since he'd had to deal with Polar Vortex, and by the looks of things, everything he and Everett had thought they knew was completely outdated. The photo of Elder Moison, centered among their greatest achievements. It felt like a memorial to a bygone era. They'd always been focused, but this level of dedication and infiltration while leaving a nonexistent footprint? No, this was different. Was Ellen in charge? She certainly was here, but who was the say this wasn't one of many cells distributed throughout the Depths and surface? And if that was true, between the Shock Unit and Polar Vortex, there wasn't anywhere safe to go. Leaving the Depths was out of the question; transport to any neighboring city would be impossible without resources and materials. Most cities outside of the Depths were worse off and weren't looking for more mouths to feed. Even if they could find a way out...

Stop. This wasn't the time to spiral. Ellen was right. For now, she had control. They had to play the game by her rules until an opening presented itself. They may not know who Ellen really was, but that didn't matter now. What that opening looked like was anyone's guess, but he had to stay in control for Piotr and Morgan.

"I don't trust them either, ever since I first got put on their detail years ago. But the facts don't have a lot to offer us. I know the Shock Unit, and if we walk out that door, we are going to get picked without a second thought, even this down Low. These guys have clearly been here for a while. With targets like us inside, we'd be halfway to surface by now in a windowless shuttle if Ellen was lying. Or whoever the hell she really is."

Piotr stopped in his tracks and responded, "So we're fucked then, is that what we're saying? We work with these assholes and hope that they don't just shit us out afterwards?"

"No, that's not what I'm saying. The fact that we're here means something. They got no love for us; why not just throw us to the wind? Protecting us has a cost and probably a high one. And if we did leave, I doubt the Shock Unit would take any of our words seriously if we got caught up and clearly—"

He gestured around the room to dozens of screens.

"—they've been busy for a long while. If I had to guess, they've had their fingers in everything we've done, and who knows how far this goes? Even if we were lucky enough to last a week out there, we couldn't go anywhere. On High, it's the Shockies, down Low, it's them. And given how embedded they are, we'd just come off sounding crazier than them to anyone we talk to. Hell, even Everett thought they'd slunk off into the darkness, and *he* is the precinct's expert on Polar Vortex."

Morgan and Piotr fell silent, their eyes closed, deep in thought. Chen knew they had to weigh their options, but what options were there? Any friends they had were through a maze of shuttle stops and cameras. Given how long they'd already been in the Pits without being raided, Polar Vortex likely owned the place. Morgan spoke first.

"Do you think they have the juice to help with Wayne? I mean, if what you're saying is right, they've been running everything since the start. If we do what they want, could they find him and set him free?"

"I don't know. All I know is that I wouldn't count on anything. We're at the end of a very short rope, and I think it's because it's our necks they wanna risk, not theirs."

Piotr spoke next. "I don't like it. I mean, what stops them from just dumping us like yesterday's tech when all's said and done?"

"Nothing. But I'll take that over being tossed out now. That gives us time to work something out. Time that only these nuts can give us. You heard Ellen, they're close to something. Something big. Based on their setup, it's been worth everything to them for years now. I mean how else could they get a tech setup this extensive and support Vandley to that extent? If they think we're close, they're not likely to throw us out on some whim. We're on a leash, but that doesn't mean we can't pull a little."

Piotr made one last circle around the room before collapsing into his chair. The metal legs scraped against the wood floor, causing Morgan to flinch and look around the room nervously.

"*Fuck.* Goddammit, Chen, you're lucky you're a detective and not a salesman." Piotr's mouth twisted into a frown. "You better have a fucking plan soon. I'm not going along with this much longer."

Morgan let out a strained breath. "That plan better include Wayne. I can't be a part of any plan that gets us out of this without him."

"*Wayne?* What the fuck, Morgan, we have our own lives to worry about. How are you supposed to help *anyone* from a ten-by-ten concrete box?"

Chen cleared his throat to interrupt. "Look, I'm not in a place to make promises. Let's start with playing along and wait for our moment. We're not even sure that's coming along yet so one step at a time, and we'll find a way to get Wayne out of this. They need us as long as we make progress, so let's focus on that for now. As soon as I see an opportunity, I will let you both know, okay?"

After a long silence, Piotr and Morgan nodded. Chen called Ellen back into the room. The smug smile still decorated her face.

"Well, you three come to some kind of understanding, or am I tossing you all out?"

Chen tried not to let the anger show on his face. "We're not stupid, Ellen. We can all see you're not hurting for resources or leads. It must've taken years to build this up without attention, even down here. You let the whole Depths still think Polar Vortex is a joke, and I'm inclined to agree. You're too scared to stick your own necks out there."

Ellen's smirk twisted into a scowl. "The cheek on you, Chen. I always did like you, but you're right. We're fucking everywhere. In the precinct, at Geraldson, in your shithole apartment, for Christ's sake. We're close. So close that if we wanted to do this loud, we could. But I figured you'd be a little more grateful for our job offer than this. Or am I wrong?"

Chen shifted in his seat and looked to Morgan and Piotr. They nodded without a word.

"No, you're not. But if the payoff is worth all the risk, we need to know. Where will we be after this? And what will happen to Wayne? He didn't deserve to get caught up in any of this. The way you treated him, what're the odds we'll be in the wind too once this is all over?"

"When this is all over, we'll have the juice to cover you three forever and your little friend. We'll get there one way or another. You're just gonna have to trust me on that. Now, what do you say?"

Morgan spoke up. "Trust you? We don't even know who *you* are. All those years we spent together in the program and cases closed. What, that was a fucking *tryout*?"

"If we fooled a bunch of detectives, who else do you think we fooled? We've got the reach you need, and I don't see the three of you having any other choice *but* to trust me. Or at least listen to what I say."

Chen took one more look around at Morgan and Piotr. If there was another way out, he didn't see it. They both nodded reluctantly as Chen turned to Ellen.

"All right, Ellen, we'll play it your way."

Ellen smiled as she turned around and brought their attention to several large boxes sitting in the corner of the room. Stacks of papers filled each to the brim, many spilling onto the floor.

"Well, now that we're outta each other's way, why don't we start with the shit we found in Vandley's place before you got there, Chen? I'll have them bring in the rest."

Ellen turned to walk into the other room. She looked back at the three of them before crossing the threshold with a half-smile.

"By the way, since we're working together, you can call me Anna."

10

They'd been sorting through pages for days. Papers littered the room, piles starting as well-defined categories, but after nearly seventy-two hours, the only clear differentiation was a pile of food receipts, a stack that was mostly words, and a mountain that was primarily calculations. Even for Morgan, one of the most educated members of Lower Crimes, the material was beyond their comprehension. Morgan and Chen had decided to keep "Project Persephone" to themselves, but even with that inside information, making any headway was impossible. They were frustrated, and "Anna" could sense it.

Every time Chen looked at her, Ellen's commanding face morphed into Anna's cold and calculating one. It was almost a relief. He'd always known there was something lurking beneath the surface. He never pushed; everyone deserved a secret. But Anna? There was something familiar about that name. If he could just get some sleep, maybe he could place it.

Piotr peeked his head from his eighth pile of the day, exasperated. "I'm not a goddamn scientist. If Morgan can't even make sense of this, how can I? This is bullshit."

Piotr swiped at his stack, knocking it over. Morgan had to jump out of the way as stacks of papers cascaded into where she had been sitting moments before. She tried to pick up her stack before sitting back down in resignation.

She heaved a sigh. "Jesus, Piotr, you know how long it took me to make that stack? But you're right. I don't know what 'Anna' thinks any of us can do. I'm a forensic analyst. Just because I went to Geraldson doesn't mean I absorbed all this weather gibberish. We need more references, more resources."

Chen looked up at Anna, who'd been manning the Fuelers for the past several days and processing their requests. She was clearly quarterbacking the operation. When she said jump, no one even had to ask how high.

"Anna, we need more transparency here. We can't just keep bringing questions to you every time we don't understand something. I think the answer to who killed Vandley is related to what's in these papers too, but this is going nowhere. Give us access to the Polar Vortex databases or at least let us out to really investigate."

"And give you access to years' worth of back-end government data? You think I'm stupid, Chen? What's to stop you three from running off with some trove of data, or even deleting it all? I'm not putting years of stealth hacks into your hands."

"Listen, it's not like we didn't try here. You've watched us shuffle papers around for three days now, and what have we got? Neat little stacks of Fuel-encrusted genius? We're not solving the case like this, Ellen. These guys need references, and I need to get out there and do what I do best. I'm no keyboard warrior, and you know it. You're all so close now; this isn't the time to hamstring us."

Anna leaned back in her chair for a few moments. "All right, I get what you're saying, but you're going to have a babysitter. You're crazier than Vandley if you think I'll let you three run buckwild without a chaperone. Morgan, Piotr, you two get supervised access to our backdoor systems. You'll have monitors from our people with each keystroke. Chen, what did you have in mind?"

Chen watched as the techs started rearranging two terminals along the far wall. Within seconds they had moved multiple monitors and chairs where the chaperones would go. Anna didn't look back for a moment.

"I think Hightower knows more than she's letting on. She's afraid, and not just for her career. Her messages were desperate, and if Vandley reached out to her, it was because he was desperate too. Now that we're off bloc on this one, I can hit her hard. She's the head of the Weather Service, after all. Hard to believe something Vandley was on to was beyond her watch, considering how close they were."

Anna leaned back in her chair and covered her hand with her mouth. She spun her chair leisurely, making relaxed eye contact with Chen as she completed each rotation.

"I see... I have always wanted to see that hardboiled flatfoot side of you, Chen, ever since you started with us. And you have a point. Those on-Highs are control freaks. I've always wanted to watch one of them sweat in real time."

"Then we're agreed. I assume that first meeting was actually you and not Vic?"

Anna smiled. "I always did like you, Chen. I always thought you got less credit than you deserved. I doubt the Weather Service will be a safe place for you to meet, so we'll bring her closer to home. Something tells me she'll be more amenable once we force her onto our turf to meet. A lot harder to lie outside of her ivory tower."

Chen tried to hide his surprise as he nodded in agreement. If they could get to someone like Hightower to come down into the Depths, they either were in deep or had something on Hightower herself. It was difficult to imagine Hightower working with Polar Vortex directly, but given the last few days, anything seemed possible. Pulling anything off without tipping Everett was a miracle in itself.

"When do you think I can talk to Hightower again?"

"I'll have it arranged in the next day or two. I'll have her meet you later in the day in the Lower City. Can't have her sniffing too close to the Pits. We'll be watching with great interest, Chen. Don't disappoint us."

Without a word, one of the tech chaperones crossed the room and handed Anna a phone. She typed a message quickly and handed the phone back to the chaperone, who returned back to their corner of the room, motionless.

"Before I go in there half-cocked, do you have messages from Vandley's side of things? I assume since Polar Vortex was bankrolling this endeavor, you'd have access to any phones he was using?"

"You'll have it. Remember, I expect a daily update after your meeting, or I'll make sure you're in a box. Our reach is High, and you breathe a word of this to anyone, your freedom is the last thing you'll have to worry about. And what a waste that would be, don't you think?"

Chen recognized the look in her eyes. It reminded him of all the times she'd had been in lockstep with down-Low leadership when he was on the beat. The times she had volunteered to take the lead on case after case. How often Vic agreed with her. At the time, he was more than happy to take a backseat and focus on the facts. Now? He shuddered at the thought of how much of what he was doing was at the behest of Polar Vortex all along.

11

Chen drew his coat around him as he left Pit Fall. He dug around in his pockets, double-checking the materials he had brought with him for his meeting with Hightower: crystalline chunks, research notes, printouts of Hightower's last messages to Vandley, now with his responses thanks to Polar Vortex's sponsored phone. His mind was spinning with the events of the last few days. The eyes he felt on him since the investigation started were all too real now, and it would be foolish to think that Anna hadn't placed a tail on him. She practically guaranteed it. Whoever she sent, they were good. He couldn't clock anyone as he made his way to the shuttle station, surrounded by faces not yet smudged with a day's work. He grabbed a seat with his back against the wall, crammed in between two older recyclers. No one seemed to glance in his direction. Chen hoped he wasn't losing his touch. He sank into the hard seat and into the collar of his coat. The weight of the Depths above made his breaths feel unnaturally slow. He tried not to fall asleep to the jerking motions of the tram.

After a winding ride with several transfers, he left the shuttle into a neighborhood known as the Junction, the upcyclers' district. Neon lights surrounded the platform and all along the narrow streets in front of him. Advertisements for upcycled tech blared their wares. There was a discordant hum of electricity as he exited the platform and onto the main street. Small homes and shops intermingled under a haphazard arrangement of lights and signs mangled together with ill-fitting parts. It was almost impossible to tell where a house ended and a shop began. Feet scraped against walkways made of a mix of stone and metal. Customers crisscrossed between stores, bargaining for parts and repairs. As he looked up, Chen could see staggered cargo shuttles descending from above at dangerous angles from the central shaft, each loaded to the brim with a mishmash of electronics in various states of disrepair. Like parasites, the shuttles dashed between the central Freight track and along ramshackle tracks of their own leading to ports where crowds of upcyclers would gather and bid on the latest available surface refuse. Then, like blood in an artery, material flowed from the ports to the Junction, ready to be assembled or sold. A cacophony of noise hummed from the storefronts and homes punctuated by the grinding of industrial cranes unloading material from the descending shuttles and loading onto decrepit shuttles headed farther down to the more desperate.

Chen never had a reason to come here. He'd always been on more violent details, and that kept him occupied in the Depths. Most crimes in the Junction were nonviolent, tech-related hackings or burglaries. The ones that were violent often had a lot of creds involved and got kicked up to the higher brass to deal with, way over his head. There was enough business to even justify a visit from on High if the crime was heinous enough. Or at least it used to be. Chen scanned the crowd and saw mostly Low Crime patrolling the crowd. He drew his collar around his face and tried to control his heartbeat.

The heat was unbearable here. The warmth from the poorly assembled electronics and the Boiler air coming from the Depths made it unseasonably hot year-round, worse during the Freeze. Even shedding most of his outer layers, Chen found himself sweating. He couldn't shake the feeling that his coat was brimming with static electricity. His hair stood on end, whether from electricity or paranoia was anyone's guess. He reached for his phone to check in with Anna and sent a message confirming his arrival after a few minutes of searching for a signal among the overloaded Junction network. He was unable to spot any tails in the crowd as he started toward the cafe where he was to meet Hightower. Chen confirmed the send before heading in the right direction.

He navigated streets claustrophobic with activity. Most people he passed were in open-air shops, fusing together tangles of metal and wires under the buzz of fluorescent lights. The smell of burning metal permeated the air. It was a wonder the place didn't burn down at any second. Small chicory stalls were arranged in any space between work areas, each with craftsmen milling around between projects. Even without the caffeine, it was more than what the Pit could afford.

He spotted their meeting point at the end of the street. It was a corner stall, comparably spacious to its surroundings with a rare fully enclosed interior. Stiff metal seats lined the interior. Windows looked out into the street. Chen could see a counter where the owner stood, taking orders and directing another busser. Patrons gathered at the counter and populated the booths and chairs. Chen tried not to draw attention to himself as he gauged the room. Just the single exit, but like many of the buildings here, the walls were thin plaster. Could be an easy exit. No one lingered at the entrance or at the edges of the street. No eyes fixed on his only point of ingress. Too many windows to try to flush out his tail. Too many ways to observe his meeting. *Joe's Junction* flickered above the door. The sign below had an unlit *Beans* portion with a glowing *Chicory* by its side. Chen hoped they didn't water it down too bad. He'd need his wits about him without having to stop by the bathroom too often.

He took a seat in a small booth along a corner wall, as planned. An uninterested man came to take his order: chicory, dense. He nursed his cup as he looked around. People filtered in and out; none made themselves notable. He checked the time on a wall clock; 5:50 blinked back at him in angry red numbers. His chicory was clearly thinned, but not too much to complain about. Ten more minutes.

* * *

Chen was on his third chicory of the evening. He'd had to order and nurse two more to stop the server from kicking him out. He resisted the urge to go to the bathroom. He couldn't afford the risk of missing Hightower and spooking her away. From Anna's messages, she'd gotten impatient but understood there was nothing to be done. He's certain her man had watched to confirm his story. As he nursed another sip, the door creaked open. Someone with an unusually large overcoat walked in with sunglasses on, collar pulled tight, and a small, new hat. He had to stop himself from getting up and shaking her hand. Hightower was more a bureaucrat than spy.

She looked around before locking eyes with Chen. Hightower crossed the stall and slid into the seat opposite him. She had sweat through her clothes, probably more than just the heat of the Junction. He struggled to stifle a laugh as she carefully removed her sunglasses. A look of recognition flashed in her eyes. Her voice was almost shrill with disbelief.

"Detective? *You're* with them too? Will there be no end to these requests? The madness? What more could you possibly want from me?"

Hightower's voice started to become sharp enough to draw attention as she started to grow more agitated. She struggled to maintain composure as blood rushed to her face. Chen motioned to the waiter from before and asked for water. She looked dehydrated from the trip, and the interruption gave her a chance to catch her breath. Hightower continued after the server walked away.

"I...I mean the gall to call me down here at a whim! Have I not done everything I've been asked to do? I...I...I—"

Chen tried to reach over to calm her, but she balked at the gesture. He could almost feel Anna's amusement as she got live updates on their meeting.

"Ms. Hightower, I can understand how seeing me again can be disconcerting. Trust me, the last few weeks have not gone the way I would've expected, but I need you to calm down. The people who have us under their thumb aren't the patient type. The longer we spend talking, the more antsy they're going to get."

Hightower took a long deep breath and took her sunglasses off. She looked twice as worn down as when Chen had last seen her. He could see her shoulders sag as she breathed out and tried to let some tension go. It was probably years since she'd been this down in the Depths and out of her protected zone on the surface.

"What do you people *want*?"

Chen let out a breath. "Ms. Hightower, I can assure you I am not one of these people, if my word means anything. What I said when we first met was the truth. I am here to solve the murder of your late friend Vandley and nothing more. It's our only way out of this."

Hightower looked at him in confusion. "How can you claim you're not one of them? You have me sitting here at a moment's notice for questioning! At my office, and here of all places! You know what kind of power that takes?"

As she spoke, Hightower tried to fix her sunglasses and put her hair in order. She appeared even more out of place the more she tried.

"You people have been relentless! Weeks at your beck and call. I've had enough. Your word is as good as the slop they serve here. Now please just get on with it so I can get back to my life."

Chen leaned back in his booth and pulled out the papers in his pocket. "I understand, Ms. Hightower, that it's hard to trust me. I wouldn't either in your position. I'll try to keep it brief. I have here the transcripts of the last texts you sent to Vandley. Today I have some of his responses that I'd like your thoughts on. I'd like to know the context of these messages."

Chen spread out a few pages in front of Hightower, drawing her attention to a few highlighted pages. As she turned through, her brow started to furrow in pain.

"Here are the messages from the last week Vandley was alive. I think you'll agree that there is a lot more for us to talk about."

You can either help me or get out of my way.

Teresa, it's too little too late. If you wanted to change my mind, you should've done it years ago.

I know everything now, Teresa. Years of my life just to uncover the truth. You kept that from me.

You can't change my mind. No one could change yours.

Remember how we started all this? We were going to change things for everyone for the better. I'd never have started this without you. It was our dream. I wish I never woke up from that.

I think something's happening tonight. I'm trusting you to have my back like you did before all this started. You're all I have left. Do the right thing, for all our sakes.

Chen could see Hightower tear up as she read the last messages. There was no way to hide the pain. It was real. She pushed the messages away as she wiped the tears from her eyes, trying to compose herself. Chen let several minutes pass before Hightower started speaking again.

"I'm well aware of what he said. Why are we dredging through this? Why make me relive the worst days of my life?"

"I'm sorry to make you do this, but this seemed uncharacteristic of him. Vandley did not seem the type to reach out for help unless he was desperate. You said so yourself. He'd always been confident in his own abilities and conclusions. He had the backing of Polar Vortex for years, so what was it he possibly needed you for? Someone whose hands were so tied it would be political suicide even to communicate with Vandley?"

Hightower squirmed in her booth. Chen could tell he had hit a nerve with that last assertion. She didn't protest the association with Polar Vortex. Seemed she knew more than she let on.

"He...thought he discovered something. Something big. He thought that with my position I could confirm some of his farther-reaching theories."

"What theories were those?"

Hightower paused for a moment and looked around. She had every reason to be paranoid, though more so at this line of questioning. "It was pretty extreme. I'm sorry to say that he was mistaken. Even if I could help him, I would compromise everything my agency does, given his questionable reputation. If I knew how bad a way he was in, I assure you, Detective, my reputation would've been the last thing on my mind."

Chen nodded slowly. Hightower did an impressive job dodging the main question. In any other circumstance, he would shake harder to see what fell out. But this theory was likely what Polar Vortex was sponsoring Vandley for. Just a little push to give Anna something, but not much more.

"I can see that he put you in a difficult position. However, he doesn't seem the type to make bold assumptions without strong data. Now I know this must be hard for you, but I believe what he was working on directly led to his death. Did he give you any indication about what he was working on?"

"No, he always had this way about him. Like he floated on the surface above you while you were in the Depths, trying to understand what the sun and sky were when all you had seen were the blazing Boilers and the light break from shuttles leaving the darkness. It was maddening, but you couldn't help but be impressed. So no, I can't say I knew what he was working on."

"I see. So then you'd have no idea what these may be?"

Chen took a small bag with crystals out of his pocket and slid it across the table. They gleamed with the flickering lights in the stalls. He made sure to leave out the bloodstained ones, but even then, he could see they got a rise out of her. She was uncomfortable and tried to hide it. Poorly. Chen could see Hightower's breath quicken as she started to speak.

"No, I have no idea what those are, why?"

"We found small pieces of these in the wound that killed Vandley. The blow appeared quick and painless. However, we have not yet been able to identify what this material is. Given his contact with you, I'm fairly certain that this has something to do with your agency. Or at least something you may know about. Now, the last time Vandley was this certain, he changed the face of our world. You were a big part of that. It's hard to imagine he wouldn't want to involve you in some way or at least trust you with the knowledge he learned."

Hightower stiffened in response. "I can assure you, Detective, that anything involving the Weather Service runs directly through me. It's the only way to survive on High, especially for a woman of my position. My head's on the block for any decision we make."

"Then you would know about Project Persephone?"

Chen was on the right track. Her face turned white with shock. Her breathing became uneven, and any sense of composure left Hightower's face. She struggled to stammer out a response:

"That's–that's just a myth, I can assure you. If anyone referred you to Project Persephone, they were leading you on a wild goose chase. Our agency and Vandley were people of science. The last thing we would do is spend our time and resources chasing ghosts from the past. I'd think even the Polar Vortex would know better than that."

Hightower took a moment to compose herself and take a sip of chicory. Her breath evened out over the next few minutes. She frowned in distaste and put the cup down.

"Now, if you have any real questions for me, can we move on from this nonsense? As you can imagine, I've had quite a long day coming this far down, and I'd rather not waste it entertaining fantastic ideas."

Chen let the silence hang in the air as he considered his options. Hightower tried to hide her discomfort, but it was clear this line of questioning had her rattled. Rattled by what, specifically? Whatever Persephone was, she wasn't biting. Chen knew he was on the right track, but whatever it was, not even the death of a friend was enough to get it out of her. Pressure wasn't going to be enough alone. He needed another angle. Chen took out his device and started to bring up his messages.

"I know how hard it must be to trust me. It must be hard to trust anyone. I know I look just like another Polar Vortex nutcase here to pressure you into giving us the information we had wanted from Vandley, but I'm here because I'm in the same corner you're in. The last time we looked into these crystals and Project Persephone, our contact, Wayne Jefferson, got taken up by the Shock Unit. Now, if I don't close this case, I'm right behind him as soon as I leave this stall. What I see across from me is someone who wants to be out from under their thumb as much as I do."

Chen found himself feeling heated at that moment. He'd been more honest than initially planned. He felt the weight of days and nights lift off his shoulders as he leaned back in his chair, taking a deep breath. He missed days on his bloc now more than ever. Uncomplicated. It was about survival then. Not too different now in that way. Hightower's face relaxed. It seemed his outburst had earned some trust.

"I...I heard about what happened to Wayne. He's a good man. I collaborated with him on some project or another. When he was set on one idea, it was hard to get him to think of anything else. He reminded me of Vandley in that way. When I heard they took him, it was like another blow. You were involved in that?"

"Not just me. He was looking into a lead for us at the time. We weren't allowed to tell him what it was about, but he was so enthusiastic about it anyway. Next time we saw him...he was being led away by those Fuel junkies just for looking into Project Persephone. We got away with what we could, but we just ran into another nightmare. One we made without even realizing. Ever since that day, I've been scared. Scared that if I can't close this case, I and everyone else involved will be next. People I know and trust. Scared that if I do close this case, I'll have nothing left to keep us safe. Now I'm not gonna make you work with me like these people do, but it's our only way forward. And I'm *motivated*. Motivated to make these people pay, and I will find a way to do it, with or without you."

The silence hung in the air. Chen had finished his chicory and continued to fidget with the cup, bringing it to his lips, expecting liquid to be there. He hoped to hide his discomfort from her as she weighed her options. There wasn't much he could offer, and Chen doubted she was foolish enough to believe otherwise. But he'd gotten enough of the smoke and mirrors, and he was betting she felt the same. Hightower broke the silence first.

"I haven't felt safe for a long time now. I've been doing what others asked for so long, it's hard to see a way out. Tell me, if I help you, how can I know I'll be safe?"

"You won't. I'm not even sure I'll be safe tomorrow. But ask yourself, are you safe now?"

Hightower considered his point. There was uncertainty in her eyes. He'd recognized that look in himself every day now. He felt like a weight on a scale in someone else's mind, only able to move the slightest inch to avoid tipping over into an uncertain future. Hightower brought him out of his thoughts.

"I'll help you. But not here, not where they decide. We're treading dangerous ground here. People have been protecting these secrets for longer than you or I know, and they won't stop at you or me to keep it under wraps. They'll restructure the whole Depths if they have to. There'll be nowhere for us to hide."

Finally, progress. He just needed enough to feed Anna to keep her interested, but not so much he became redundant. Or worse, to make her impatient and throw caution to the wind.

"Thank you, Ms. Hightower. I don't know how we'll get out of this yet, but we will find it. I don't know about you, but I'm tired of running."

"Please, call me Teresa. If we're on a sinking ship together, we might as well drop the pretense."

"Okay, Teresa. Since you know the pressure we're under, I can't leave here with nothing. They'll expect some results from allowing me off the range. It doesn't have to be anything important. We need something important enough to deserve further investigation but not enough for them to act."

Teresa considered the proposition for a moment. She slid the coffee cup back and forth between her hands, leaving scratch marks in the recycled table.

"What do they know about Persephone?"

"Nothing yet. I thought it prudent to hold that information back. We were able to get the information before Wayne was taken up."

"Good, then for now give them that. Those crystals are connected to what Vandley was working on and Persephone, so I imagine that will satisfy them for now. The reference itself is so old it'll probably lead them to the university or Weather Service. Somewhere I can get ahead of them with enough of a heads-up. I doubt they even have the reach to go through the physical microfilms we have on surface without making some noise."

Chen mulled this over. Teresa had a good point. It was clear Anna and Polar Vortex had spent years of funding and effort on Vandley and his work. As much as Anna tried to present a strong front, Polar Vortex was on a precipice. They had the resources to find out the truth behind Persephone, but it would cost them everything they'd built. If Chen gave them Persephone, there was a good chance it was enough information to whet their curiosity without the confidence to activate their hidden resources. Chen doubted they'd be willing to risk all this energy until the truth was within their grasp.

"Then we have a plan. I'll report back on Persephone and its link to Vandley's murder. Given how much risk they've taken to recruit us rather than freeze us out, it'll be hard for Polar Vortex not to bite. I'll need some details so they know where to start looking. If what you're saying is right, I agree it'll be hard for them to get the information outright."

"Okay. I have a few ideas on leads to present that would force them to surface for what they need. At the least, it should buy us both time to plan our next steps. Given how closely the families guard Persephone, I doubt they have anyone in place to get it easily."

Chen nodded in agreement. He tried to resist scanning his surroundings for his tail.

"I'm certain our meeting is being monitored as we speak. Why don't we spend a little more time here before I have to report in, and I'll make sure Anna knows this is one step away from what they need."

Chen and Teresa spent another hour animating a conversation that was long over. At first, they swapped childhood stories, Teresa about growing up in the Pits, Chen on growing up with the sun. Why they had diverged from their destined paths. They passed the papers between them back and forth and tried to let their nerves dissipate. Teresa even surprised him by appearing emotional now and then. She was a quick study.

Chen looked up at the clock and wrapped it up. They made it look as good as it was going to get. Teresa left first for a surface-bound shuttle with Chen following suit sometime later, going back deep into the Depths. Still no sign of his sitter.

Chen made sure to send an update text to Anna as he boarded the shuttle for the Pits. He could see the lights of the Junction fade and the heat quickly melted away as it became nothing more than lights in the distance. The shuttle wound and wound as Chen tried to avoid bumping into the muddied passengers next to him. Try as he might, his coat became dirtier through contact. He tried to wipe the filth off his jacket but only succeeded in getting his own hands crusted with recycled scraps and electronic grease. He smudged his phone as he sent updates to Piotr and Morgan on their secure line. The spots made it harder to read the messages as he sent them and replied to their queries. They were nervous, and he couldn't blame them. Hardly a plan at all yet.

He thought about what he would say to Anna. Rehearsed it many times over. He never could predict her. She always felt assured of something, regardless of what happened with the cases that came through Low Crimes. Now he knew why. Nothing that they worked on together had ever really mattered. Nothing but this. Everything she did worked toward some higher purpose. Chen was almost jealous of that kind of certainty. Right now, he couldn't even be sure he'd be waking up to the dark overhead of the Depths or a concrete ceiling. He kept rehearsing, but it never felt right. A little too much information there, a little underselling there. Chen leaned back on the window. Piotr and Morgan had no good ideas either.

He wasn't faring much better. Chen tried to use the relative quiet of the ride to come up with a better idea. Any idea. Anything to get them out from under the thumb of...everyone. His skull tapped gently against the glass as the shuttle wound down along the track. Chen felt his brain rattle with desperation. Every path he set aside ended up with them either in a concrete box or worse. As his hands wandered toward his phone to check for messages, he brushed up against the photo of Elder Moison. He brought it out and studied it. How *had* Polar Vortex continued without their guiding light? He cleaned the grease off the photograph and tucked it into his breast pocket. He was interested in what Anna had to say about it. The question was how to bring it up without catching a bullet.

Chen looked up as the shuttle pulled in toward the Pits. The people around him had been gradually replaced by recyclers coming off their last long shift. His coat had bumped up against enough people that he blended in. As he walked through the Fuel-dense air, he repeated his information one more time. Didn't sound great. He walked up to the stoop of the Pits and looked up at the dark, dilapidated building in front of him. If there was anything picking had trained him for, it was preparing as best you could but getting fucked anyway.

12

"What the fuck is Project Persephone, Chen?"

Anna didn't try to hide her irritation as she went through the data. It'd been a few hours since he got back. She had Piotr and the other members working at a breakneck pace, sifting through the noise. It was almost refreshing to see her true face after working with her for so long. He could always tell there was something boiling beneath the surface. It probably didn't help that Chen had intentionally tossed some of his most pivotal notes into a Boiler on the way back after committing them to memory. They'd have to work a little harder to find the connections that Wayne had dug up through microfilm. Those copies were old enough to be physical only. To get any further, Polar Vortex would have to get a little more skin in the game.

"Whatever it is, it's on the right track for what you people want. It's clearly the key to Vandley's murder and whatever Polar Vortex was sponsoring him for. You expect Hightower to give up the goat so easily? It's obviously her last bargaining chip."

Anna stood up from her chair and walked across the room to where Chen was leaning against the wall. He could feel the heat of her breath on his face as she spoke.

"Don't get smart with me. Don't forget, we keep you from a concrete box. If I were you, I'd be happy to get any yard time at all."

She went back to her table at the center of the room and took a seat. Piotr and the other data miners continued to work furiously behind her at a bank of computer monitors. Morgan sat in the far corner of the room, looking through the minimal printouts that Polar Vortex was able to find. Morgan looked up at Chen now and then with concern. Chen gave her as reassuring a nod as he could muster before continuing.

"All the same, she gets the message. You're in control, but if you choke up on her, she's gonna act desperately and not always in the way you want. I'm not saying we give her all the space she needs, but a few days will make the difference. After all, you people have waited years, and now you wanna rush these last few days? When you're so close?"

Ellen sat back in her chair and started to relax. She eyed Chen suspiciously as she let out a terse reply. "She has three days, Chen. Three days or our people throw caution to the wind, and we won't need you then. And you know how I'd hate to see you go. Let her know the clock is ticking."

Chen swallowed and nodded. He made a point to bring his phone out and message Teresa about the timeline. It was less time than he would've liked but more than they probably could have hoped for. He turned to Morgan and Piotr as he waited for a reply.

"How's the search for Persephone?"

Piotr turned around from the glow of his computer. His thin face accentuated the bags under his eyes. Adversity was part of Chen's training, not Piotr or Morgan's.

"Fucking thin. We've got rare references here and there, but I have a feeling it's *old*. We've got the most connections through the archives of Geraldson University before they were even named after those industrial pricks. We're talking real early Freeze days. There's some real hilarious ideas in there for keeping humanity alive."

"Anything useful come up?"

"Like I said, most are either vague, single-word references or heavily redacted. They're throughout the on-High databases, but the epicenter is definitely at Geraldson. Based on the age and the packrats those government types are, I'm betting there's a stash of info that's been gathering dust for an age. It's definitely there, but getting to it is gonna be more than just hacking into it. "

Anna turned her attention to Piotr. The tech sitters sat up straighter to attention in reflex.

"What do you mean more than hacking?"

"The saying goes that physical access is total access. The backdoors we're using here are powerful, but if I can connect into the mainframe at Geraldson, then I'll be able to locate either the original directory or at least where the records are housed. That's not even a guarantee. If it's as old as I'm guessing, it may be hard copy only."

"Sounds like a lot of guesswork to me."

"Yeah, it fucking would be. I've been in the Depths all my life. I couldn't tell you worth a damn how they organize things up there. But the fact that we are finding references at all does mean it exists somewhere. And the fact that the university itself is probably as old as the information we're looking for, there's a high likelihood it's the next jumping-off point to find the real deal."

"Fucking English, Piotr. How high a chance are we talking?"

"What I'm *saying* is that somehow, if we connect into the mainframe of the university, there's *some* chance that they hold the keys to the kingdom. And if we're lucky, we'll know which door it unlocks."

Anna put her hand over her mouth as she considered Piotr's logic. As she turned around, the techs resumed their slouching positions and continued typing manically at their keyboards.

"That *is* thin. Real thin. We don't have people deep enough to access something that old and secure. What exactly do you need for this little pet project?"

"This is probably surface stuff, at least surface-adjacent. We can't do anything from down here. If you can get me access, I think we have a shot."

"Now that will be...problematic. We're pretty good at shielding you from the Shockies while you're all in the Depths, but on surface? That's another story. None of you can just gallivant from the shuttle stop, given that your little buddy Wayne was already picked up there. And I've grown attached to our little group."

Morgan flinched at Wayne's mention, trying to hide her hate. Piotr continued, getting more animated.

"That's the rub, I don't think you need to get us to surface. Big institutions like Geraldson often require expansive servers to store and process data. Tech like that gets hot. Anyone who's been to my neck of the woods knows that. When I worked at Junction, we didn't have a choice. We had no space and no control over the Boiler system. We spent half our time dealing with heat management and restarting our system whenever some other schmuck would set up too close to us. These richies have the creds to make that choice. While their main building is heated with a custom Boiler system, they're able to store their tech adjacent to that system, making it much easier to regulate. They're able to set up racks and racks of servers to their heart's content, and since it's removed from the Boiler mains, they can expand whenever they need the space. It's really something only a Junction kid could dream of—"

Piotr was getting livelier. There was a twinkle in his eye as the corners of his mouth turned up into a fiendish smile. Piotr had run this idea with Chen before this. It was a solid plan, but reining in his excitement was next to impossible.

"Jesus Christ, Piotr, get to the point before we have to give you a private room. What is it that you *need*?"

Piotr stopped short and cleared his throat. "Okay, okay. So what do these rich fucks do? You can't very well sully the beautiful landscape of the impressive facility. Besides, how would you expand if your building is restrained by pedestrian concerns? No, they put their database in a fucking hole next to their fancy campus. A hole where the temperature is just barely regulated so their tech doesn't seize up. There, they use the natural Freeze temps to keep everything running smoothly while also giving themselves infinite space."

Piotr rose from his desk and threw a sheet of paper in front of Anna, who leaned back in surprise. Piotr drew a crude rectangle labeled *Geraldson* and another halfway across the page labeled *Servers*. Piotr then shaded in the space underneath. Anna even let out a smile. His enthusiasm was contagious.

"There's a maintenance connection to the main building surrounded by transmission cables for easy access. There's a thin layer of dirt between where the Depths start and that maintenance tunnel ends. It's incredibly efficient and for our purposes leaves a concentrated point of access. For those with less than noble purposes."

Piotr drew a line between the two structures to illustrate his point and returned to his chair, catching his breath. Chen saw him smile wider than in all the years he'd come to know him. He had to admit, the plan was daring. There was clearly upside for Piotr living out some kind of Junction boy fantasy. Chen watched as the gears turned in Anna's face. He could feel his heart thumping. He hoped the plan itself was too extreme for Ellen to bite quickly. If she acted on this too fast, his and Teresa's timetable would get a whole lot tighter. Anna looked up to Piotr after several minutes of consideration.

"I'd love this idea more if it didn't involve so many moving parts and the fact that we are clearly making some kind of childhood dream come true for you."

Piotr let slide another impish grin. "I'd be lying if I said I wasn't stoked at the idea. I do think we could pull this off if you can get us up there safely, fantasies aside."

Anna got up from her chair and sat at the edge next to Piotr, letting a grin take over her face as well. "So, you're telling me you want the manpower and resources to get you close to surface, nearest where the Shockies are present, on the possibility that you can tap into a network for ancient data that might lead us to the next unknown step?"

Piotr rested his hands on the table. His legs drummed uncontrollably with excitement. "We're technically not even on the surface. We'd still be in the Depths, where I assume your reach is the strongest."

The room stood still for several minutes. Piotr's foot echoed through the silence, increasing in frequency.

"Would it help that you'd be making me the happiest I've been in a long time?"

Anna let out a strong laugh. Chen and Morgan visibly twitched. They weren't used to seeing her so animated, at least in a positive way. Her eyes moved between Piotr and Chen as she spoke next. Chen had a bad feeling rising in his stomach.

"I can't make any promises until we run the numbers, but I'm interested. We're near the finish line now, and I'm getting *antsy*. Will Teresa and Chen pull through? Will we pull off a heist worthy of film in the next few days first? I don't know, but as long as we get us where we need to go, I'm in!"

She punctuated her excitement with another laugh that shook the thin walls of the room. Chen felt it vibrate through his body. His heart skipped a beat as Anna continued.

"I *like* this, Piotr. We've kept all our efforts under wraps for so long, it's refreshing to get our hands dirty. We're gonna need blueprints, manpower, and a whole lot of luck. Chen, message Teresa, let her know that either she gets us the data we need or we'll get it without her. If she feels nervous now, remind her how ready I am to hang her out to dry."

Chen swallowed hard. He knew there was a chance that this plan of half measures could backfire, but never this hard. Piotr gave him a sideways glance as Anna continued to pace the length of the room, sending messages back and forth and rallying the people around her. A cacophony of typing filled the room as they began retrieving data around Geraldson University. The ridiculousness of the plan was meant to get her to stop and think. Instead, it had only excited her. Chen had a sinking feeling that this plan of Piotr's might actually work, and worse, if he was right, it would be inevitable that Polar Vortex would get what they needed without Teresa or Chen.

"I'll let her know, but we should keep the line open with her in case the information we get is incomplete. It's a little early to be popping corks, don't you think?"

"Don't be such a buzzkill, Chen. After all, you'll be on the heist too. I'd prefer this to blow up in your faces instead of mine."

Of course. Chen felt his face flush. Where the hell was Teresa? He tried to hide his distress as he got up to message Teresa. He sped out of the room, making sure to avoid eye contact with Anna. This time, she responded immediately.

That's insane, how am I meant to deliver such complete information in such a short time! I'd draw too much suspicion! And once I do, what exactly guarantees my safety? These people have only threatened me with ruin.

I'll find a way to get you to ground. Look, we have no choice now. You're going to have to get the microfilms loud. I'll find a way to keep us both safe, but I need something too. Can you get the microfilm to me?

I think so. Those maintenance tunnels are hardly monitored, and if I'm taking a risk as it is. I just need to know I'll be safe.

You will be. We have two days until they can get the pieces together, and we WILL have a plan by then. You'll have to do your best to trust me.

Chen could sense that Teresa knew more than she was letting on. He couldn't blame her. He still wasn't sure if Morgan or Piotr would approve of picking up another stray in their plan. He'd have to make a bet that the information she possessed would give them the edge they needed over Polar Vortex. Given the lengths that Teresa went to protect it and how far Polar Vortex went to get it, it wasn't hard to believe. These nuts were close to something big. That kind of juice could change the power dynamic in their favor. Or so he hoped.

There was a long pause between messages as Chen walked to a window and looked outside. Despite being hidden here in the Pits, he'd felt more exposed than ever before. He couldn't help but look to every corner of the claustrophobic streets below him and the infinite murkiness above. He felt suffocated by both, struggling to breathe, his knuckles whitening with tension. He closed his eyes but only felt the pressure accumulate on the back of his eyelids until he was forced to open them. He felt his phone buzz in his hand, stopping him short of crushing it to smithereens.

I suppose I have no choice.

✳ ✳ ✳

Chen dodged between Polar Vortex techs as they rushed around the room. Piotr had been quarterbacking over the last day, coordinating the data gathering around the Geraldson heist. Anna moved from room to room, communicating on phones handed to her by a couple of assistants that stayed in a ten-foot radius. Even Morgan was providing details of the building in her time there: exits, nighttime staffing, security. If Chen wasn't a hostage, he'd feel almost offended at how useless he was.

Teresa hadn't updated him since last night. He'd made some progress on the exit strategy, but he found himself ruminating rather than making progress. In his experience, it was best to take another look at it after an hour or two. There was another puzzle to turn over.

Chen watched Anna take a phone to an adjacent room while her assistants stayed behind. He followed after her, clutching the photo of Moison in his hand.

Anna gave him a sideways glance as he entered the room. Chen took a seat until she finished her conversation and took a seat next to him. She hadn't slept all night, but it only showed in the bags under her eyes. Excitement made her appear refreshed.

"I'm surprised you have time to follow me around, Chen. Don't you have a job to do?"

"I'm not much of a tech guy. I'm more boots on the ground. What's the plan there?"

"Ha, nice try, Chen. I'd hate for some unfortunate leak to happen and set our plans back; maybe give you and Hightower some breathing room to win this race."

"Can't blame a guy for trying."

"Actually, I can. The others at the precinct might not see it, but I do. I know you're smarter than you let on, Chen. Known since we started working together all those years ago. What's the deal. You worried about Hightower? You ready to risk Morgan and Piotr for some on High bureaucrat that ditched her closest friend the second it got inconvenient? Or you gonna stop beating around the bush and tell me why you're really here?"

Chen turned to look at Anna. She had an impatient look. He always knew the same about her. There was more under the surface. Even now, he'd bet Anna had only shown a fraction of her determination. Her conviction. Chen brought out Moison's booking photo that Everett had given him. He saw her face wince as he smoothed the wrinkles and held it out in front of her.

"Where did you get that from?"

"Everett. When we were still treating this like a legit case. I remember thinking how clear the Polar Vortex angle was after looking through Vandley's apartment. How he hid those receipts for me to find. And how quickly the lead dried up. Everett was convinced that y'all were gone. That there was no way Polar Vortex could coordinate an effort so quiet. Certainly not without this man."

Anna reached to take the photo from Chen. Her eyes narrowed, and the corner of her mouth tightened. She seemed angry. Chen's instincts told him to push. The real Anna was just under the surface.

"There a point to all this, Chen?"

"Everett believed that if this guy Moison was still in charge, there was no way Polar Vortex could stay so organized and so quiet at the same time. That his ego wouldn't allow it."

"His *ego*?"

Anna's face had twisted in frustration. Her voice cracked. Grief and anger were plain to see. She rose from her chair and began pacing the far side of the room. After a few minutes, she turned to face Chen and tore the photograph into pieces. He'd seen the real Anna. Surprisingly, there was more sadness than he would've guessed.

"This is the way you've always seen us. Criminals, crackpots, fools. The way he was booed out of lecture halls, arrested at protests, and mocked in the media. He was Clifton to the police, Elder to Polar Vortex. He was *father* to me."

Chen felt himself tense up. She'd raised her voice briefly, but the commotion in the other room continued, disciplined as always. This was more personal than he could've imagined. Dedication that could only come from blood. Anna wiped a tear from her eye as she composed herself. She smoothed out her jacket and straightened her back before meeting Chen's gaze with cold calculation.

"You think ego got us here? Got *you* here? No. I let Polar Vortex continue to be the butt of everyone's jokes. Let Everett think that we died off without our 'cult leader' at the helm. All for this. All so we could crawl so far up the Depths's ass that they can't tell where they end and where we begin. Tell me, Chen, are we a fucking *joke* to you now?"

She paused to catch her breath.

"All he wanted to do was reveal the truth about the world. A truth he knew, we *all* knew, even before your little hero Vandley. After his damn countdown, we saw the same discontent in Vandley that we've had since our group's inception. That this 'Freeze'? It's shit. My father thought that once the countdown happened, the public would have no choice but to believe us. Then he thought that Vandley speaking out against it would be enough. That reason and science would win out against all this goddamn *ignorance*. But he was wrong. Dead wrong. You leave people to make their own conclusions and reasonable assertions, they'll disappoint you every time."

Anna crossed the room in a few calm steps and stood right over Chen. He couldn't stop himself from flinching. Not from fear, but from her presence overwhelming his own. It was clear why these people followed her.

"But that's over now. No more lectures. No more protests. We tried to bring truth to the Depths, but that's ass backwards. I'm bringing the Depths to the truth in a way that can't be ignored. We're going to turn this godforsaken place upside down."

Chen felt a shiver run down his spine. Anna turned to walk back into the room where the planning was underway. She turned at the doorway to look back at Chen. An unnatural glow from the other room's monitor cast deep shadows on her face. Now it made sense. Only a cause this personal could drive Anna this far underground. Let her father's cause languish as everyone's punching bag. Now that they were on the precipice, Chen could feel that this was more than just bringing people the truth. She was right: they were so integrated in the government, there was no telling how far this went. They might as well *be* the government.

Anna looked back at Chen before going back into the other room. Her eyes were smoldering coals. Her breathing was steady with conviction.

"Now get back to work."

13

Piotr could hardly contain himself. Chen watched as he flew from room to room examining blueprints, assembling a massive amount of gear, and speaking with Anna in loud, excited tones. It took Piotr just one restless night to convince Anna it was possible, but you'd think it'd only been a few short hours. He summoned energy from places Chen could only dream of, even with Fuel. He could see how close Polar Vortex was to bringing years of planning to fruition based on how animated Anna's face was. The dull faces of the other Vortex members had suddenly shifted to excitement and nervousness. He even heard some of them speculating, a rare break from their extreme discipline. After the death of Vandley, the pieces they'd been gathering in secret were finally being assembled again, and the energy in the room was palpable. The more excited the room became, the more Chen could feel his own nervousness rise. He'd gotten the details of a plan worked through with Teresa, but to say it was risky was an understatement. There were too many variables to Chen's liking, but given the desperate drive for success Polar Vortex had initiated, it was the best Chen and Teresa had to work with.

He walked over to the corner of the room where Morgan sat and took a seat across from her. She looked twice as tired as he felt. Neither of them had slept well in days. It was already difficult planning the data infiltration in concert with Piotr and Ellen, but weaving his own cooperation with Teresa into the mix had led to a lot of eyes-wide-open nights. Luckily, Fuel was readily available at every moment for the few hours he had. He had to keep Morgan in the dark. She was preoccupied with interpreting the scientific data Polar Vortex was mining and pointing them in the right direction, and any more subterfuge was likely to cause a mental breakdown. Despite how well she hid it, Chen had known her long enough to see the signs.

"You look like shit, Chen. Red eyes, dry tongue, and skin falling like snow from your nose. When's the last time you slept without Fuel to help?"

Looked like it was a two-way street. She still had the energy to be concerned about him.

"I'd rather not say. I know you hate to see your hard work go to waste."

"Ditch the tough guy act. I'm serious, Chen. After what happened to Wayne, I haven't been able to see things the same way. I can't lose another friend of mine right in front of me. Not when I could do something about it."

Chen tried to relax and let out a breath. It was easy to forget that Morgan was a doctor, not a detective. She hadn't signed up for anything like this, least of all losing a friend in the process.

"I get it, Morgan, believe me, I do. I've lost people before in the line of duty. Lost myself even. Honestly, I've been running on fumes for days. This whole...heist? It's nuts even by their standards. If it was just that, I'd have trouble getting shut eye, but I am working on something. Something for all of us. I know you're worried, but I promise, this won't be forever. We'll get out of this. "

"And how's that, Chen? What's your master plan for getting us out of this?"

Chen felt nauseous. He had thought about telling Morgan and Piotr. Morgan especially, after everything she'd done for him in the past. But it was too soon. Too early. There were too many variables that could get more than just himself killed, or worse if this went sideways. He'd tell them, but not until he was sure they were walking into a certain future together and not the precipice.

"I...I can't say yet. If it blows up in my face, then I want it to just be *my* face. Ellen knows what I'm capable of, and I doubt she'd go straight to disavowing you and Piotr if there's a shred of use left in either of you. They're close, and they won't risk losing any lead or edge they can get. I'll make sure of that."

Morgan took a deep breath and got up. She put her hands on the back of her head and looked down at Chen, exhausted. "I'm tired, Chen. Tired of playing some game where my friends and I are just tools to be used. I want out of this, but not if the price is too high. Not if that price is your life. If you think keeping me and Piotr in the dark is for the best, that's fine. I know you want out of this as much as we do. I'll go along with it only if you promise me you're not on some hero streak. No more sacrifices, Chen. No more loss."

Morgan's expression was cold, hard. He'd never seen her this way before. It was reassuring.

"No heroics, that I can promise you. Do I look like a hero?"

Morgan let out a smile and laughed. Chen felt a chuckle coming on.

"Not one I'd want to save me, that's for sure."

She stood there for another few minutes, looking through Chen. If he had to guess, she was probably seeing Wayne in some sort of concrete cell. He wished he could tell her what was happening to him, but no one really knew for sure. Chen wasn't sure if it was more comforting or just another thing that ate at Morgan as she looked up at the ceiling for answers night after night. Anna's voice rang out from the next room. Chen heard the sound of feet shuffling to snap to attention.

"You two done braiding each other's hair in there? Get out here."

Chen stood up and followed Morgan into the other room. Piotr and Anna were gathered around a large table with a map in the center. Next to them was another member of Polar Vortex he didn't recognize, tall, lanky, but with strong forearms showing through his rolled-up sleeves. Tattoos extended up to his neck, which flexed as he nodded to Chen and Morgan. The room was a mess. Papers, maps, and half-soaked rags littered the space. Chen felt like he had walked straight into an unlit Boiler. In the center of it all was Piotr. He hadn't changed in the last two days. Bags weighed down his face, sitting right on top of his pasty skin and budding five o'clock shadow. Ink stained his sleeves and hands as he beckoned everyone to join him around the center table. Despite all appearances, he sounded energetic. The enthusiasm spread around the room. Even the sitters on the outskirts couldn't help but peek at the scene laid out on the center table. Anna didn't even admonish them as Piotr began to speak.

"Gentlemen and gentleladies. This is what the last day and a half have been building up to. As you all know, we're here to tap into those snots on High, particularly the esteemed Geraldson University. Whatever this Project Persephone is, it's clear that Geraldson's got the goods, and we wanna make sure they share. So welcome to the heist of the century!"

Piotr paused and extended his arms out with flair. He was having so much fun that even Anna held in her comments with a smile. It would almost be comical if their lives weren't on the line. Piotr took a moment to read the room and continued unabashed.

"You think Polar Vortex of all people would appreciate showmanship. Anyway, what we've found is that they keep their data center off-campus, underground and connected through a single utility tunnel for maintenance. This allows them to keep their data centers cool enough to run without ruining their precious aesthetic and keep their fuel costs low. This also means that a significant portion of that maintenance tunnel runs underground here."

Piotr's finger pointed at the massive Geraldson complex on the map and traced its way along a connecting line sloping gently downward until it delved under the surface before terminating in an expansive data center, represented by a crude depiction of Piotr's. His hand then traced backward about a quarter of the way before stopping near where two lines ran closely parallel.

"Here is where our new friend comes in. This line running parallel represents a decommissioned shuttle track. It was part of a very early system before Geraldson became as big as it is and expanded its campus over it. This is the point where the two tunnels run parallel to each other close enough that we can blow through with relative ease before accessing the data line side. Luckily, the wires carrying Geraldson's data run along the outside of the concrete encasing, like the inner membrane of an egg. Think of the catwalk that workers use as the yolk. These wires carry most of the data that Geraldson uses. Given its age, they will likely have access to the information we need. The tangle of wires is thick enough that we should be able to tap into the wires physically without any visibility to anyone inside."

Piotr took a step back from the table and surveyed the room. His toothy grin caused some of the onlooking sitters to smile themselves.

"I'll hold here for any applause, praise, and or questions from the peanut gallery."

Piotr looked up from the map, face as bright as the Junction.

Chen voiced a concern. "What's the security? We're just in and out without anyone seeing us?"

"Glad you asked, Chen. The data tunnel itself has security inlaid on the concrete shell. We'll have to take that part slowly to avoid the sensors peppered throughout. Even the smallest nodes emit an electric signal, so as long as we scan twice before drilling, we should be fine. As for inside, there is a patrol that makes rounds every hour. However, since the catwalk they use inside is metal, their footsteps should echo as they patrol. The wires provide enough cover so they don't see us, but we'll be able to hear where they are and vice versa. If we don't make too much noise, we should be good to go."

"And how do you know all this? They publish their security details in a newsletter?"

"Practically speaking, yes. With our dear friends at Polar Vortex that work at Geraldson as well as the back-door access we have to the system, we gathered enough information that we might as well work there."

"What about our security? These old tunnels often have recyclers who aged out physically or seasonals without work for the cycle. What's gonna stop some curious Fuelers from asking questions?"

Anna responded with a smirk. "We got you covered on that one, Chen. Forgotten spaces with forgotten people? That's Polar Vortex territory. We'll make sure no one interrupts for as long as you all need."

"I assume it's our skins on the line?"

"You'd assume right. Small team, small exposure. Jeremy will be there to make sure you all play nice together. He might not look the part, but he's an expert babysitter. He'll make sure you three respect your bedtime. We'll be expecting an electronic upload parallel to the progress Piotr makes so we're all on the same page. If there are any sudden hiccups in upload speed or if we don't like what we see, Jeremy here is authorized to send you to bed without dinner."

Chen looked at Jeremy. Their gazes met steadily, without emotion. He was an operator. Chen and Teresa's plan would have to be executed with a minimal number of steps. Even then, the risk of exposure was high. Chen hoped Jeremy was as excited internally as Anna was externally about the potential success of their plan. That was the only advantage they had.

"Naturally. Who's on the team, exactly?"

"You, Piotr, Jeremy. Morgan will verify the data live from base to the best of her ability. Your security will be there and invisible. Transportation to the tunnel will be covered from the Shockies. You'll be safe every step of the way. The trip back? Maybe if you give a gold star performance, I'll give you the confirmation that you two are safe to return once the download is complete to my satisfaction."

Piotr's expression faltered slightly into a face of concern before shifting into a more serious countenance. He had been so caught up in the planning that he forgot about the stakes.

"Given the amount of data Geraldson processes and how long they've been around, it's a strong contender for what we need. Especially after the Shockies came down on Wayne the way they did. It's going to work."

Morgan whispered so low only Chen could hear, "It has to."

Anna's face brightened as she stood back from the table and clapped her hands. The others around the room sat straight up to attention. "Well, team, we've got a plan. It's now or never for all of us, especially for you three. You've got two hours of rest before I get our people into place. I'm looking for the performance of a lifetime."

With that, Anna turned around and began coordinating with those around the room. Chen and Morgan stepped back from the table and walked to an adjoining room. There was a window at the far end with security features old enough that it opened. They spent a long moment looking outside at the dark streets interrupted by distant flickers coming from Boilers spread out on the dark landscape. The Depths extended infinitely above them. Chen could see a small bright light in the distance that he now knew as the Junction. It glowed hot and white, an anomaly in the background that he'd grown accustomed to. Otherwise, it was just inky blackness all the way to a surface neither of them could see.

Chen turned to one side and sent a message to Teresa. It would be hours before she responded. He could tell the stress was getting to her, and there was still a lot of prep on her end. Her messages were getting more spread out, erratic. Chen didn't know how much went into her side of things, but it needed to be fast. He instinctively ran his hand over his phone. He had felt phantom buzzes at all times of the day. Another false alarm. Teresa's messages came at all hours of the day and night. He hoped that she still had her wits about her through all the stress. There wasn't much he could be certain of at this point. And there certainly wasn't any choice in the matter.

He squinted, trying to pierce through the roof the Depths and into the surface above. He remembered leaving the bloc because of what he felt now. No choices, no certainty, no mobility. He wondered how it came to be this way. Maybe he was just naive enough to believe all the promises the program had to offer. Or just all the promises he made himself without really knowing. He turned to Morgan, who looked back with a haggard expression.

"No more heroes, Chen. Promise me."

"I promise."

14

Chen had just gotten a few minutes to close his eyes before Anna startled him awake. She was clapping wildly with excitement that only Piotr could match.

"All right, team, enough beauty sleep. There's no saving that face of yours, Chen, so stop trying and get up. It's the start of a new day for us all."

Chen rose slowly. His back spasmed in protest along with his neck. Morgan watched him like a hawk every time he reached for his handkerchief. He tried to remind himself that she meant well, though he wasn't sure they had that luxury. Chen looked over to her. Morgan rubbed her eyes and sat at the edge of her cot. He could tell sleep had escaped her too.

"Jesus, Anna, I haven't seen enthusiasm from you in the years we were at the precinct. Now you're like a schoolgirl?"

"Mock all you want, Chen, it's not my ass out on the line today. We haven't been this close in years, and I just got a *feeling*. We're *close*. And then this whole charade will be over for all of us. Frankly, no longer babysitting you three will be a relief. This thumb we've all been under, everyone will finally know the truth. Of course I'm fucking *excited*."

"You and me both, Anna." Chen got up from his cot and walked to the foot of his bed. He picked up his bag and slumped it over his shoulder. It was heavier than usual. He'd been quietly assembling a bug-out bag as best he could but only got as far as a few days' worth of provisions and what little creds he had on him. It was hard to do anything substantial under Anna's watchful eye. He hoped it didn't have to last him long. Chen turned toward Morgan and nodded. She gave a tired shrug in response.

Piotr was in the main room, nervously eyeing the map and making notes. His eyes darted between the map and his own gear. He obviously had not taken advantage of the few hours of sleep afforded to them. A small mountain of equipment sat in the corner. Screens and laptops were stuffed precariously into a large hiking bag. Wires poked out at all angles. It seemed impossible to wear with any degree of comfort, even split among the three of them.

"Sleep at all, Piotr?"

"What do you think, Chen?" Piotr widened his bloodshot eyes for effect. "Ain't it enough for me to just work on all this bullshit—" He sidled closer to Chen and whispered, "But *our* bullshit too?"

Piotr quickly checked their surroundings before covertly reaching into his pocket and handing Chen a small electronic device. It was about the size of a mouse, with a few lights and buttons hastily assembled onto base made of scraps. Chen placed it gingerly in a hidden interior pocket in his coat.

"Yeah, well we can rest when we're done. I'll make sure it's worth it."

"We *will* be done, right? These toys can only keep me entertained for so long."

Chen stopped to linger on his thoughts before answering. Days of planning and coordinating flooded his mind. All hinging on several minutes of diversion and deception. It was all he could do to utter a soft, "Right."

Piotr broke away and attempted to look nonchalant, reassessing the gear and maps laid out on the table and floor. Chen waited as the last of their group, Jeremy, came to join them at the central table. He was dressed much as they were, casual and like they belonged with the ignored. He looked well rested compared with Chen and Piotr. He didn't acknowledge the rest of them and nodded at Anna as she came up to them. As Chen suspected, a real operator. Anna's gleeful energy was almost infectious if his freedom wasn't on the line.

"All right, we've gone over the plan ad nauseum, so let's get in the right space. You all know what's on the line today. We are on the precipice. Everything we've worked for. It's been years of dedication from every part of Polar Vortex, and it *will* be worth it. As for you three, my good mood might turn into goodwill depending on what happens up there. So don't disappoint me. Remember, Morgan will be here with us to monitor the data stream live. We know what we're looking at, so don't try to blow smoke up our ass. Now move out."

Anna rapped the table for emphasis. Everyone in the room let out a collective breath. The three of them gathered their effects and prepared to leave for the shuttle stop. Piotr shouldered a smaller pack loaded with multiple devices. Jeremy lifted a large duffle bag laden with heavy tools that rattled with each step. Chen tried to blend his bug-out bag with the rest of the wires and screens he was responsible for. After running through his checks, he nodded at Jeremy and Piotr to signal he was ready. Morgan looked at Chen and Piotr as they stood at the door. Her gaze sparked with concern before quickly being replaced by exhaustion. She sat back down and turned toward the screen behind her, where several Fuelers sat typing furiously. Anna had her placed in a central spot against the wall, showing she was more prisoner than cooperator. He hoped he'd have a chance to see her again soon.

Chen walked out of the Pits behind Jeremy and Piotr. The air was heavy with fuel today; it must be especially cold on the surface. He could feel the oppressive heat of the Boilers as fuel was shoved in at an accelerated pace. They were concentrated near the Pits, where the recyclers lived and worked, sending heat to those above through a rattling system of pipes and heat stops where smaller Boilers topped off the air. When Chen had worked late shifts here, he used to stare up at the heating system in awe. Now it just looked like a desperate attempt to control the unmanageable.

They boarded the shuttle stop in a tram near the back. It was always crowded this far in the Depths, but Anna had assured them their security started immediately on the shuttle so long as they followed her instructions. Chen could feel a crush of bodies surrounding them, wondering who among them was their cover. No eyes seemed to wander their way as the shuttle left the station and careened carelessly, winding upward.

Chen watched as the shuttle wound around the circumference of the central tower and toward the surface. As they passed each stop, people shuffled to their destinations. None of them seemed to make eye contact with Chen, though he couldn't trust much of his paranoid instincts. No familiar faces seemed to stay on with them. Did Anna have that diverse a following?

They passed the infinite abyss of the recycler districts and the lights of the Junction as surface drew closer. The crowds shifted slowly from those with heavily recycled wear to office types in upcycled clothing. The bumps of the ride smoothed out as they ascended the central tunnel until they were just a few stops shy of Geraldson. Chen was certain they were being watched, but he couldn't clock anyone remotely inquisitive. Their gear drew some curious stares as the ride itself passed without incident, even under the surveillance of the near-surface stations. It was the first time Chen had been farther than the Junction since the Shockies were looking for him, and it felt as straightforward as when the investigation started. Anna wasn't lying; Polar Vortex had the tech and the juice to protect them. If they chose to.

They left the tram along with a few other passengers and began walking along the boarding platform. They stuck out in the crowd of scientists and administrators, but Jeremy's gruff exterior ensured their glances were brief. Piotr led them along the station, walking parallel to the shuttle, until they reached a rusty gate.

Signs hung at odd angles, warning against access or loitering. Most knew these areas were home to the desperate and made special care to avoid eye contact. A lock that was put in long ago hung broken from someone years past who first discovered this hidden haven. Lights flickered at uneven intervals from the ceiling, reaching into the dark maw before them. Condensation dripped from the ceiling through the thin layer of metal and dirt that separated barely heated air from the frozen landscape above. Jeremy wordlessly pushed the gate open, ushered them through, and closed the gate.

The space seemed abandoned until Chen's eyes adjusted to the lack of light. He blinked to clear his vision and saw curious eyes peering back at him, the faces disheveled and gaunt. The air here was significantly cooler. Someone had repurposed an old ventilation fan near the entrance to provide a constant flow of warm Boiler air. Though with their relative distance from the source, it was still frigid enough for the group to cinch their coats tight. Chen had rousted vagrants in similar spaces deeper in the Depths, though he never felt good about it. At best it was kicking people when they were down. The irony ran through his mind as the darkness slowly enveloped them the farther they went.

As the group progressed, they caught furtive, curious glances. There was a mix of newer tech and older materials that you'd typically see beyond salvage. Some were clearly taken from the odds and ends that fell off a passing freight shuttle, but most were near the end of their usefulness. Coats were an assembly of multiple threadbare items roughly knit or melted together, nearly impossible to secure against the wind. Most of the people they passed only offered a brief stare before looking back down on their meager possessions. Occasionally a group of children would shadow them for a short distance before losing interest. Chen instinctively patted his pockets to make sure none of his possessions were lifted. Piotr pointed up ahead toward a section of old power supply track on the ceiling. Chen recognized it as an outdated system from the previous shuttles. Jeremy looked behind them and nodded at a huddled group of people staying warm around a metal drum fire. They nodded back silently and turned their attention back the way they came.

Chen followed Piotr's arm as his colleague spoke. Piotr was pointing toward a spot on the ceiling much like the others they had passed.

"That's the spot where the tunnels run closest together. If we punch through here, we should be able to access the hardline into Geraldson. Jeremy, if you would."

Jeremy took the lead and approached the spot Piotr pointed at. He opened a ladder and turned to Piotr, who nodded. Jeremy took out a small chisel and carved a small hole in the ceiling. Chunks of rock sprinkled the floor as Jeremy made progress through the concrete. He blew the debris aside and inserted a small package of plastique explosive. Jeremy then placed a plastic bowl stuffed with cushioning around the explosive and taped it in place. He held up five fingers and counted down until a small *pop* made Chen jump. Jeremy removed the bowl from the spot in the ceiling and signaled for the group to come closer.

They approached the hole carefully as Jeremy put a finger to his lips. Chen looked up and could see a metal wall gleaming back at him. He could feel the heat as he reached up on his tiptoes to touch its surface. It reminded him of the Junction and its tech. Piotr stopped him before he made contact.

"Try not to knock too loud. Any noise above a certain threshold reverberates through that whole maintenance tunnel. We've got twenty minutes before the next patrol comes through. Jeremy, do your thing."

Jeremy grunted in affirmation and took out a set of smaller cutting tools. He attached adhesive mats around the exposed metal before beginning to slowly cut at the metal above them. Painfully slow. The mats dampened most of the vibrations as he cut his way through, making a hole just large enough for a person to fit through. After about fifteen minutes of moving mats along the cut, Jeremy broke through to the other side. Hot air blasted through the opening, gently blowing Jeremy's hair as he made the last cut. He handed off the metal plate to Chen as he started putting his tools away. It was hot to the touch. Chen could feel his fingers shake and his breath quicken in anticipation. He reached instinctively for his pocket but felt paper instead of the fabric he had been expecting. He pulled it out to read: *Remember your promise, Chen.*

He suppressed a laugh. Morgan could never help herself. He steeled his nerves and looked up in time to see Jeremy step back. A tangle of exposed wires was above him, like the exposed nervous system of some technological organism. He knew from the schematics that there was separation between the wires and the catwalk inside, but it was impossible to tell from the wall of circuitry. Without knowing the schematics, you could assume they had just punched a hole into a solid tunnel of electric thread.

Piotr bumped up against Chen's shoulder and broke his thoughts. Piotr drew Chen's attention to a thin space between the metal casing and the mess of wires inside. There was just enough space for Piotr and his gear to lay flat. Chen began handing off electronics to Piotr, who slid them into the space between. Piotr took his time making his set up perfect. He threw a long wire back to Chen, who hooked it up to a nearby signal booster. Chen watched as three green lights blinked to life. He signed Piotr with a thumbs-up. He took a moment to forward a message to Teresa: *Be ready.*

Piotr took a moment to close his eyes and steady himself. The entire structure sloped imperceptibly toward the three of them. Piotr tucked his feet first as he grabbed at the wires above, as if entering a slide, and turned to face the rest of them before hanging a timer off the edge set to one hour. They held their breath as a soft clang of footsteps passed up above them. The guard above was coming through for his pass. Several minutes later, they echoed again, heading in the other direction. Chen let his breath out. He'd been unconsciously holding it until the guard had passed by.

Piotr started the timer and began furiously splicing wires open, holding tools between his teeth as he reached deep into the tangle. Chen watched as Piotr's arms disappeared to the shoulder, bringing wire after wire out. He occasionally clipped one off to the side after examination, collecting a thick rope of cable off to his side. Piotr took a deep breath and closed his eyes, centering himself before pulling a set of pliers out and frantically splicing through and connecting his system to each wire sequentially.

Chen's eyes could barely tolerate the red, fluorescent numbers as they vibrated back at him, counting the seconds down. He could see Jeremy holding a headset to his ear with a placid look on his face, unblinking and unconcerned. He was responding to an unknown voice every few minutes, likely confirming progress. Twenty minutes passed as Piotr clawed and scraped, stopping now and then to attend to multiple devices around him. Despite the tension, his smile was contagious. He was having the time of his life.

After forty minutes had passed, Piotr stopped to look back at Jeremy. He gave a thumbs-up and started a second timer next to the first. Ten minutes started to count down as Jeremy pressed the receiver closer to his ear. Jeremy whispered in an excited tone. For the first time, he showed a soft smile as he gave the affirmative back to Piotr. They'd found what they were here for. There wasn't much time now. Chen gripped his phone tight as he messaged Teresa: *Ten minutes.*

Chen tried to hide his nervousness. The last days of planning were on the line. His foot tapped impatiently on the concrete floor, echoing softly through the tunnel. Fortunately, Jeremy was too focused to notice. This had to be it. He waited nervously as the timer dragged past five minutes. An eternity passed as the angry, red numbers ticked slowly past two minutes. Chen could feel his breath catch in his chest as his phone buzzed in response.

I was able to access the maintenance tunnel hatch. It's in place.

He willed a sense of relief, but tightness in his muscles quickly took its place. Thirty seconds left. There could be no mistake in timing, or there would be no trip back for any of them. Ten seconds. Chen could see Piotr's body tense like a snake. He swore he could hear the sweat drip off his chin and onto the floor as the timer finished counting down. Jeremy was clutching the headset to his face so tight, his knuckles were white. His eyes were glued to the screen in front of him. Chen couldn't read his face outside of the excitement. Four dazzling zeroes blinked at them for less than a millisecond before they started moving. Jeremy finished packing his equipment as Piotr wiggled his way out of the space, a small laptop clutched tightly to his chest. Chen moved up quickly and started handing off Piotr's equipment to him. He tried to simulate a sense of urgency but couldn't stop himself from stealing glances up the tunnel. He needed every second delay. His phone was still as questions crowded his mind. Where was it? Had he missed it? Had Teresa failed? *Where.*

As he moved up to empty the last of Piotr's equipment, he could see a small cloth sack slide down the edge of the pipe. It was moving so slowly, he thought he was imagining things. It came to rest just within arm's reach. That was it. She'd placed all their hopes on no one asking twice if the head of the Weather Service needed the tunnel to herself. And for once something went *right*.

He stole a look behind him and saw that Jeremy and Piotr were busy packing the last of their things. They wouldn't be busy for long. While they were occupied, he snuck a glance at the papers inside. There was an accordion folder labeled *Persephone* with rough sketches, blueprints, and a large red Confidential stamp emblazoned across each page. His heart quickened. He had it. He made a note of the page numbers, odds only. Clever. Basically useless to a schmuck like him without the rest. Teresa was probably holding on to the rest as insurance. Before jumping back down, he put the accordion folder into the hem of a pocket he had sewed into the lining of his jacket. It couldn't have been more than five pounds, but he could feel the weight of it shift back and forth as they made their way back through the maintenance tunnel. It felt like it would throw him off balance at any second.

The trip back was a blur. His mind buzzed with anticipation. Chen worked to stop himself from anxiously outpacing the rest of the group. Their shadows dropped all pretext. They ran alongside them through the darkness, passing face after disinterested face. They were as excited as Jeremy was. Nothing left to hide.

Chen could feel the warmth of the shuttle station embrace him as they crossed the rusted gate that separated old from new. Faces around him blended in a paranoid mush. Chen tensed as the shuttles approached the stop. Piotr struggled to even his breathing as his face glowed from their success. They entered the shuttle headed toward the Depths as the chime rang, indicating the doors were closing. Piotr and Chen's eyes met briefly before a large smile ran across Piotr's face.

"Fuck them all, Chen."

Then, before anyone could react, Chen dashed through the closing doors and into the shuttle on the opposite side. The doors closed around him as Jeremy's expression twisted into one of shock and rage. He tried to pull the doors in front of him apart without success. Their Polar Vortex shadows tried to do the same for the doors in front of Chen, but their thin frames failed to find the grip necessary. They clawed and scraped at the door as the other passengers held their breath in fear. Some had enough sense to transfer to adjacent trams. Chen could see Piotr's laughing face as Jeremy turned toward him, squaring his body as he grabbed Piotr's collar tight. Chen felt his throat clench tight as the first blow fell on Piotr's delighted expression. Blood ran freely down his nose, dripping onto the tram floor. Chen felt the jerk of the shuttle as it left the station and the roar of the on board Boilers as they breached the surface. He was alone in the tram. Most of the others had gotten their wits about them and moved as far away as they could before the shuttle blasted to ground level.

It was days since he'd seen the sun. The light was blinding. He tried to take a seat and relax but found it impossible despite the fatigue coursing through his body. He could feel his phone vibrate angrily as the messages from Anna came through.

You think this is funny, Chen?

What are you playing at, you fuck? The data we extracted is fucking odds and ends! You fucking knew this would happen, didn't you?

Enjoy that look of surface cause it's the last light you'll ever FUCKING SEE! You won't make it another step before the Shockies are all over you.

We don't NEED you anymore! ANY of you! What do you think is going to happen to your friends Morgan and Piotr? That's blood on YOUR hands if you don't get back in the Depths right fucking now!

Chen wiped the dryness off his nose and mouth as he typed his reply.

Without me, you have nothing. If anything happens to Morgan or Piotr, you have nothing. You want to finish this case? Then you'll need the data I have. I have the only physical copy. If I get a hint of you Polar nutjobs near me, it's going up in flames. Then what will you have to show for all those years of work? All those years of creds, hopes, nutjob dreams? Fucking nothing. Count on it.

Chen put his phone in his pocket. He could feel Anna's anger through his device, but he was spent. He knew she wouldn't risk lifting the protection around him until she was sure what he said was true. And it was. Once they verified Chen had the data, they couldn't risk him getting picked up. Him, Morgan, or Piotr. Just a little more time.

He patted the bulk under his jacket where *Persephone* was. Its mass reassured him as he turned to look out the window of his shuttle. He watched as endless stretches of farmland covered in thick, opaque plastic sheets surrounded him. They absorbed what little sunlight was available each Freeze to try to keep the weight of snow and ice down, but it only went so far. He knew from experience that the land underneath was dead. The sheets made it salvageable for next year, but any real picker knew the truth: the surface died little by little each cycle round.

He used to hate taking this route. It reminded him too much of where he came from, of what he was trying to leave behind. He'd stay awake counting down the minutes, trying to stretch the time between his trips from his bloc to the Depths for supplies. But now, it was all he could do to stay awake. It would've been weeks since his bloc retired the machinery for the winter and insulated the ground. He'd usually be in the shed by now, repairing the damage from a cycle barely completed. A job that weeks ago he'd rather have forgotten than linger on. Now, under the free open sky, he let his thoughts wander into the infinite space above as the shuttle passed a sign reading *Bloc 409*.

15

Chen exited the shuttle stop and into a furious wind tunnel of hail and ice. His fellow passengers exited the tram, moving stiffly through multiple layers of clothing. It reminded him of his first few Freezes as a child when he had to move the equipment in for his father to winterize. The high winds stopped them from giving him too close a look despite his underdressed state. He thanked whatever luck he had left and moved quickly into an adjacent parking lot, where rows of buses sat idling next to one another. The lot was empty. Pickers with any sense or forward planning would have no need to move between the Depths and surface for supply runs this late in the cycle, but there were always some who thought they were smarter than the countdown. Chen boarded a bus and tried to stay warm. The on-board Boiler tried its best, but surface dwellers were used to low fuel rations. It'd been over a decade since he had to give it a thought.

Chen patted the envelope in his jacket as he cinched it tighter in an effort to stay warm. He could feel the packet start to freeze into his skin, becoming a part of him. He looked out the window as a sea of white expanded in front of him. He used to be able to recognize where he was by the buildings he saw. The Lopez's winter shed on the corner would signal he could fall asleep without missing his stop. A bump rough enough to wake him up would mean he should stay awake. If he slept longer, then he risked having to stay at a neighbor's bloc until the bus passed by in the opposite direction. Not anymore. Instead, a vast alien landscape stared back at him with silent judgment. He'd been gone a long time, and the land knew it. There was little conversation around him. Even in his paranoid state, he could tell his fellow passengers were spent. Fuel canisters sat at their feet, shifting with each turn. Bags of provisions rattled as the bus made its way along icy paths with reckless abandon. He scanned the half dozen people riding with him. Their eyes were fixed on the floor, rarely looking up to confirm each passing stop. He recognized the resigned look on their faces.

Chen tried to stay vigilant by watching the landscape. Acres of land covered in insulating plastic sheets stretched beyond the horizon. When the Freezes had first started, much of the land Chen saw was privatized by the families in control now. Farmers had essentially been sharecroppers for a generation now. Temperatures varied from a cold winter to an artic blast. The government had given way to industry to try to solve the problem faster than bureaucracy could, but with concessions that reverberated for years to come. They dressed up the deal as a lesson in necessary evil. Without the families stepping in, they'd have lost everything to the uncertainty of the next cycle. The Depths got built, but ownership was the luxury of those up top. Chen thought about how his family and bloc had worked the land of others for generations, controlled by a need for survival. How even in the Depths, his meager rent went to some oligarch in a long line of landlords. He wondered how far that control went now.

Chen's eyes began to close as the bus came to a stop. He hardly registered that this was his stop before dashing out of the closing doors. He struggled to maintain his balance as he emerged onto a flat concrete block with a sign reading *Bloc 409 - Grid C*. It hung at an extreme angle that should've fallen long ago if not for stubbornness. The bus left Chen in a cloud of exhaust and ice chunks, leaving him alone with his thoughts. He had a long walk ahead of him between covered fields. It'd be a close one with the clothes he had on.

His mind wandered to the messages Anna had sent him. They were angry, desperate. By now, Piotr would've returned to nut-case central. Chen hoped an earful was all Piotr was getting from her, but he knew better. Based on what he saw, Polar Vortex didn't run on empty threats. Chen hoped his own threat was enough to promise them a modicum of safety. The messages had finally stopped an hour ago, he assumed after Anna forced Morgan and Piotr to examine the data and realized his assertions were more than just a bluff. If he had calculated wrong, he doubted Anna would've wasted the calories moving her fingers across a keyboard to scare him. Not to mention the Shock Unit would've picked him up long before he exited the shuttle if his protection was off the table. Now that he was moving through the blocs, surveillance would be a fraction of what'd be subject to in the Depths. He was safe, at least from unnatural forces. For now.

Only a few minutes in and Chen could no longer feel his face. His fingers flexed in his gloves, trying to banish the stiffness. They'd lost sensation long ago. The envelope seemed to get heavier with each step. It helped to ease his mind of paranoia as his eyes shifted back and forth over the plain, flat landscape. He'd see anyone coming from a mile away. A large, familiar building drew closer on the horizon as his feet tried to keep purchase over the slick ice. The metallic roof gleamed as the rest of the wooden structure took up more of his vision until there was nothing else. He knocked gently on the tall steel barn door in front of him. It echoed as he waited.

Teresa drew the door open a crack. Her eyes were wide, red, and shifted quickly back and forth as she opened the door. A blast of warm air hit Chen in the face, though not warm enough to bring any feeling back. Chen scanned the surroundings. Machines and picker gear took up most of the floor space with the tallest machines sprinkled in between. The tarps and floors were covered with dust, save for the trail Teresa had left in her wake from the door and the corner between machines where she'd been lying low. The air inside wasn't exactly warm, but compared to where Chen entered from, it felt like a sauna. He followed Teresa a short distance to an area where she had scavenged an unused tarp into a makeshift bedroll. She turned around slowly and addressed Chen:

"I didn't think you'd show."

"Honestly, I wasn't sure either. Though not from lack of trying. From what Anna's been threatening me with, we should be safe for now. I let my brother know to keep my father away from the shed. Not much reason for him to come here this time of cycle anyhow. Given Polar Vortex's reach, I'm worried that they'll opt to go loud once they realize we have what they need. And it won't be pretty."

"I've been thinking the same. Given the short notice, I couldn't scrub the original scans as thoroughly as I could've before pulling the hard copies. I tried to give them enough of a hint so that they knew we weren't bluffing, but I fear I went a little far. I agree that it's only a matter of time before they put enough together to know who to pressure and how."

There was a long moment of silence as they sat down on the bundled tarps Teresa had gathered. Chen tried to warm himself by pulling dusty cloth around him, but they'd been sitting there for months and had already absorbed the temperature of their surroundings. He tried to stop shivering, to no avail. It was probably more than just the cold. Teresa spoke as she looked around the shed.

"So this is your bloc? Your family's shed?"

"Yeah. Our family's been here for a generation or two. Don't worry about visitors. I let my brother know to steer everyone clear, and my bloc's always been cohesive. We've never had a problem with stealing or breaking in."

"Did you come up through the mobility program?"

"Yep, part of the first class. And now I'm here again."

Teresa took a moment to process this as she looked on the stacks of machines and parts.

"You know, it's funny. You were exactly what we pictured all those years ago when Richard and I were just recyclers dreaming of the countdown. That one day, the countdown would let someone like you make a choice outside what their family had done. What society expected of them."

"Yeah, well no offense, but I ain't exactly back here of my own volition, Teresa."

Chen knew he offended her, but he didn't care. Here he was, back on his bloc, bringing an uncertain danger along with him. For years, she had known something was wrong and did nothing about it.

"Listen, Teresa, I know trust only goes so far, but our backs are against the wall here. The second they put all this together is the second our safety is gone. There's enough surveillance even up here that the Shock Unit can find us, and I doubt that Anna would make them do it the hard way. You have to loop me in on what's going on."

Chen watched as Teresa shifted uncomfortably. She was almost there. He could sense it.

"Do you know what you're asking me to do, Chen? If you think these past few weeks have been hard, it's been much harder than that. On High, down Low, there hasn't been a moment's rest for me since this whole thing started with that damn countdown. Vandley and I, we started all this together deep in the Depths. Two recyclers watching each year go by with hundreds of others, not knowing whether we'd gambled right and got in line for picking jobs that season or if we'd starve through another until the next Freeze. This was supposed to bring an end to uncertainty. For all of us, but certainly for the ones who needed it most. Now look where we are. What all this got Richard."

"Teresa, I wish I knew, but I can't unless you tell me. I mean, this is my bloc we're on. My home. I have known uncertainty, and that's one of the reasons I'm investigating here with you and not picking anymore. Vandley gave me and many others that. An end to uncertainty. If you're telling me that he was killed trying to do the same, I would really like to know."

Chen watched as Teresa alternated between tense and relaxed. She reached behind her and pulled out a matching folder to Chen's and signaled to him to bring out his. He handed her his half, which had been slightly bent from him pressing it too tightly to his chest. He could feel the strength of her grip as she took it from him and began combining it with hers. It seemed to take nearly half an hour before she flipped through the pages and with a sigh of satisfaction placed it on the ground between them. The heating system creaked with effort as another blast of air blew through the barn as she began to speak.

"This is now the only full copy of Project Persephone that I know of. This is what it's all been about since long before us, before the countdown. Back in the early days of the Freeze. This is what Richard was killed over."

Teresa took a moment to steady herself as her breath caught. Chen reached out to comfort her, but she held her hand up to continue.

"The countdown predicts no natural phenomenon. It tracks *this*."

Teresa picked up the dense collection of papers for emphasis before slamming it on the ground in frustration.

"This *monstrosity*. This system that's been in place since after the first dozen Freezes. Back when each cycle brought the world to its knees and they were throwing money at any project with a chance of success. We were all led to believe they died in the cradle. But they didn't. Not Persephone. Persephone's been with us ever since. It's been in our lives, our fear, our *atmosphere*. And the worst part it, I've known about since the early *fucking* predictions and said *nothing*. Nothing! And now? Now it's cost me everything!"

Teresa swiped at the papers on the floor, scattering them along the tarp underneath them. She breathed heavily as Chen watched the tension leave her body with each heave. Her breath fogged the air around her as the secrets that boiled her from within were released.

"What do you mean the countdown predicts this? Persephone?"

"Yes, it's all been Persephone. If you remember the references to terraforming that Wayne was caught with, Persephone was part of a much larger project the weather bureau funded back when periods between Freezes were devastating. Before they had the Depths, weather-tolerant crops, before they had anything. They tried to change the environment itself in a desperate ploy for control. Dirt more amenable to agriculture, season management for predictable picks, even cloud management for increased periods of sunlight. Persephone was the only viable solution to fall out of that desperation. Freeze management. They found a compound that when released in a controlled fashion through layers of atmosphere could trigger a Freeze. With experimentation, they found that if they triggered a Freeze frequently enough, no natural ones would occur in between. Eventually, they found a cadence that offered enough predictability to build the Depths without making anybody suspicious."

Teresa took a deep breath and wiped tears of frustration from her eyes. Chen was still processing the ramifications. Teresa could see his confusion and drew the conclusions for him.

"Over the years, Persephone became more than what it was intended to be. The families that funded it all? They've taken our uncertain future and replaced it with their certain success. Crop prices crashing? Freeze. Maintenance requests not hitting quotas? Freeze. They claim for some greater good that always aligns with their own interests. So here we are, in a world built by them, controlled by them, with rules we all follow without even realizing it."

Chen felt like his heart had stopped. His head swirled with possibilities and questions. All of this, all their uncertainty, all their fear. Manufactured? Created? How could this be possible?

"That's...that's insane. I mean how could I even believe this? Who...who would even be able to pull this off for so long? I mean it's ridiculous! This amount of control without anyone knowing?"

"It's everyone at the top, Chen. The industrialists. The Geraldsons, the O'Rileys, the list goes on. Descendants of the early backers of those desperate projects. They were part of the early research projects and the ones reaping the benefits today. It was all because of this. And now? Every cycle they meet to discuss the next release of Persephone freeze. Every cycle, they talk about the pros of the last cycle and when they should activate the next. Market data, Fuel consumption, materials, all calculated and optimized. I've been in those meetings. They act like stewards to humanity's progress! All that misery? It's another number to them. Everything pick you've done? Every Boiler that's low on Fuel? All research to them. And ever since that countdown...it's been me too."

Chen felt himself growing agitated. Everything she was saying, it was beyond comprehension. It sounded like Polar Vortex rhetoric. Polar Vortex...at that moment Chen remembered what Anna had said. About how their and Vandley's goals happened to align. About how the Depths ignored any truth that was inconvenient. He always wondered what that meant. Now he knew. Now he knew what audience Vandley had found. An audience primed to believe him from the start.

"Is that why Vandley disappeared after his comments? Is that how he became such an embarrassment to on High?"

"Yes. He spent years trying to scream the truth to whoever would believe him. After years of countdowns, he finally caught on. The theories he set in motion, the calculations he put in place. Richard knew there were only a few ways it could work indefinitely. So, he begged the public. He pleaded with the Bureau. Finally, he came to me. Nothing. When he stopped making his assertions to the media, I had hoped he had lost steam. No, I knew better than that. I just wished it was true. I found out too late that he finally had someone's ear to bend."

Chen could feel the shame wash over Teresa. He saw it now. She had lost everything. To go from working with her friend to give the world around them certainty, to perpetrating a sham in one fell swoop. It must have been maddening. But still, based on what she was saying, one question kept at the back of his mind.

"How could on High even be sure? I mean if they've been behind each cycle, why keep it going for so long? Would there even be a natural Freeze again without them?"

"That's the million-cred question, Chen. That's the argument they live on. That uncertainty. That without them we'd be tossed back in the stone age in just a few cycles without their predictable administration of Persephone. That it's for the greater good. It just happens that their good is always a part of it."

"And you? Doesn't this whole thing buck against what you and Vandley fought for? What he kept fighting for?"

Teresa slumped over at Chen's assertion. He's sure she'd asked herself that same question for years now.

"Yes. Yes, it does. After the first few predictions, they decided to loop me in. They thought it was only a matter of time before I caught on, given my position. And they needed at least one half of the all-star countdown team to maintain credibility. Richard knew without being told, but they assumed the bad press would be enough to kill his theories in the crib. He always needed me to get people to listen."

Teresa looked down. Her shoulders slumped. She seemed to melt into the floor. Her voice returned in a low whisper. "And that's the burden I'll carry for the rest of my life."

Chen let the words hang as Teresa gathered herself. He was impressed with how composed she could become. The pressure of the last number of years was enough to break anyone. Probably practice for her.

"He reached out to me about a few months ago. He was calm. Confident. Everything he was when he created the countdown. He figured it all out through raw effort. I knew that about Richard ever since we met down in the Pits—"

Teresa let a smile tug at the corner of her mouth. She looked up to the corner of the room, through today and into a long gone past.

"He'd always been that way. Richard called me to let me know that Polar Vortex had been supporting him for years and called for confirmation of what he already figured out. He even had a sample of the compound Polar Vortex intercepted for him to cinch it. He knew it all. Even correctly guessed that I couldn't still be the head of the Weather Service without being looped in. He wanted to give me one last chance to do the right thing. To help our dream become a reality for everyone. I remember how disappointed he sounded that first night, that I would go along with something so...insidious all these years. I thought I could handle it, but it just reminded me of everything I'd compromised over the years."

"How did this all lead to his death?"

Teresa pinched the bridge of her nose between her fingers. Her voice lowered to a whisper of guilt and strain. "I...I couldn't give him what he wanted. Ever since I became privy to Persephone, the scrutiny became constant. But my reactions told him everything he needed to know. Richard tried to get me to do the right thing. Reminded me of the dream we tried to build together and how we had a second chance to do it again. He knew without me he didn't have an ounce of credibility. But...but I just couldn't. I said what they always say, that without what they were doing, we'd be lost. That the people would stand behind the devil they knew rather than risk some unknown horror. Every justification I had repeated to myself I threw at him. He brushed them off like the lies they were. I don't know if I ever really believed them."

Teresa got up and started pacing back and forth. Her energy started to become more and more nervous.

"Richard kept pushing for a few more months, reminding me it was the right thing to do. How it was wrong to continue living the lie. Things I'd stopped saying to myself years ago. But I just couldn't. I told him and myself it was too dangerous. That people wouldn't believe it anyway. It just sounds like the same drivel Polar Vortex had been peddling for decades. But I could never pull that kind of crap with Richard. All he wanted was to get the truth out there, but he knew that Polar Vortex would just use this information to their advantage. He feared he'd just be replacing one evil with another. But with all they'd invested in him, they wouldn't take no for an answer. Polar Vortex knew he'd contacted me, but as much as they can pressure me, they can't compel me without arousing too much suspicion. Richard knew they wouldn't wait much longer, so he contacted me the night he died. He knew he was out of time, that if he didn't give them what they wanted, that they would...force my hand."

Chen took a seat as a wave of realization washed over him. Disparate pieces slammed together at an uncomfortable speed. The conclusion slipped out before he even realized he was speaking.

"They killed him. They killed him and assigned the case to themselves, knowing that without the legitimacy of Lower Crimes, no one would talk to just another nutcase. They needed investigators like me so that all they worked for all these years wouldn't go to waste if their assets started asking too many questions. They knew they were just toeing the line to the truth. And they knew it would scare you enough to take them seriously."

Teresa nodded slowly and let out a gasp. "Yes. Yes, and it worked. They haven't left me alone for weeks now. After Wayne was picked up, suspicion from on High has been turned up to eleven. They know there's a leak, and they know it's someone outside their ranks. Worst of all, I can't look in the mirror without seeing a disappointment. Richard's words have been echoing in my head nonstop. When you came to investigate, I feared that you were just another dog of Polar Vortex. But now, this..." She pointed to the papers on the floor. "This could be our last chance to do the right thing."

"*Our* chance? What are you talking about?"

"When you came to me with your plan to escape, it felt like redemption. We have the opportunity to make this right. This can't have all been for nothing. Richard can't have died for nothing."

Her look of shame and guilt were gone. She looked confident. Not a shred of desperation. Like Morgan. So driven by some sense of justice that it overrode their sense of survival. It was crazy.

"Teresa, when's the last time you slept? You've been consumed with guilt for weeks, maybe months now. You're not thinking straight. We just got out, and we have to focus on *staying* out."

"Chen, why did you bring me here? You're clearly capable enough to get out. I'm sure you could've gotten out without concerning yourself with me. Maybe even left to a different city. But you didn't, and I think I know why. You've got that same instinct that Richard had. A penchant for the truth. A drive so strong, you'd pursue it no matter the cost. And now here it is, and you want to turn away? If you're the person I think you are, you can't."

Chen felt himself growing hot despite the temperature. He took his coat off. He needed space, needed air. He almost drew the barn door open to leave, but Teresa stopped him in time before he froze to death outside. The look in her eyes was strong, determined. It made him nauseous. Who did she think she was? Pushing her guilt onto him? After all he did? After all he went through to get her here? Chen turned and rushed off in the other direction to the far end of the barn. To his relief, she did not follow.

The machines towered above him as he tried to catch his breath. He put his hands on the top of his head and tried to think. Just to think. He reached into his pocket but found only the crumpled note Morgan had left. Morgan, Piotr. He thought of them down in the Pits, waiting for news, waiting for Wayne. He gripped the sides of his head as if it was about to explode. This was just a case. A case like any other. When did it become so much more than this?

She was right. If he really wanted to, he could've been on another bloc hiding out. Even made it out of the Depths and to some neighboring country with their own Freeze proof-city. He was resourceful. He was smart. But damn it all, she was right. He wasn't selfish.

Before he knew it, Chen had walked near the back of the building. The towering machines gave way to a low-lit area with workbenches gathered messily in a corner. Tools of all sizes hung from the pegboards jammed into the corner. It was messy, disorganized. Chen felt a familiar itch in his head. It was a welcome distraction.

He took a seat on a dusty swivel chair in front of the nearest pegboard. Despite being inches taller and dozens of pounds heavier than when he last sat there, it felt familiar. He never did like working on maintenance every cycle, but he was the best at it. No one could refurb the sorter like he could with countdown to spare, though it never left him time to do much else. He reached out and started pulling tools off the shelf. Pliers of different sizes mixed in with socket wrenches missing their corresponding heads. There were more scuff marks on them than he remembered.

He could see his brother organizing the shelf in his absence, picking up the tools in a rushed and careless way as the countdown blipped through the bloc's collective consciousness. Chen could see him running back and forth between the workbench and the machines that needed attention. He could see his brother scuffing the wrenches as he haphazardly switched between pieces of machines that needed constant upkeep and prep for each Freeze. He could see him desperately trying to fill out order forms for anything they couldn't stretch longer. There was never enough time, no matter when the countdown seemed to start. God help them if they came up short. The Geraldson logo glared back at him from the industrial pickers. He could make out the O'Riley factory set from under the dents that had accumulated from stretching their tools just another cycle too long.

He'd left years ago to join the program. He could be selfish. Where was that Chen now?

His hand moved up the unnatural curve on an O'Riley wrench. He'd bent it many cycles ago, shortly before he left. He remembered the heated arguments. How his contributions meant more than his wants. How he had slammed the wrench on a table. How upset his father looked when he stormed out the door and into the cold. How that once that fucking countdown began, nothing else really mattered.

Chen stopped himself in the middle of organizing the socket heads. His father would probably have had a heart attack if he came in here and saw things as they used to be. Best not to involve them if he could avoid it. His brother already did more than Chen was comfortable with. He did his best to replace things as they were, though it was easier said than done given the state of disarray he had found it in. He wiped the dust evenly off. There'd be little reason for them to come in here until the thaw started, so the filth would replace itself in time. Chen pushed himself back from the desk and got up, taking out the device Piotr had sent him away with.

In his hand was a smooth, handheld device, much like his own phone. Piotr had explained it to him in strenuous detail, but Chen only paid attention to the basics. After spending so long in the back end of the on-High system and seeing how Polar Vortex interfaced with it, Piotr had gotten a feel for the surveillance system that stayed vigilant for offenders such as themselves. Piotr marveled at the total control they exercised. If Chen stepped foot on any shuttle or any central surface structure, he'd be in a concrete coffin within the hour. Anywhere above the Pits, he'd have a generous half day at best. The Pits themselves were Polar Vortex controlled, so as far as Chen was concerned, he might as well step on the blazing sun. As Piotr colorfully put it, "Chen my man, you are monumentally fucked when you get outta here. Why don't you let old Piotr unfuck you a little."

Chen laughed as he remembered the shit-eating grin on his face. He turned the device over and couldn't suppress a smile as he remembered Piotr's explanation:

"This little black beauty will scrub you live. You'll be like a little smudge on their fancy ass monitors. Obviously, they won't take that long without asking questions, but with creativity, you should be able to duck in and out of their field of view and buy yourself even more time before they figure you out. Then they'll be on you like pickers on the thaw."

He sent a message through their secured line, updating them on the events he'd learned so far. Chen doubted they'd be able to send a message soon without drawing suspicion, so he headed back to the front of the shed, where Teresa sat quietly on the floor next to the newly stacked Persephone blueprints. She looked up at him briefly as he took a seat next to her.

"So, Teresa, what'd you have in mind exactly for these bastards?"

16

Chen's head was spinning. Teresa had walked him through her plan half a dozen times by now, but when Chen tried to do it himself, his head filled with the details, many way over his head. Even without looking outside, he could tell the sun had set hours ago. They'd been at it nonstop. He tried to strip more detail away until he understood the bare bones. Teresa was clearly tired but had the patience of a saint. Chen felt like a child being held back after class for extra lessons.

"Teresa, all due respect, but you really gotta talk to me like I'm not an egghead. We've been at this for hours, and you're talking to me like I'm a graduate student. You gotta dumb it down even more."

Teresa smiled patiently as she stood up from the ground and began pacing. It'd been a long night, but her energy showed no sign of slowing. Chen watched as she morphed from professor speaking on their specialty to a babysitter patiently explaining why Chen couldn't eat a snack before bed.

"That's fair. I've thought about this nonstop since our meeting at the Junction. I'll do my best. Okay, so back to basics. The weather service collects data around the clock through a series of weather balloons. Imagine a child accidentally releasing their birthday balloons into the sky. That's much like what the Weather

Service did years ago, except these are too expensive to just lose. These weather balloons are tied together and distributed through multiple layers of the atmosphere. They were installed during the time of Persephone in a desperate attempt to predict the weather. They've sat there ever since, taking in the gas all around us for study."

"Hold on, hold on. Why would they keep these balloons out for so long? I thought money ran out a long time ago? What would be the point of the upkeep for a project that ultimately didn't work?"

"Today, the main story is that the university system continued to support these antiquities due to their relatively low upkeep in the hope that we'd have some use for the data. They've set up labs, supported research grants, and made careers for people to lend credibility to this idea. Then Richard comes along, and they've got the perfect reason not only for keeping the balloons around, but also to upgrade them to their hearts' content in the public eye. Richard's theory was first based on the data gathered through this system, and no one was the wiser until Richard spent more time gathering the alleged 'natural' phenomena. It became the perfect cover, at least for a while."

"Okay, I'm following so far. The balloons started as a defunct project that ostensibly limped on in the name of science. That's the lie we're fed so far. What are they actually doing?"

"Exactly, Chen. The balloons are the distribution system for the crystalline substance that initially brought you into my office. When they decide to trigger a Freeze, they send a signal through the tethering system that keeps the balloons from floating off. This triggers the balloons to release their payload and start the Freeze process. Since Richard came around, they've been able to upgrade their designs. Depending on how much or how quickly they release this material, it can alter how long or how cold the upcoming Freeze is. It was the perfect system, or so they thought. Because Richard based his calculations on this balloon system, it was only a matter of time before he caught on to what his predictions truly followed. Ironically, the more they experimented, the more varied the data became. That's what got Richard on their trail."

"Wait, wait, they can control how long they last now? How can they treat our lives so...casually?"

Chen felt his neck grow hot with rage. He thought about how many close Freezes there were in the years before he left. How tense things were every Freeze where the calculations came close. How every Freeze he cinched his coat tight and wondered how loose his brother's coat was fitting after the previous cycle. It was beyond control. It was megalomania. Teresa noticed his distress and offered a sympathetic smile.

"I'm sorry, Chen. That's how they treat all our lives. I'm sorry I was part of the system that ran your life and so many others. Before I joined, they ran my life too, not to mention how they keep the Depths as the preeminent economic powerhouse in the world. Now it's no excuse, but we finally have a chance. If I know how you're feeling, then you're ready to nail these bastards to the wall."

Teresa looked excited. For the first time, he saw another victim in Teresa. A victim like him. Another who had lacked control all their life and finally had a chance to take it back. He'd never seen her so animated before. He could feel his own anger channel into her quivering movements. Chen nodded to her to continue.

"Now, there's one clear weak point in all this. The yoke they hold over the Depths lies in that system. Ever since Richard gave them carte blanche to play with their toys in public, they've put more resources into it, modifying it, improving it. They've turned it back into a bona fide research project. And every research project needs researchers."

"Okay, I get they're rich and powerful beyond all belief, but there's no way they can keep something like that under wraps. I know scientists. Even Richard needed a team and a sponsor. How can they stop people from talking about the project of the century, even if they could hide the money?"

"Yes, you are correct. The amount of money they sank into it needs a team to make use of it. At first, they tried to covertly divert university projects to the cause. A little siloed team here, a redirection of a funded project there. For a while it satiated their desire for advancement, but they never knew where to stop. That kind of separation made it impossible to get any real work done. It was a high risk of exposure for very little gain. So, they turned to extrajudicial means of recruitment."

The realization hit like a truck. Efficient and cruel. Emblematic of the oligarchy of families that lived above everyone.

"Extrajudicial? Wait, you can't be talking about the Shockies?"

"That's exactly who I'm talking about. We've all heard the stories. The boogeymen of those on High sent to spirit away hardened criminals and kids who break curfew alike. We all expect those taken never to be seen again, but why leave such a valuable resource to waste? A diverse set of delinquents with desirable skills weren't going to be sitting long."

Chen's eyebrows lifted in realization.

"Wayne?"

Teresa nodded.

"Wayne, among many others. These people, they needed everyone. Mechanics, engineers, researchers, sanitation. They built a little town around this thing. Well, more accurately a town around the base of the thing where they're anchored to surface. It's nested inside the Weather Bureau campus, where another nondescript government building is unlikely to draw attention. I'm sure you're aware that the families hold a lot of sway. Most don't know that since they funded the early research, the government has all but ceded power to the families' descendants. Government buildings are simply extensions of their property."

It'd been the worst-kept secret how powerful the industrial families were, but to hear how deep it ran firsthand was disturbing.

"A whole town around this thing? All right under our noses for years. Why just the base? I mean why not populate it up the chain or establish an entirely different organization?"

"Too risky. They're all about control. The only way to keep control is to restrict access. Chaperones go up with staff anytime the system needs updating or maintaining. Even the ones with the longest tenure have two guards minimum each time they travel up."

"Why do you even know all this? I mean, sure, they had to clue you in once they realized they could only hide it from you for so long, but it seems unnecessarily perilous to give you this much detail."

"You forget I'm a researcher at heart. I was only promoted after working for decades with Richard on the model. By that point, our progress had gotten so far, it would've been suspicious to the public if they squashed it without explanation. I'd been on news program after news program extolling the benefits of predicting the Freezes and how that would launch the Depths into the future. My exposure had become so public by that point that they figured I was better used than kept in the dark. And for years, I'm sad to say they were right. Once I denounced Richard's comments and chose to protect the Weather Service, they knew they had me where they wanted me."

"And now? I assume you can't just disappear without drawing suspicion."

"Not for long. I'm high up enough to get some breathing room, but the only ones with true freedom are the families. They'll catch on soon enough, especially since after picking up Wayne for sniffing too close. They'll want to check the physical files, and I had to wave my badge around to retrieve them. I don't think it'll be a far reach for them to link Richard's murder, Wayne's suspicions, and my absence as their worst fears. They'll circle the wagons and move to damage control. No protection throughout the Depths will be enough to save us. Which is why we need to act now before they put the pieces together."

"Act how? As far as I can tell, they've got us by the short hairs no matter how you look at it."

"Their control works twofold. It would be trivial for them to discredit anyone bringing Persephone to light. I mean, it sounds as crazy as what Polar Vortex has been saying for years to the point where the rhetoric defeats itself. Then there's the system itself. As magnanimous as they claim to be, money underlies everything. With their research, they've made many self-interested choices based on fuel outlooks, materials goods, and how it all affects their bottom line. While I struggle to say they'd resort to despotism should we blow the cover off, I wouldn't totally rule it out. A long Freeze would be enough to set back any coup for decades to come. Panic breeds desperation, and desperation is where they are strongest. I wouldn't be surprised if Richard came to the same conclusions."

Chen shuddered to think what Anna would do with this information. With how deeply they'd infiltrated, he wouldn't be shocked if they could turn over enough of the staff until the power they exerted was total. Given how much they'd invested into Vandley, he doubted exposing the truth would recoup that kind of loss and dedication. Anna seemed dead set on revealing the truth, but anger that intense could lead to unpredictable decisions. He knew they didn't have long until they too pieced together what Chen had known only for the last day or so. Teresa was right: they needed to be stopped. All of them.

"I agree with you, Teresa, they need to be stopped. Whether it's on High or Polar Vortex, there can be no good so long as this system exists. So, what's your plan here? I'm no scientist, remember."

"The key lies in the weather balloon system. They're unoccupied for several hours a day once maintenance is done and the 'Shockies,' as you call them, turn over shifts. They're tethered through a heavily reinforced cable anchored at the far corner of the Weather Service campus. It's held firm since the early days, so upgrades to it have been largely ignored for more profit-driven endeavors. With good timing and good fortune, we can release the entire chain of balloons into the upper atmosphere. Sure, they can communicate with it wirelessly, but without regular maintenance, fuel, and Persephone supplies, Freezes will quickly fall out of sync with projections. Then our story about Persephone will be much harder to discredit once we release the papers."

It was a daring plan, to say the least. To go into the heart of the Weather Service where their surveillance was strongest and destroy the monster from within. It was almost a fantasy. But given their time limitations, fantasy was the only chance they had.

"I follow you so far. It's a desperate plan, but I don't have anything better. So, what happens then? I mean, the next cycle could start months or even weeks from the end of this Freeze, right?"

Teresa shifted uncomfortably at that question. He could see her mind working to formulate an answer to his satisfaction, but he doubted that one existed.

"Yes, Chen, you're right. We'd be rocketing everyone we knew into an uncertain future. Even with all their resources, I doubt on High could make a weather balloon chain fast enough to avert the chaos that would affect their bottom line. I doubt even Richard could tell you what would happen next. But it would be uncertain for *all* of us. Not just those on High or Polar Vortex. I couldn't tell you if the sun would shine next month or even tomorrow. But it would give us a chance to try again. A chance for people like me to make predictions for the good of all and not just the few."

"Isn't Persephone just a tool? Why destroy the thing itself? It's not without merit, couldn't someone else use this thing for the betterment of everyone?"

"And who would that be, Chen? The scientists working on it? Polar Vortex? Forget about the fact that we'd have no time to credibly explain the system to the public without sounding like a couple of cranks. Who would you trust to handle this system? Not to mention that since we'd have to hand over control quickly to fight on High, we'd have to do it without the chance for public scrutiny."

Chen racked his brain. Anna claimed that the truth was paramount, but Chen had only known her true self for a week at best. That level of control, especially without public scrutiny, was a heady drug. And despite her assertions, the death of her father made her intentions less than pure.

The scientists in charge were essentially prisoners. They deserved justice and freedom, but he wouldn't be surprised if revenge was high on their priority list. And what better way to exact revenge than to turn on High's best tool against them? Either way, the Depths would pay the price. It had to be a price worth paying, and Chen couldn't see that being the case with anyone in charge.

"This is fucking insane. You're telling me that we either help to continue a system that has controlled everyone's lives for the sake of predictability, or we buy our freedom not knowing what the price ultimately will be? There must be another way. I mean, what kind of choice is that?"

Teresa sat back down as she stopped pacing around the room. For the first time in hours, she looked exhausted. He'd finally understood, but they'd come no closer to an agreement. She sat with her back straight and looked at Chen with unwavering conviction.

"There isn't one. I've spent countless hours and late nights thinking about what I could do. About who could take over, how to reveal the truth realistically without sending everyone into chaos. Or just how to escape. Especially when Richard left, any idea I had failed from the start without someone else's support. I've been in a fog for years now. Richard's death has cleared my mind for the first time in over a decade. Events are in motion, Chen. If we do nothing, someone will hold this system over the Depths and there will be nothing anyone can do. When someone holds all the cards, you have to change the rules. This is our chance to make sure everyone lives in the same uncertainty they foisted on us for all this time."

"And what about Piotr and Morgan? We wouldn't be talking together if it wasn't for them. What happens when we outmode everything that Polar Vortex has been working for? They won't have a use for them any longer, and I doubt Anna is the understanding type."

"I've been thinking a lot about that these last few nights, and I've got a solution for that. All we need is time, and time is something I can buy us. I'll take our complete copy of the plans and approach Anna about taking their place. She knows my usefulness. Having both the plans and myself to interpret them will be too big a resource to turn down."

Chen felt himself shiver at the thought. He turned to Teresa with an incredulous expression. "Teresa, I can't let you do that. Before I left, I promised Morgan there'd be no more heroes. No more sacrifices. She's already inconsolable after they made off with Wayne. She'll never agree to this."

Teresa's brow furrowed in annoyance. "Then don't give her a choice. Given Wayne's resourcefulness and intellect, I'm almost certain he's there, right now, researching Persephone at their beck and call. Our sabotage of Persephone is certainly his only hope out. During the time it takes for us to work out an exchange with Anna, I need you to make sure that the information I have becomes worthless. If we time this right, Morgan and Piotr will be halfway to surface and I'll be halfway down before Morgan knows what the price was. Then there will be no system and no choice but to reveal the truth."

"And what exactly are you buying me time for? How do I fit into all of this?"

"I'm asking you to destroy the distribution system. It's the only way to make sure these Persephone plans can only be used for exposing them rather than a route to power. I'd guess we have three days before Polar Vortex pieces together the information, or those on High connect the dots and freeze me out. I have to act now to give you the window to use my credentials and Piotr's device to access the control panel and manually override the anchor that keeps them in place."

Chen looked up and met Teresa's gaze. She was serious. Serious about a plan that sounded borderline suicidal. "*What?* You expect me to personally go to one of the most well-known and well-guarded government offices on High? How do I even get in the door?"

"You won't. I will."

Teresa reached into her pocket and produced a lanyard with a badge attached to the end. She turned the badge to face Chen. He could see a younger version of Teresa looking hopefully back at him. At the bottom in capitalized red letters read *EXECUTIVE ACCESS*.

"This badge is just short of total access. It'll get you where you need to go."

"And what happens when they realize I'm not Teresa Hightower? Or after I destroy the system?"

"They won't. There is a series of entrances near the maintenance side that are monitored primarily through video. The tapes are routinely reviewed to double-check against badge access, but not live. It's usually done on a shift-by-shift basis. If we're quick enough, you'll be in and out before they have a chance to see you as Teresa, the walking smudge."

Chen felt himself making tight fists without realizing. He'd gripped his palms so hard without realizing that there were small bloody marks from where his nails broke the skin. He couldn't tell if he was still seething about the system itself or the plan itself. Credit to Teresa, she wasn't sugarcoating anything. The best of circumstances had Chen escaping the surface by a hair's breadth.

"We're? What do you mean if *we're* quick enough?"

Teresa's expression softened as she noticed how tired he looked. How defeated. Though he wasn't trying hard to hide anything.

"Yes, Chen, *you're*. Listen, I know what I'm asking you to consider is 'off bloc,' as you say. Hell, it's in the fucking stratosphere. But we don't have a lot of time to make this happen and even less to decide. Take the night. Talk it over with Piotr and Morgan. They've as much a right to this as you do. But please, don't delay. We don't have the time."

With that comment, Teresa rose and moved away from Chen, taking the Persephone papers with her. She moved with the energy of passion. Something Chen lacked.

This plan was certifiable. A plan of extremes born of guilt and need, with him at the center of it all. Chen had meant what he said. He was certainly not hero material.

He moved toward the end of the building. For insulation purposes, there were no windows in the back, but he headed toward the repair corner and sat in his old stool to get some perspective. He remembered many late nights sitting here before each Freeze, frantically trying to repair old machinery or make an amalgam of old parts so they could delay another order to Geraldson Co. Sometimes he'd take a few minutes to look up at the corner of the ceiling and imagine a window into the outside so that the cold, inky blackness of the sky could swallow him and this entire shed. Somewhere without a red blinking clock, without the smell of Fuel, without responsibility or expectation. Or monotony. The last few days had him yearning for that predictability again. He looked up in that corner now, and a fluorescent light hummed back artificially at him. It offered no dark corners to hide.

Chen pulled out his phone to access the secure chat Piotr had set up but hesitated to type. He could almost picture what Piotr would say with that shit-eating grin on his face:

"Fucking do it, Chen. Fuck those pricks surface side. They don't deserve this much thought. They fucking never thought about us."

Morgan? He wasn't so sure. He didn't feel good about deceiving her, but he knew that without a guarantee for Wayne, she'd be hard to predict. Ever since that moment they snuck out of Geraldson together, her conviction had strengthened like iron. Where that conviction led her, Chen doubted even she knew. At least Teresa had a vision, even if it was insane.

He could feel his head pound and his body ache. It'd been nearly two days since he last used Fuel, and it was starting to show. His hands shook and his vision blurred. This was hardly the longest he'd laid off the cloth, but Morgan had seen him through withdrawals in much more predictable times. Chen could feel his mind start to clear from the haze he'd been in the last few weeks. He could hardly remember the last time his sleep wasn't initiated by smothering his own mouth and nose. He thought about what he was going to say to Piotr and Morgan, what to type as the cursor blinked back at him expectantly. Chen began to type.

Have a plan, not sure if you're going to like it. Persephone, it's all real, they've controlled it all for so long now. The cycles, it's been them all along, Geraldsons, O'Rileys, the fucking cabal at the top. Teresa wants us to tear it all down. She...

Chen rubbed his eyes, but it did not help the message read any better. It needed more work. He read the message half a dozen times. His eyes crossed as he tried to edit and make it sound less ominous, but there wasn't really a way he could see to do it. His fingers felt heavy, followed quickly by his eyelids. His head slumped forward on the stool as his gentle snores rattled the old stool as they did many cycles ago.

17

Chen was falling through the Depths. His body was weightless along the central Freight line, shuttles traveling around the circumference of the central shaft, winding around him like the mechanism of an ancient clock. He could see Morgan being shuttled from her university studies and to the morgue, resigned. He could see his brother Nate running counter to her to the surface, burdened with bags of replacement parts. He looked as exhausted as Chen remembered, fighting the countdown clock like everyone around him. He watched as a Freight trams flew toward him at an alarming speed. Desperate people were glued to the sides like parasites, trying to reach inside for any part that was salvageable. He could hear the rattle of surface wreckage as the Freight shed pieces to its attached passengers. As the bottom of the Depths came up, he threw his arms in front of himself. His body punched through the floor as the cycle of shuttles started again. The shuttles full of stressed faces, the Freight full of the wealthy's garbage.

Chen awoke with a start. He instinctively started reaching for the tools in front of him, racing against the clock. He had already started reorganizing the wrenches to their sockets before he realized what was going on. His neck throbbed. Many cycles ago, he could sleep in that upright position without much fuss. Chen looked at the time. His device glared back at him, flickering 10:57.

He unlocked his screen with a pending message to Morgan and Piotr unsent. He let out a sigh, realizing that he had fallen asleep before messaging Morgan and Piotr about the plan. There were a few queries from them asking for updates, but nothing since late last night. He doubted that Anna was giving them real peace since his escape; they were likely acting as her mouthpiece. He hoped that rest would clear his mind enough to decide. The cold overhead lights mocked his naivety. He'd talk with Teresa first before planning a more detailed message.

Chen rubbed the back of his neck slowly as he rose and started moving toward the front of the shed where Teresa was sleeping. His footsteps echoed louder as he moved toward the more wide-open space where the larger machinery was housed. His breath fogged as he rounded the corner and called for Teresa.

"Teresa, I hope you could get comfortable. I know how hard it is to sleep in here when it's all environmentally controlled for machines and not people..."

As Chen rounded the corner, an empty tarp stared back at him, undisturbed. He looked around for signs of a struggle or disturbance. The layers of dust were only broken by two sets of footsteps, calmly reflecting the recent past. He could see Teresa's footsteps burn a path in the ground before heading toward the shed door. He could feel his breath catch in his throat as he noticed a stack of papers placed neatly on a machine's seat next to him, carefully weighed down with a spare part to prevent their disturbance. He tried to stay calm as he read the top page:

Chen,

I'm sorry. I tried to wait for your decision, I really did. But I've never been more certain about anything in my life. This must be how Richard felt the last time he called me. I wish I had the same conviction as I do now. Then maybe all this could've been avoided. I've contacted Anna and set the plan in motion. As you read this, I'll be on my way into the Depths, and Morgan and Piotr should be on their way up. I've hidden half of Persephone and promised to reveal its location once Morgan and Piotr are safe. I doubt I'll hold out as long as Richard did under their scrutiny. You'll find my badge and directions to the entrance I spoke about yesterday to Persephone. I wanted to give you a choice, I really did. But I realized there's no time for that now. The Depths deserve this chance, and you're the person to give it to them. So please, do the right thing.

Teresa Hightower

Chen gripped both sides of the letter until the paper tore at the edges. He read and reread until the words lost meaning. He ran to the back and tried to calm down but found himself ripping tools off the pegboard. He tried to stop as he began throwing everything into disarray. He lost control of his body. His mind told him to stop, but his arms wouldn't listen. Metal clanked on concrete as tools littered the floor around him. He was angrier than he ever remembered. When the pegboard was empty, he took the stool and began beating it against the ground until the metal warped in a way that even he couldn't fix.

How could she *do* this to him? This was his *life*, his *bloc*, *all* of their lives. Ever since he was young. The needs of the many over the needs of the few. HIS needs. He grabbed the warped wrench and beat the desk with it until it snapped in half.

Sorry? What a load of *shit*. Who wouldn't be *sorry* after their indecision got their friend killed? And for what? Just to push their agenda on someone else after their guilt got too much to bear? And now he was to pay the price? What sanctimonious *bullshit*.

Chen reached into his pocket and again only found the crumpled note from Morgan. He screamed in frustration and tore it up, scattering the pieces across the floor. What the *fuck* was he supposed to do now?

Chen paced the shed, trying to steady himself. His breath formed a constant trail behind him, mirroring the lines in the dust formed as he walked. Teresa was long gone by now. She probably hadn't slept at all last night. She'd put a lot of thought into leaving him with nothing. Persephone was gone. Remembering the conviction in her eyes, odds were she was telling the truth about her plan. If she was smart, and she was, it'd be too late to reach out to Morgan and Piotr. They'd have left the Pits by now, making any message to them pointless.

Nothing there. Teresa's crusade wasn't his own. He solved the case. As soon as Anna confirmed the Persephone information, Chen doubted she'd bother coming after him. She might even feel generous enough to continue his protection. Or at the very least give him enough time to come up with another plan to disappear. He could do it with Morgan and Piotr. Tell them where he was, plan where they were going next. He doubted Piotr aspired to be some sort of revolutionary. Morgan...they'd find a way to get to Wayne. She'd understand. They couldn't help him from inside a concrete box. Maybe Anna would be magnanimous enough after realizing Polar Vortex's goals to release Wayne and extend their protection. Though he knew that was wishful thinking at best.

There was always the chance that Anna followed through on her promise. Like Teresa said, it was only a matter of time before Polar Vortex would find the truth, considering how far Vandley had got them. And now she was serving it to them on a silver platter. Their infiltration probably went farther than Chen realized.

That was assuming that Anna stayed on-brand with the original Polar Vortex her father had built. And that was a big if. The Polar Vortex that Chen knew, that anyone outside the group knew, was gone. Science-based fanatics were replaced by military zealots. In the years since her father's death, Polar Vortex now looked more like the Shock Unit than a group interested in revealing the truth. There was a chance he was wrong, but could the Depths rely on just a chance?

Chen cracked the shed open and let the freezing air hit his face. His breath caught in his throat as his face grew numb and forced a moment of clarity. He took a few breaths before closing the door and taking a seat on the tarp.

Goddammit.

Chen grabbed the stack of papers Teresa had left for him. On top of the pile was a badge reading:

Teresa Hightower

Head of the Weather Service

EXECUTIVE ACCESS

She gazed back at him from the badge with a look of optimism that he didn't share. The look of someone who hadn't lost anything yet. Chen found a neatly folded map underneath and laid it out on the tarp. Before him sat a detailed floor plan of the ground level of the Weather Service. A large, transparent watermark of the Weather Service logo embossed the background with CONFIDENTIAL stamped along the side. Chen realized that she had taken this with her on her way out of the Weather Bureau. All of yesterday's conversation, presenting her logic. All fucking theater. This was always the plan, whether Chen wanted it or not. He swallowed his anger and began studying the map.

The campus was sprawling, nearly fifty acres all spread along the surface. There was an immense building that took up nearly the entire north border of the map flanked by two rotund Boilers. Chen recognized it as the building where he had first met Teresa. It was the main administrative building where most of the high-ranking bureaucrats and researchers spent their time. Long lines extended out from it like spokes from a hub, each flanked at regular intervals with residential-size Boilers. It kept transit between buildings warm throughout each cycle. Teresa had marked these as walkways with warnings scribbled in red: ALWAYS UNDER GUARD. Given that they were just at the start of a Freeze, these halls were likely used at all hours of the day. At arbitrary spots, these walkways diverged and met with smaller, ancillary buildings in a complex spider web of bureaucracy. A small building near the southwest corner was circled and labeled Anchor Controls.

Chen followed a line backward from the building and through the campus. It formed a meandering path between the building alleys, through several loading bays, and eventually ending near the shuttle stop at the southwest end of the map. Besides some small heat shelters in the loading bays, the path was completely outside. Of course. Teresa had conveniently left that out of her plan's description.

Doing some quick calculations, Chen estimated that the entire trip one way would take about twenty minutes at a brisk pace. And given the time of year, brisk meant not freezing to death. He could tell at a glance that this path was meant to limit exposure to surveillance, but even with short breaks inside the small heat stations, it would be tight. With economical movement, he could avoid spending more than ten continuous minutes exposed. He'd seen many pickers lose more than just a finger that way.

Chen flipped through the instructions on how to operate the balloon anchor controls. Teresa was right; the tech was outdated. There seemed to be no redundancy built in once the main switch was flipped. After decades of dominance, why wouldn't the families be overconfident? They had nature on their side. She'd drawn some crude stick figures denoting two guards posted outside the entrance in a heated station and a principal engineer sitting at the central control panel. *Eleven p.m.* was handwritten and labeled as guard turnover. Normal procedure indicated that one guard reviewed the previous shift's video logs to compare ID scans to faces, but Teresa noted that the night shift often sped this process up by having both guards review tapes at once. If he was lucky, they'd wave him through with little scrutiny.

Chen began pacing the length of the building. He studied the materials over and over until he could see himself going through the motions of Teresa's plan. He was desperate to come up with an alternative, but as the clock against the wall ticked down to sunset, his mind could only draw blanks. She could be halfway to the Pits now, maybe farther if she had left before sunrise. There simply wasn't any time left.

He imagined Morgan and Piotr standing on the shuttle, trying not to fall over from exhaustion as it curved upward through the central shaft. He could see Teresa clutching her package tightly to her chest winding the opposite way. She looked almost peaceful. Assured in her plan. Far from how he felt now.

He thought about how confused Morgan and Piotr would be once they arrived at an empty shed on surface. Better to let Nate know about more unexpected guests. He'd asked enough of his brother already, but Chen knew that if he said it was important, Nate would get it done. He'd made the place hospitable enough without asking too many questions. Chen left a note for Piotr and Morgan explaining what he could without alarming them too much. They just needed to lie low and trust his brother on this. He recorded a message while packing the little he needed.

Chen gathered his clothes and stuffed the map into his hidden pocket. He patted Piotr's device for comfort as he drew the door open and let the ice sting his face as he headed toward ground transport. There wasn't a heat shelter there, but he didn't mind. He felt like he was burning from the inside out.

Chen checked the time and estimated that he'd have some wiggle room to walk through the steps in his head on the shuttle before reaching the Weather Service. He watched as the sun set over the horizon and the ambient temperature tumbled to dangerous levels. His brother would be settling in about now, his dad probably up with a soft light in the living area, calculating food reserves and parts. It didn't matter how many times his father ran the numbers, it never reassured him. He could hear the transport's miniature Boiler struggle to life as it kicked up a cloud of dust and ice on its way to him.

18

Chen struggled to control his paranoia as the shuttle rocked back and forth. He sat at the rear end of his compartment facing the rest of the car. Scientists crowded the tram in front of him and paid him no mind, but it didn't help much. The transport ride went smoothly as expected. He was getting closer to their territory now.

Chen glanced at the cameras in the carriage, one directly in front of him in the upper corner and another one directly above him. He was in a relative blind spot for now. Those promised to be harder to come by as he got closer. The ride before didn't have a camera to worry about, but the closer he got to the Weather Service, the denser the coverage was bound to become. Chen likely still had Polar Vortex coverage for now, but once Teresa got to the Pits, the odds of keeping it decreased dramatically. He'd be last cycle's news.

He cradled the device Piotr had given him in his pocket. He'd activated it shortly before coming on the shuttle. He'd have to keep the activations economical to avoid suspicion, though it seemed impossible as he pulled into the station and he spotted three cameras even before exiting the shuttle. Chen got up and tried to mingle with the scientists as they squeezed to exit the platform. The station itself had an outdated government feel. A large glass dome offered an unobstructed view of the sky. The dark sky was broken up in the distance by the main weather service building, which divided the sky in two with ominous brick piercing the airspace above. Chen could see the hint of two massive Boilers omitting a red-hot glow. The sight shook him enough to cause him to hesitate before shaking it off. He moved quickly and tried to shield himself with the crowd as he rushed to a utility exit near shuttle maintenance. Surface-level security was still a few stops away, and maintenance teams didn't routinely patrol until then either. Usually.

Chen took out his device and turned his flashlight on. His light extended a paltry distance into the maw of the tunnel gaping before him. He looked above and saw no signs of cameras in the passage ahead. He took a moment to switch off his device. It was hot with effort. This tunnel was relatively deserted compared with the one near Geraldson, likely due to increased government security near the actual system. He doubted any recyclers lived this close to the shuttle stop. It was too much risk of getting caught with very little gain. Chen moved ahead, his steps echoing as he tried to stay close to the wall. According to Teresa's blueprints, there should be an exit spilling directly into surface for external maintenance. Every so often, a shuttle running nearby shook the walls of the tunnel, causing dust and ice particles to fall onto the track. There was a small rail system to allow maintenance crews easy access to where they needed to go. Legally, these small shuttles needed to keep their light on while running to prevent collisions. During a Freeze, these were more guidelines than rules. That meant that whenever the tunnel shook, Chen had to slow to a crawl and keep ready to hide should a crew ride through at the worst time.

Chen felt along until his hand brushed up against a cold metal handle. He could feel his sweat freeze slightly as he checked his reference map. This was it. He took a few minutes to clasp his coat tight and wrap a scarf around his nose and mouth. Any exposed skin would cut his time outside in half. He double-checked to make sure Piotr's device was activated before putting on gloves so thick he lost all tactile sensation. As an oncoming shuttle shook the ground beneath him. Chen pushed the door open, and a wall of icy wind greeted him.

He had less than a second to appreciate the frozen tundra laid out in front of him before he had to squint against the force of the Freeze. Keeping his eyes open could mean partial vision loss in minutes, blindness in ten. Chen struggled to push the door closed against its frozen latch before gazing out into the violent, stormy night for the next landmark. He scanned the whiteout conditions for a sign. Any sign. A red light blinked steadily in the distance. According to the map, it was several hundred feet away, but the weather distorted the distance to appear much farther. Combating the Freeze was as much mental as it was physical. He needed to trust the map. He knew from picking days that he needed to hurry to the heat shelter. Once he lost his sense of urgency, he knew he was done for, and they'd be arresting his frozen corpse in the morning.

He recalled many of his emergency shed trips on his old bloc and focused on putting one foot in front of the other. The distance wasn't too different, but he had been much younger then and more confident in his body's recovery abilities. Chen kept his head down as he walked, glancing only momentarily at the light ahead of him to make sure he was headed in the right direction. Even if there was someone out here doing maintenance, he doubted they'd be able to see each other until they were practically touching. He struggled to steady himself as his foot hit a patch of hidden ice under the snow. He reached out onto the ground before he lost his balance. Chen knew that a fall could be fatal, especially if snow made its way into his coat. He'd been to plenty of memorials for just that. As his body started to feel paradoxically warm and his mind was convincing him to take a seat, he could see the snow change to a red hue as his head hit the phone-booth-sized heat shelter in front of him. Chen could feel the radiation of the lamp inside. He fumbled desperately to open the door as a wave of hot air greeted him.

He collapsed onto the small wooden bench. The door slammed shut automatically to conserve heat, nearly pinching one of his fingers off. He moved his finger and toes steadily as the blood slowly pulsed with his heartbeat through his body. He removed his scarf and let the hot light above bathe his skin. Steam rose from all over his body as ice turned to water vapor. Chen hardly noticed the camera in the corner in his relief. He sat there for a few minutes, forgetting why he was there and the longer walk ahead of him to the next shelter. He struggled to pull the map out of his pocket with his fingers feeling so raw. As far as he could tell, he was headed in the right direction. He could see another red light nearly due west of his position. It flickered in the distance. As he got up and gathered his things, he noticed a white light approaching steadily from the east, where he'd just come from. It seemed to rise and fall rhythmically, as with a person's steps. It followed the path he had taken Not good. He tried to control his breath to conserve energy and avert an outright panic.

Chen tried to stay calm as he dressed for the next leg in his journey. No time to rest. He'd have to hurry on this next leg without fully replenishing his body heat. Had the hatch he used been attached to a sensor? Did they send someone to investigate, and they noticed his steps in the snow? Were the heat shelters themselves monitored, and the smudge he was drew too much attention? He didn't know, but he couldn't stay to find out. While he was certain they couldn't see him from that distance, he tried to open the door to the shelter nonchalantly and began trudging toward his next oasis.

Halfway through his journey, Chen saw a set of tracks leading toward the shelter he was heading for. He was able to make good time shadowing the steps in front of him, but that didn't stop questions from invading his mind. Was he following the steps of a security sweep he had tripped? There wasn't time to find an alternative. Five more minutes out here and there'd be permanent nerve damage, and it was another fifteen minutes until the stop after this one. About ten steps from the door, he saw that the heat shelter was occupied.

He couldn't tell from this distance what the person was wearing or if they were busy repairing the shelter itself, but from his numb feet he knew there wasn't another option. The next stop was the anchor point, and that was easily double the distance he had just walked. This shelter was meant to be his last drink of heat before the final push. He made doubly sure to pat Piotr's device before gently rapping on the door.

The woman inside jumped in surprise. Her face softened as she noticed Chen shivering and made way to allow the door to open and Chen to step inside. She was dressed in branded Geraldson coat and scarf. Before she turned around, Chen noticed MAINTE-NANCE emblazoned across the back of her coat. He could feel her concern mixed with skepticism at Chen's state of dress. Nothing too shabby, but clearly upcycled, if not recycled fully. He tried to gauge the right amount of eye contact as he turned to close the door behind him and face her.

"Th–thank you so much for letting me in. I'm not sure how much longer I would've lasted out there. I'm sorry to barge in like this."

"It–it's fine. I didn't expect to get a heater this late in the night in this kind of weather. Don't you people usually stay somewhere else? They called us out here like it was some kind of five-alarm fire. Woke me up from my first sleep on shift in weeks."

She looked like she'd been on the job for years. Chen recognized a veteran night shift worker when he saw one. Antisocial on the job. Annoyed by any call that had wakened her from sleep. Her curiosity shifted to annoyance as she turned to face him, waiting for answers. He hoped that she was more likely to make Chen the morning shift's problem rather than her own.

"I'm sorry to do this, ma'am, it's just that the shuttle tunnels weren't safe for me. Pissed off the wrong self-proclaimed king of the tunnel or the like. Didn't have swipes for the shuttle down Low, so I went where I could. 'Bout got outta Dodge before they threw me out somewhere even less friendly. I saw the hatch and came out straight into the Freeze, trying to find what heat I could."

Chen watched as her annoyance turned to tired resignation. Right on the money. She rolled her eyes as she responded.

"I see, so nowhere else to go? And it's Martha, not 'ma'am.'"

"Sorry, Martha. And yes, nowhere else to go. I promise as soon as the sun comes up, I'll trudge my way back to the shuttle where I came from, like I wasn't even here. Won't even take up space that's being used. If you're here, I won't be."

Martha made it a point of giving Chen a sideways glance as she pulled out her radio. She clicked on the receiver and spoke. "This is Martha, notifying all channels. I found the source of the disturbance. An alarm was tripped by falling debris. I'm working on the repair now, please acknowledge."

She let go of the transmission button. Static dominated the channel for a few seconds before an unknown part responded. "Copy that. Security sweep canceled. Stay warm out there, Martha."

Martha tucked her walkie into her waist and turned to face Chen. "All right, but you gotta promise to cheese it if you see someone in a heat shelter or heading toward one. Otherwise, they'll wake our asses back up again, and I'd prefer to sleep the rest of my shift."

"I promise, starting now. I'll head right out as soon as my fingers aren't blue."

"Good. Now is it safe to assume you were the one that tripped the proximity sensor on that shuttle hatch?"

"Yes, that one's on me. I'm sorry for waking you earlier, won't happen again."

"Okay. I got a colleague headed toward me walking along the path you left. I'll let him know that I took care of it. Hopefully we can both get some rest tonight. But you gotta be outta here at first light or I'll make sure dayshift do a full sweep. And *they'll* be well rested. Security's not known to be kind up here with you folks."

Martha put a hand to her hip and looked at him with a critical eye. She wouldn't stand for her sleep to be interrupted again. Better not to end up in a cell out of spite.

"That won't happen, Martha, trust me. I don't plan to be here longer than I need to be. Heard too many stories of the on High crime squad. I'm not looking to be a part of that."

"Okay. Well you look warm enough to me. Get outta here and I'll get on the radio. Oh, and do a better job sweeping up your trail. I could follow you with my eyes closed from what you left coming in here. I'll stay behind and let my coworker know it was a false alarm. Other people won't be so friendly, so give the shelters a wide berth. Just make sure to find your warmth off campus before the sun comes up."

Martha motioned toward the door as she turned back to working on the shelter. Chen rubbed his hands together one last time before donning his gloves and clothes. He hoped she'd keep her word. He couldn't check his map, so he pointed himself as west as he could manage and headed toward what he hoped was the far edge of the campus. He dragged his feet slightly and tried to create a less obvious path. He hoped this was enough to keep Martha off his back without spending too long in the Freeze. After a few agonizing minutes, Chen looked up and saw two bright white lights glaring at him through the snow. If memory served, this should be the guard's shelter right before the anchor point. He tried to find the weather balloons that were likely above him, but the cloud cover had intensified, and all he saw was a cold, unfeeling emptiness above.

As Chen approached, he saw the building come into view. In front of him was the guard station, essentially two heat shelters welded together. It had windows to allow for a 360-degree view of their surroundings, which was more for show than anything else in this weather. He could see a dark shape looming in the background, presumably the anchor building he was here to sabotage. It was hard to make out any details, but there was a small green light near a nondescript metallic door. Likely the keypad he had to scan into. Chen could see two guards in the station, an older-looking woman leaning comfortably back in a chair while a younger man stooped forward in a seated position, looking much more focused. Both had their eyes fixed to a screen in front of them. He could see the reflections of a screen dancing in their half-focused eyes as he got closer.

He tried to keep his distance as he approached the small stairway heading toward the building. Chen could feel the heat from pavement warmers that kept the worst of the ice from freezing the stairs. It must take a lot of energy to keep the heat consistent from the campus's central Boilers. It was a luxury few could experience, even when he lived on surface. Still, he felt unsteady as the guards turned to look at him. The older one spoke first while the younger quickly returned to reviewing the screen in front of him.

"Hold it. What they got you coming in for this late in this weather? I thought you government types were all nine-to-fivers."

She chuckled at her own comment. Her counterpart did not. He had the focus of someone new to the job. Chen did his best to smile through his scarf and offer a small laugh. She had the comfort of seniority. That played in his favor.

"Yeah, maybe if you're my boss or my boss's boss. Got the call right as they were clocking out. They put a maintenance cycle through, and it's gonna take another set of eyes in there. My eyes to be exact."

"Figures. What's with the outfit? They call you in without any overtime either or something?"

"Maybe if they got their shit together first. You know how it is. Some asshole forgot to sign form 23C or something, and now I gotta hop in here and save my boss's ass, or I'll be going down with the ship. Gotta log in a project that was supposed to be done weeks ago. Especially can't show up in my uni. Too many questions that are inconvenient for those up above."

Chen watched as the senior security guard considered his story. She watched for any sign of nervousness and leaned forward, exerting a soft pressure. Chen almost started sweating trying to suppress his urge to run. After a couple of minutes, her shoulders relaxed and she returned to a laid-back position in her chair.

"Damn, fuck those guys. I can barely see you shivering. You must've been out here for a while now. All right, go on inside but check in with us in the next half hour. Otherwise, we're coming in."

Chen nodded and walked quickly to the door. He pulled out Teresa's badge and placed it against the cold metal pad. The feeling in his hand was nearly gone. He was cutting it close, and the guard had eaten up most of his time. The light blinked green, and Chen quickly pushed inside, letting the warm air enter his lungs.

After taking a few breaths, he turned around and took in the interior. It looked even more outdated than the plans looked. The overhead lights were flickering with an artificial glow. The antechamber was little more than a concrete box with a bench to dress for each shift. Up a set of stairs directly in front of him, Chen could see a mess of panels and wires along the two walls to his left and right. Small bulbs blinked at random intervals, and several even flashed red with urgency. There were labels hanging off wires on the ceiling where someone, likely decades ago, had made a futile attempt to bring order to the chaos. He heard a chair squeak as someone in the next room rose. Cautious footsteps echoed him as Chen tried to compose himself. Given how unglamorous this position was, he was reasonably confident that a new hire would be placed here, especially on the night shift. Even odds he'd be able to talk his way through this or even muscle his way if need be. The engineer was likely some kind of egghead without much fighting spirit. He shook the frost off his coat and started taking his hat off, trying his best to look friendly.

"Hey, man, sorry to bug you in the middle of the night. They sent me from on High to do some routine maintenance they forgot to schedule. You know how it is with the anchor point, always getting the scraps and..."

"Chen? Chen is that you? What are *you* doing here?"

Chen failed to hide his shock as Wayne rounded the corner.

19

Chen stood there in shock. Minutes seemed to pass before his mind started to bounce back. Wayne looked thin. He remembered that he often skipped meals, but even then. Thinner than he remembered, more than just eating less. There was clear malnutrition. He could see the peaks of his cheekbones rise as his thinned eyebrows rose in confusion.

"Chen?"

His voice punched through his mental fog. Chen pretended to brush some frost off his coat as he tried to form words.

"*Wayne*? What are *you* doing here?"

Wayne let out a light laugh. It triggered a coughing fit that went on for several seconds. Chen could see his ribs rise and fall through his shirt. It looked painful.

"I asked you first. I'm pretty sure between the two of us, I've more of a right to be here than you."

Chen rubbed his temples. Ever since this case started, nothing had been straightforward. Why start now?

"They had you on Persephone this whole time? Morgan was worried the worst had happened to you since the Shock Unit took you!"

"Well, I'd say Morgan's not too far off. I haven't been here the whole time. They start off most of the 'workforce' in orientation.

Way too civil a word to describe what happens. This hasn't been the most gratifying experience in my life, even with cutting-edge research. And what about you? *You* know about Persephone? Is that why you're here?"

"Not for very long, but long enough to know why I need to be here. And you? They got you working on this monstrosity?"

"In a manner of speaking. As you can see, I'm a bit of a glorified babysitter at the moment. Bit too fresh a face to trust with the good stuff. Sleep doesn't come to me easily these days, so it's not the worst being on night shift. The Shock Unit doesn't make sleep a priority of theirs. Well, it's good to see a friendly face. At least, that's what I hope."

The "orientation," as Wayne put it, drew up images of the early days of the Freeze. Workers being forced to construct the Depths at a manic pace with little to no pay. Subsistence wages if you were lucky, a cot and three squares if you weren't. But now wasn't the time to dwell.

"Honestly, it's been a long time since I knew what was going on anymore. Do you think we can sit down? It looks like we could both need it."

"Sure, if you can follow me into my little palace."

Wayne turned and motioned Chen to follow. His movements seemed in slow motion. One leg dragged slightly behind him, leaving a small streak in the dust on the floor. They entered the next room. It reminded Chen of an old film, a small, circular control room with one of those semicircular control panels one might see in an ancient nuclear safety video. The walls were minimalistic. A central panel blinked lazily in response to some data gathering Chen would never understand. Wayne lowered himself slowly into a swivel chair in the center and gestured toward a stiff metal one next to him. He spun around almost whimsically as Chen took a seat, taking his larger coats and thick pants off. It was pleasantly warm.

"Welcome to my humble abode. To be honest with you, time has lost all meaning, but if I had to guess, I've probably been here for...nearly a week?"

"Not a bad estimate, though my sense of time hasn't been the best either. I think since we spoke it's been a few weeks? Maybe a little longer."

"Ah, I see. I heard you speak about Morgan in the present tense. Is she doing well? Did she make it out okay?"

Wayne's eye turned to Chen in concern. Chen could tell that even in his poor state, Wayne thought of Morgan as much as she thought of him.

"In a manner of speaking. She should be working her way up the Depths right now. Probably better off than either of us, if I had to guess. She's been worried about you, as always."

"Good. Good. She'd be disappointed that I haven't kept up with my nutrition."

Wayne closed his eyes at the news and leaned back. His thin frame made no sound as it shifted the chair, despite the old metal. He was so thin, it made Chen uncomfortable. He couldn't help but think of what could do that to a man.

"And you, Wayne? What's happened to you?"

At that Wayne sat up. His eyes shot open, and a slight panic crossed his face. Chen could see he was somewhere else, reliving whatever horror had happened to him. Chen knew the Shock Unit was rough, but to see it in person, in someone he knew... He took a few deep breaths before speaking again.

"A little too soon for details, I think. Suffice to say that it wasn't long before I was ready to help with their little Persephone project. Before they took me away, I had started to suspect the worst despite how ridiculous it all sounded. I always had more imagination than the average researcher. By the time I was ready to...cooperate, I had enough basic information that they saw the use in me. And that's what really matters to them. Usefulness. My imagination became my undoing. They still felt I needed convincing first, of course. Once they felt sure I wasn't going to run off, my 'orientation' was finally over."

"Teresa did say that since the countdown they were a lot more active in chewing people up before spitting them out. That their research division was able to really get going once the countdown got so much attention."

"Hightower? Figures she'd be in on it too. That bitch. It's hard to surprise me nowadays. Don't have the energy for it."

Chen flinched at Wayne's harsh language. It felt bitter and un-characteristic of the Wayne he had met at the university.

"And what do they have you do here all night long?"

"Like I said, babysitting. Making sure enough of these lights stay green and reporting anything strange that happens overnight. You never answered my question. What are *you* doing here?"

Chen shifted uncomfortably in his seat. Last time he saw Wayne, his nervous energy had made him easy to read. This Wayne? He looked too tired to care about anything. Chen was sure the Shock Unit had ways of beating the fight out of you. He wasn't comfortable with the idea of going through Wayne after all he had put him through.

"Honestly, Wayne, I question why I'm here at all."

"Come on, Chen. Half-truths? I think I deserve a little more than that considering how I ended up here. Wasn't my informa-tion of use to the investigation? Did it help you solve that little murder of yours?"

Chen cleared his throat loudly. Wayne was right. He was owed more than what Chen was giving him. "I'm here to tear it all down, Wayne. All of it. Persephone, on High, all the bullshit."

Wayne let out a full laugh, one that made his skeletal body rattle and scrape against itself. It put Chen at ease for a moment. Wayne looked a lot like when Chen had first met him, entertained and curious.

"*You*? I hardly took you for the unsung folk hero type. Well, you gonna push through the last agent of the big bad before setting off a chain of events out of anyone's control? I gotta tell you, I don't think I'll give you a fight worth singing about."

Chen couldn't help but laugh in response. It was a nice change of pace to let go in front of someone who had no reason to hide their feelings. Even if amplified his guilt tenfold. He was beginning to feel part of what Morgan had been bearing for days now.

"You'd be right. You know, Morgan said the same thing to me after you were taken. No more heroes. And you couldn't find a worse candidate than me."

"So why go this far?"

"To be honest, I find myself without much of a choice. Looking back, it's been that way since the beginning. I guess I can't really escape it."

"Ah, well, I know what that's like. So, what's this eleventh-hour plan you find yourself in the middle of? Safe to say it's got something to do with the balloon system?"

"Safe to say so. Funny enough, it was Teresa's idea. She tells me that the controls to release the balloon chain are right here. That panel over there, in fact, according to the plans she took."

Chen motioned to the wall, where he had spotted a pair of metal handles before sitting down. He knew by instinct Wayne wouldn't be able to stop him if he just made a dash for them. But like Wayne said, he deserved better.

"So, what'll you do, Chen? Play the hero?"

"I don't know. What happens to you if I do?"

"I'm not sure, though probably nothing good. I may be an overqualified sitter, but it'd be safe to assume I'd get caught up in it nonetheless. It all tends to roll downhill, if you remember. That's been going around from what I hear, getting chewed up in other's machinations. I'll be on the chopping block with a lot of others. Those guards out there included."

Chen leaned back and took a moment to deliberate. He'd never known on High to be particularly generous or understanding. He could only assume that directly meddling with the families' affairs would be far worse for anyone involved.

"You could come with me. I don't plan on sticking around afterward, and the guards outside looked half asleep on my way in. I doubt they finished their video review yet, and you wouldn't be noticed until well into the morning shift."

"Ha, why do you think that is? This place isn't just my prison; it's my oasis. They make a point to confiscate any clothes they find that aren't already on my back. I mean, look at me."

Wayne hammered the point home by lifting his shirt, showing how oversized it was on him. At a glance, Chen estimated that Wayne had shrunk to half the weight of when they originally met. The wind alone would knock him off his feet and freeze him shortly after.

"I doubt my feet would carry me more than thirty feet before I collapsed in the snow."

Chen rubbed his eyes in frustration. Of course. It was clean, efficient, and effective. Every decision they made, the collateral always fell at someone else's feet. Every step Chen took was along a path someone else had laid in front of him. Polar Vortex, Teresa, and now on High. Each step planned meticulously for a scheme someone else had in mind.

Chen got up and walked the perimeter of the room. He was in a cage of manufactured certainty. They all were. It was bullshit. All of it. Chen could feel Wayne's eyes follow him slowly as he paced. Each step echoed in the small room until it seemed to blend in a deafening crescendo. His heart pulsed in his eardrums as he tried to find a way out. Out of this room. Out of this system. Out of the box they had put him in. He looked at Wayne, and empty eyes stared back at him. Chen let out a growl of anger as he sat down with a thud in the chair across from Wayne. He took Piotr's device out of his pocket and tossed it into Wayne's lap. Wayne looked at it in confusion.

"What is this?"

"It's my ticket out of here. Or was. It scrubs you from surveillance. I've used it sparingly so I could make a return trip. Your return trip."

"What are you talking about?"

"I'm tired, Wayne. I haven't had any say in this since the start. Turns out none of us have. I left my bloc to find an escape. Load of good that did. And now I'm here to do a job, but I'm gonna do it my way, not anyone else's. I'm releasing these balloons, and you won't be paying the price again. Take my clothes, take this device, meet Morgan and Piotr on my old bloc. And tell Morgan I'm sorry I couldn't keep my word."

Silence hung as Wayne pocketed Piotr's device. Chen hoped to see some fire in his eyes at the thought of escape. Instead, they were as devoid of feeling as they had been a few minutes ago.

"And you're ready to pay that price? You're not even sure what the cost is. Let me tell you, Chen, it's goddamn steep."

"Only one way to find out, Wayne. I'm just certain I can't afford to leave you here. This is my choice to make, and I'm asking you to take it."

Wayne closed his eyes and took a moment to process what Chen had said. Then he got up slowly, looking more spry than Chen had expected. Wayne dressed in Chen's clothing and examined Piotr's device. He found the button on the side and watched as a light turned green atop its smooth finish. Wayne left a trail in the dust as he walked toward the exit. He stopped in the doorway separating the control room for the entrance.

"You know this doesn't make us square."

"It's not you I'm trying to square with."

Wayne nodded and rapped the doorframe. "Good luck, Chen."

Chen nodded in response, but Wayne had already turned to leave. He wasn't sure how long he sat in the chair, watching the control lights flutter before him. It almost lulled him to sleep. He thought about Morgan and Piotr, probably entering his family's shed by now, alone and confused. He thought about how Wayne's appearance would probably shock them. Chen imagined Morgan's face, animated for the first time in a long while. Maybe even crying. Chen imagined Teresa arriving at the Pits flanked by Polar Vortex. Anna's shit-eating grin in a moment of triumph that wouldn't last. His mind lingered on his brother. How haggard he probably was this deep in a Freeze. How he was risking everything by helping Chen and his friends. How Nate never hesitated to make those kinds of choices. For the first time, Chen knew how that felt.

Chen got up from the chair and headed toward the corner of the room and the panel. He unceremoniously pulled both down in unison. A red light blared overhead, spinning a warning only he saw. The ground seemed to shake. He imagined the balloons overhead flying untethered and free into the upper atmosphere with nothing to weigh them down. He knew the feeling.

Chen crossed back into the central panel and sat down in Wayne's place. Alarms blared throughout the room. Lights insisted angrily for his attention on the panels in front of him. A clock nested on the wall in front of him. It counted down to the next shift. He paid it no mind.

20

The rest of that night was a blur of noise and movement. Chen had closed his eyes and remembered the sound of the alarm being interrupted by the door opening. Heavy boots sounded through the room. He had just enough time to see half a dozen Shock Unit soldiers surround him before they covered his face with a black sack. Chen struggled out of instinct, trying to shake free of the arms controlling him. This was quickly met with a blow to the stomach that doubled him over. He could feel people on either side of him pick him up by the arms and drag him out of the room. He felt a blast of frigid air as they dragged him through the snow and ice into a waiting car. They did not dress him.

Chen could hear hushed voices speak from the front seat. They sounded muffled, likely from a partition between the back and front. They had the heat on full blast for their own comfort, but they did leave the window cracked out of spite. He'd done much the same for suspects in the back of his patrol car when he was certain of their guilt. The Freeze was bad cop enough for most.

Chen tossed back and forth as they wound through unknown streets. He had been tracking their turns and keeping time before the noises outside gradually became more muffled. Probably underground now. Given how little noise he heard, it was likely off the beaten path. He gave up marking turns after that.

He wasn't sure how long they'd been traveling before they finally stopped. The driver got out without a word and pulled Chen out of the seat onto a concrete floor. It was quiet. Disturbingly so. Not even a hum of overhead lights broke the monotony as they lifted him again and started to drag him along. His feet scraped against the even floor beneath him for what felt like half a mile before they came to a stop.

The temperature was comfortable, clearly centrally controlled, unlike most of the Depths. He wasn't familiar with any place like that underground. There wasn't any hint of a breeze. He could hear the scratching of a pen and a grunt of affirmation as a metal door creaked open in front of him. A short distance later, he was thrown to the ground. Footsteps receded back from where they came.

Chen took a few deep breaths before getting up. He undid the latch where they had secured the bag on his head and slowly took it off. Wherever he was, it was dark. They had refined their interrogation techniques, starting with effective disorientation. He got up and felt his way around the room. It wasn't far from what he had imagined. Four concrete walls, all right angles, a little smaller than Vandley's apartment where Polar Vortex had stashed him away. He imagined a camera watching him from a corner equipped with night vision. Chen tried to suppress his fear so they wouldn't have the satisfaction.

Vandley. It was just a case. How did it end up like this? There was a thin blanket in the center of the room paired with a bucket. Otherwise, things were bare. He sat down and tried to warm himself by wrapping the sheet around him. Somehow it seemed to invite an impossible breeze. He tried to listen, but besides the slight rumble of the ground whenever someone walked past, there was nothing. No protests, no conversation, no screaming even. Somehow it just made Chen more nervous.

He could feel his eyelids get heavy. Time passed without indication. He quickly fell asleep.

✳ ✳ ✳

Chen awoke with a start. Light spilled into the room through a small slit in the door, about eye level. He tried to determine what time it was, but it was impossible. A gruff voice spoke to him in a matter-of-fact tone.

"Who sent you?"

"Wh–what? Sent me?"

"Who. Sent. You."

There was no anger or frustration in his voice. He spoke slower, as if they didn't speak the same language. His demeanor was calm, as if tutoring Chen rather than interrogating him.

"Listen, it's too late. Persephone is down and there's no getting it back. Keeping me here will do you no good. So let me—"

Chen was interrupted by the sound of something hitting the concrete floor. The slit closed with a clang and bathed him in darkness once more. Chen crawled forward on his hands and knees. His hands grasped a small round shape. He knew it well. It was a potato, much like the ones he had planted since he was a young man. He could feel the ridges and picture it in front of him. Chen began eating it slowly but quickly started scarfing it down. He could feel a slight breeze tussle his hair from above. It was cold. Freeze-cold. He quickly slid to the center of the room and covered himself the best he could, but it was pointless. The outside air surrounded the space efficiently from all sides. The room was quickly freezing. He'd learned about Freeze torture in school. How it was used against early dissenters of the Depths. The books chalked it up to a desperate government, but it was heavily implied that was when the families started exerting their control. They learned the hard way to reserve hard control for the worst dissenters in the quiet of their private spaces. Dissenters like Chen.

He turned to one side to try to preserve half of his body heat. Sleep was slow to come.

21

Chen tried to keep track of the days with potato skins. One strip per day, assuming that his captors passed through daily for questioning. He estimated that it took about ten potato skin days before he succumbed to hunger. His interrogator seemed to come on a schedule he could only guesstimate, so far asking the same question for a brief few minutes before leaving as anonymously as he came.

Who sent you? Who sent you? Who sent you?

They never raised their voice. Never tried to intimidate him. Just asked patiently day after day, each time dropping the bare minimum in calories.

He thought about screaming Teresa's name back. About saying anything at least to hear a different question flung at him. The repetition was maddening. Sleep had turned from slow to impossible. Whoever his interviewer was, they kept the temperature just warm enough to avoid permanent damage but cold enough that rest only came in fits and starts. His captor always seemed to come right when he'd had enough, when he stopped shivering and oblivion was on his doorstep. If he had to guess, they probably calculated his caloric needs down so that each potato kept him alive. Only just. They had worked out the specifics long before taking him in.

Chen's attention was drawn to the slot sliding open. Light burned his retinas as the voice he'd come to know asked the first new question in days.

"Are you ready to talk?"

A different question. Did they sense weakness? Chen was so bewildered, he hardly had time to respond before the slot was closed.

"I'v–I've *been* talking, someone just needs to *listen*."

"Are. You Ready. To Talk."

The same chiding tone, like being spoken to by a babysitter.

"Like I've been *saying*, I can talk, I just need someone who—NO!"

Chen leapt up as the light left the room. The sudden darkness caused him to misjudge the distance. He felt a pulling sensation in his wrist as it collided with the door. The cold stopped the worst of the pain. He banged on the door, regardless, until both his wrists flopped uselessly. He could hardly get his hands around the potato that sat under him.

Chen dragged himself back to the center of the room as the vents above opened and let in Freeze air. How long was this cycle supposed to last anyway? Hadn't he stopped all this? Wasn't it all supposed to be over? What was the point of it all?

* * *

Chen had no idea how long it'd been. Could've been days or weeks. He'd given up on keeping track with potato skins a long time ago. It wasn't worth the waste in calories. He hadn't felt his fingers or toes in so long, he worried they'd fallen off. It was impossible to tell in the perpetual darkness they kept him in.

He hadn't changed clothes since coming in. He could tell they hung looser than they ever had. Even more than the leanest cycles back on bloc. He couldn't remember the questions they'd asked him anymore. All he knew was that they weren't to their satisfaction. He vaguely remembered even agreeing to answer any questions they wanted a few times, to no avail. It did no good. Just potatoes and darkness. When the slot opened this time, he hardly reacted at all and remained on the floor. There was a pause before a potato pushed itself through and the same voice followed soon after.

"Are you ready to talk?"

Chen could hardly bring himself to move, much less speak. He'd been a few calories from death for weeks now. He had no idea what they could want from him. Anything important he did had already happened. Anyone important he knew should either be in charge or in an adjacent box. There was nothing left.

"Yes...yes. Please, yes."

The slot didn't close immediately. There was a brief pause before the voice answered.

"I think you are too."

The door opened for the first time since Chen had been thrown in. The light was blinding. He couldn't even squint against it. Two men took him from either side and stood him up. He didn't have the energy to fight or even stand, so they dragged him. The hallway was warm, so warm he could hardly stand it. The concrete floor below him moved at a brisk pace as they turned down another hall. Chen saw his toes in the light. Blue but not black. A small mercy. He tried to look up, but his neck flopped around without strength.

After a short distance, they forced him into a metal chair. He was sitting at a table with a similar chair across from him, empty. There was a one-way mirror on the opposite wall. After a few minutes, a calm, well-dressed man entered the room from behind him. He was older, with salt-and-pepper hair decorating the top of his plain expression. Nondescript in every way. Chen watched his reflection as the man walked in front of him and then quietly sat down and took a folder out of his briefcase. He didn't recognize the man looking back. The folder had Chen's full name and picture stapled to the front. He turned the pages with little interest.

He gave off a patient air, like waiting in line at the shuttle stop. He spoke in a low voice.

"Good to see you, Detective Chen. I've been waiting for you to get ready to talk."

Chen's anger rushed through his body as he weakly protested. "I've *been* ready. Ready for who knows how long. What do you people want from me? Why now?"

Chen's voice rasped as a coughing fit took over. This was the most animated he'd been in weeks, and it was a lot to handle. The other man responded slowly and deliberately.

"No, no. Now you're ready. Talking is a two-way street. It's my job to know when you'll listen. And I've been at this a long time."

"Listen to what? I thought you people wanted to know who sent me, what I did?"

"Let's not dwell in the past, Chen. We've got what we needed. Sure, I would've appreciated if you helped us get the facts a little faster, but it all worked out in the end. Teresa, Polar Vortex, Anna even. The whole plan. Very elegant, if I might add, though I would've expected nothing else from Teresa Hightower. You're a different story. You? You seem to be caught up in something way above your pay grade. And look where that got you. Do these people really deserve your loyalty?"

Chen let his head fall onto the table. He felt a wave of exhaustion crowd out the indignation. Where was Teresa anyway?

"Then what do you people *want* from me?"

"We'd like to know if you're ready to be of use to us."

"Use? What kind of use?"

Through all this, the other man looked unbothered, like he'd read the script of their conversation well beforehand, and it was going just as anticipated. Chen realized many people had sat in this chair before him. Wayne too.

"That's for us to worry about. We just need to know if you're ready or not?"

"If I could just get some idea—"

At that comment, the older man closed the folder in front of him. No annoyance, no anger. No emotion. Just another day on the job.

"It's okay, Chen. Don't worry about it. Why don't you have more time to think about it? Perhaps I misjudged you. You've got more grit than most that come through here."

The older man nodded at the two-way mirror. He began packing up a briefcase, much like Chen remembered doing at the end of a long day, just waiting to get home. It was frustratingly casual.

"I hope we can work together soon. I'd hate to lose an asset like you. Take him."

Chen felt his heart race. His chest felt like it was going to explode with anxiety.

"No, wait, I'm ready, please—"

Chen was interrupted by the same two men who had dragged him into the room. They stood him up and started hauling him back from the direction he came. Chen remembered muttering words of protest, but he couldn't be sure. He hung his head low and watched the same concrete floor pass him by as they tossed him back in his dark cell. In those few minutes, some feeling had returned to his hands and feet. It made returning to the cold much more painful. Chen felt his body deflate as he tried to pull the thin blanket over him. The vent above whirred as it opened to let in the Freeze.

22

Chen had been getting bits of sleep here and there for some time now. Or at least periods of unconsciousness. Every time he'd settle in for longer than a few hours, the vent seemed to kick on or his body spent his last calorie, waking him up in biological desperation. The daily cadence of questioning had dropped off quickly after their last meeting, from what he could tell. Whether that was because they thought his will was stronger than it felt, or his usefulness had expired, he didn't know. All he knew was steady monotony. Slot opens, potato falls, slot closes. Day after day after day.

He'd been ready to be "of use" for weeks now. Or at least he thought he was. He was determined to stop asking questions; that seemed to end the conversation on the spot. Chen had given up on seeing that well-dressed man again and just hoped that something would change. Anything.

Then, for the first time, the monotony stopped. No indifferent steps, no rude, blinding light. Instead, it opened slowly, almost gently. Instead of a harsh, artificial glow, a soft yellow light filtered through. It swept the room back and forth with purpose until it fell gently on his back. A flashlight? A soft voice gently probed into his mind. It asked more than just one question. It sounded almost concerned. It sounded like—

"M–Morgan?"

"Chen! Chen it's you! Over here, can I get some help? *Please!*"

Chen could hear the door open as Morgan stepped into the room. He heard footsteps running down the hall as Morgan laid a blanket over him. It was almost too warm, like he was being swaddled for the first time in his life. He felt like he'd burn up in ash at any second. She turned him over carefully and supported his back with her arm. He didn't know how much weight he had lost, only that it was shockingly easy for her to manipulate his body. She seemed to be dressed in doctor's clothes. He hadn't seen her like that in who knows how long. She looked worried. Worried, but good. The bags under her eyes had taken a softer look, and she looked like she'd rested at some point. She looked healthy, even. That was good.

"Wha–what're you doing here? Didn't you make it out? Did they make you work for them?"

Morgan's eyes welled up. He probably sounded so weak. Chen listened as she tried to compose herself enough to speak.

"Yes, Chen, I made it out. We all did. And you're an asshole for it. Arriving in that shed, getting the story from your brother of all people. How you two are related is a medical mystery."

"Wouldn't want to do anything out of character."

Chen felt a laugh work its way up his chest, which then morphed into a coughing spasm. His body wracked itself in a painful effort to try to stop. He had no moisture left.

"Woah, Chen, woah. Give it a rest. Paramedics are on the way. I know this must be confusing, but I'll explain everything when you're better, okay?"

"That a promise?"

Morgan smiled. Tears ran along the corners of her mouth and soaked the blanket. They fell on his face and moistened him where tears would be if he had any left.

"That's a promise."

Chen felt his eyes grow heavy as people flooded the cell. They loaded him onto a stretcher and wheeled him out into the hallway.

For the first time, he watched the ceiling as the lights above blurred into a long streak. He closed his eyes to the glare and fell into a deep, dreamless sleep.

23

Chen felt his body stir. His eyelids were stuck together. He must have been asleep for a while. He heard beeping machines around him as he made mental body checks. His fingers and toes seemed intact. Lucky that he'd be able to feel them at all considering what he'd been through. The air he breathed in was warm. He could hear the hustle of employees running back and forth through a hallway in the distance. Chen heard a gasp and retreating footsteps followed shortly after by a rush of activity. He felt hands probing all around him, checking his arm where a pain told him an IV was, and little bumps around his knees and elbows. His lips had fused together, preventing him from protesting.

Fingers pried his eyes open. Someone shined a bright light between his eyes, darting back and forth. He heard a grunt of affirmation and a rush of orders from a woman's voice in the room. Everything sounded so far away. He heard a few more voices whispering and footsteps leaving the room. Chen felt an unnatural sense of rest come over him as he slowly lost consciousness.

His body felt heavy. Heavier than it ever had. This time his eyes opened without resistance. The light was blinding. Someone had washed him, to his surprise. He was in a clean set of patient wear. He instinctively held his arm up to block the glare and saw a mess of wires and tubes come up with it. Chen felt points of pain from where IVs stuck out, but they felt distant and alien. A familiar voice broke his thoughts.

"Welcome back, Chen."

He turned his head to face her. She was sitting on a stool at his bedside, stethoscope around her neck. *DR. MORGAN* was embroidered above her lab coat's pocket. *Reintegration Unit* was stitched underneath her name. She was in a button-down and pants. How long had it been?

"Morgan? Wh–where am I?"

"I thought you were a detective, Chen? Gone for weeks and on ice? You're in the goddamn hospital. Where else would you be?"

"Ha-ha, you know most people would take it easy on someone who's lucky to still have their extremities."

"I might have more empathy if I wasn't looking at a liar. I mean, Jesus, Chen, when we got to that shed and Wayne looked back at us? I didn't know what to think. It's not like I wanted Wayne back if you paid that price. I'm surprised your brother put up with us as long as he did."

"I'm sorry, Morgan, I really am. I tried to keep my promise, but it felt like the only way. The only way to do the right thing for once in this whole damn case."

"Ha, the case? Chen, this stopped being a case a long time ago. Everything's different now after what you did. You missed the biggest of the tidal waves you caused, but the damage is still ongoing."

"Damage? What did I miss?"

"Everything. Chen, the Depths won't be the same ever again. On High tried to keep it covered as long as they could, but they couldn't do much in the face of the Persephone papers. Hightower promoted that story to high heaven. It was the talk of the Depths for weeks. They tried to discredit her, but given her history, it was hard to hush up. Especially after she presented Persephone crystals for study."

Chen used a remote by his hand to elevate the head of the bed. His head was swirling with questions. Most of all, a sense of relief washed over him. It wasn't for nothing. They had made it out. And Teresa was right, they couldn't cover it all up fast enough.

"How did she get them to buy it all so fast?"

"Well, the popular theory is that public sympathy surged after Vandley's death was revealed. Hightower then rode that wave and made her story ironclad."

"Makes sense, it's a good story. Too good a story. What do you think?"

"Personally, I think Polar Vortex ran interference the whole way. Without them, something tells me those crystals would've disappeared long before they made it to the lab for analysis. Or Hightower would be in a pine box under mysterious circumstances."

Chen scrunched his brow in confusion. If he had any energy, he'd be angry instead.

"Polar Vortex? Why would Anna or any of them keep going after all we did? They lost the payoff of a lifetime. What's in it for them?"

Morgan shifted in her seat. She left his gaze for a moment. Chen could feel her tense up before explaining further. "Like I said, Chen, a lot has changed. The whole system's out of whack. After Persephone was revealed, everyone, the entire Depths, could be heard calling for change. Real change. There were calls to make Teresa the head of the Weather Service again and they felt obligated to agree. When she was reinstated, she tried to blow the whole thing wide open."

"Tried?"

"She hit a brick wall soon after that. The families circled the wagons and put every cred they had into publicity stunts, counter stories, even bloc sponsorships. The goodwill it bought went a long way, but not enough for all. Some of those on High didn't survive the scandal. The Geraldsons got the worst of it. Nobody would buy their farming equipment. Competitors flooded in, and confidence in their business plummeted. They sold everything that wasn't tied down. The university even got renamed, but it didn't help. It's called College of the Depths now, totally public. That got the other families to rally. They offered the Geraldsons as the sacrificial lamb. Considering how far their family dates back, it wasn't a hard sell. After that, the cycle ended and the calls for change quieted as people started getting ready for whatever comes next."

"So, the public got their pound of flesh. Makes sense. The creds make for a pretty good cushion. What's Teresa been doing now?"

"Trying to reestablish public trust. She's determined to make the Weather Service live up to the promise it was established on. To work for the public good. She's been almost painfully honest with everyone. How they weren't sure what the cycles would be like again. How there might never even be one again. She's been trying to make Freeze industries a more available public good to cushion the uncertainty, but it's been hard. Nobody knows how much to buy, how much to prep, and Hightower's been trying to make the best of it."

"I'm surprised the remaining families would let that happen."

"Oh, they didn't. It's been a fight tooth and nail but one Teresa has been happy to do. She's become the Depths' most fervent voice. If she had her way, the families would give up their shares to a central public agency. Probably won't happen, but she thinks anything other than what we have now is a step in the right direction."

"And Anna? What about her and Polar Vortex?"

Chen could see Morgan tense. Not good news.

"After the release of the balloons, they had to come to an understanding. Anna wasn't going to just let her go after all she'd done. Early on, Teresa tried to bring them out to the public eye. In subtle ways at first. But given how much Persephone sounds like everything they'd been hawking for decades, most people saw them as some kind of unsung heroes. I wouldn't call them mainstream, but Polar Vortex got enough support that they aren't hiding in the Pits as much as they used to. Many of their former agents have announced their allegiance in the government and kept their jobs because of how implicated they are in Hightower's redesign of the

Depths. They became impossible to shake. Given their level of infiltration, Teresa decided to bring them into the fold."

Chen sat upright much too fast. He felt something crack in his back, and his vision swam. He was on the verge of vomiting before Morgan leaned forward and gently coaxed him back down.

"*Bring them in*? How could she do that? After all they've done? After what they've done to Vandley? To us?"

A monitor next to him started to beep faster. He felt something near his ribs pop. Morgan pressed a button on the monitor to silence the alarm before sitting back down.

"Chen, you can't get excited like that. You'll pass out from exhaustion! Your body hasn't stored a real calorie in who knows how long. We've been giving you steady IV nutrition, but if we go overboard, you'll end up worse off than when we started. And that's saying something. You want the doctors rushing in here again to put you to sleep?"

Chen could feel his head swirl. He could feel adrenaline coursing through his body, warming him from the inside out. He took some deep breaths to try to slow his heart rate. The monitors next to him slowly returned to green.

"Goddammit, Morgan, how could you of all people go along with this? After what happened to the three of us? I know Piotr didn't want this shit. Where is he?"

At this, Morgan looked visibly upset. Her face turned red before she took some breaths of her own. He'd offended her.

"Look, Chen, I'm not happy about it either, but don't think for a second I'm 'going along with it.' I'm here as long as I'm doing good. I've spent the last months rehabilitating everyone who went through Freeze torture with the Shock Unit. I've built up a lot of trust with everyone, and the moment Hightower or Anna break that trust, I'll be there to turn the tide."

Morgan took a moment to gather herself. She'd been gripping the edge of bed until her knuckles turned white. It'd been a while since Chen was able to get underneath her skin like that, accidental or not.

"As for Piotr, he's one step ahead of me, even. He folded in with some former Polar Vortex hackers. Said they had the best toys. Many in Polar Vortex weren't fans of how publicly they became part of the system they'd been fighting for so long. Them, disillusioned, can you believe it? Anyway, they'd been on some hacktivism kick for a while now. Revealing incriminating papers, bad actors, all the history they tried to hide. Probably got way more where that came from. He's got a serious cache against everyone on High, enough to make any of them blush. They've been a thorn in everyone's side, Teresa included. Can't say I blame them."

Chen tried to sit back and relax. He knew nutjobs like that back in the patrol days. Some people were in the fight just for the fight itself, not for what came after. He couldn't shake the feeling that he'd woken up to the same shit on a different day.

"Sounds like y'all got it all figured out, huh? The sun's coming out, everything's warming now, that the idea?"

Morgan let out a heavy sigh as she made eye contact with Chen. "Hardly. We exited this cycle, but we have no idea when the next one will hit. Tell you the truth, we're all nervous, Chen. Blocs have been rationing like never before. You can feel the tension in the Depths. Everyone seems to be in a rush without a real destination. The Depths haven't been in this kind of predicament in decades. Since before the early Freeze days. Sure, technology's better. The people aren't."

"I can't blame them. Before I left my bloc, we felt the same each cycle, even with the countdown. Without it, it's gotta be much worse."

"Predictions are grim. High prices as a result of hoarding, increased pressure on recyclers for parts. Other cities are calling for reparations for the havoc Persephone wrecked on their economies. Probably going to get worse before it gets better. It's a lot of change all at once, and you know how the Depths react to that."

"Yeah, I do, Morgan. It's not good."

"To put it lightly. Teresa's been trying her best, but it's hard to get everyone on the same playbook. High prices are good for on High, making Freeze goods public has a lot of backing but seems economically suspect at best. And we got a lot of people screaming doomsday in the public square, almost like the second coming of Polar Vortex. It's taken a lot of effort to stop it from devolving."

"And Wayne?"

Chen saw tears well up in Morgan's eyes before she wiped them away. It took a few minutes for her to begin speaking again. Best not to press her any further than he'd already done.

"He hasn't been the same. He tried to go back to the university as a teacher, but the effort of day-to-day work was a lot on him physically. Especially to be back where it all started. He even did a stint at the Weather Service, trying to research how the future cycles are going to be. Wayne was there maybe a month before moving on. I lost contact with him after that. He's asked us to leave him alone, and it's been the hardest thing for me to do."

Chen had seen a few people like that in the force, eyes glazed over, each step weighed down with a listlessness nothing could cure. They never lasted long, and they never stayed in contact. It was always too painful for everyone involved.

"I'm sorry, Morgan. I tried my best, but I knew when I saw him that night, he wasn't the same. You were right, no one needs more heroics."

"It's okay, Chen. Your heart was in the right place. And I still hope it is. That's another reason why I'm here."

Chen bristled visibly at Morgan's statement. She noticed and put her hand on his. He did not feel the comfort he hoped.

"Should've known you're not just here for my sunny disposition."

"Chen, I'm your doctor now. And your friend. I'm here for your health and to make sure you get what you need. The Depths owe you a debt they'll never know about. When we found you, I tried to keep you under wraps for as long as I could. But on High found out eventually, and with Anna in as deep as she is, they're interested in you. Now that you've woken up, they'll want a meeting once you're healthy. I can hold them off for a little longer, but it won't hold up to a second opinion. I just want you to be ready. Whatever it is, I'm here with you."

Chen closed his eyes in frustration. Every time he thought he'd reached the end, it just began again. He couldn't escape no matter how hard he tried. His temples pulsed. He could feel his heartbeat in his ears. He looked down and pressed the nurse call button.

"Thanks, Morgan. For everything. You know, when they were picking me up that night I thought about Wayne, Piotr, and you. I'd imagined you all reuniting in that shed in relief. I didn't have a lot of happy memories there, but that thought kept me going the longest in that box."

"Well, I'm sorry to have disappointed you, Chen."

"Not at all. From what I heard, that's the warmest that shed has been in decades."

Morgan smiled gently. A sense of calm washed over him.

"Then I'm glad I was here when you woke up. I'll do my best to delay them, so get your strength up. I'll even upgrade you to a soft diet soon. And the good news, you're just in time for some fresh bean coffee. Hightower's given us the funding to last until we've made all their former prisoners whole. I'll make sure you get some high-quality calories while you're here."

"Thanks, Morgan. You know, I like you as my doc."

"Turns out I'm not so bad at keeping people alive either. Like riding a bike. Lucky for you, you weren't my first test case."

Chen laughed as he drew the blankets up to his neck. He wiggled into the bed. It felt almost too soft. He saw Morgan's lips move but felt himself drift off. A nurse entered the room and injected something into his IV. He felt his body fall through the floor as the world cradled him to sleep.

24

He'd been in the hospital for ten days now. With Morgan's care, he'd put on a startling amount of weight, almost half of what he'd lost. He'd come to learn that the Shock Unit had him for months. They'd proceeded on with business as usual until it was clear the command structure was changing. It didn't take long for them to change their tune. They were survivalists, like everyone else.

Chen had just settled in from a stint in physical therapy before a nurse came in. Morgan had lifted the moratorium on visitors to his room, and the nurse wanted to know if he was ready for his first caller. A familiar voice sounded from the hallway.

"He doesn't have a choice!"

Nate rushed past the startled nurse and into the chair beside Chen's bed. His expression changed from amusement to concern as he took in Chen's condition.

"Jesus, Alec. What happened to you? You look like you went through the Freeze cycle of the century!"

Chen turned to face Nate. He could see the worry lines deepen as he waited for Chen to answer. It felt like just weeks ago that they were together in the Depths, catching up. He'd forgotten all he asked of Nate without explanation. He was long overdue.

"You could say that. I haven't been this slim since that Freeze when we were ten."

"How could this happen? Was it the Shock Unit? Dr. Morgan told me about what happened, but I didn't think it was this bad."

Chen felt himself wince. It would make sense that Morgan would notify his next of kin, especially since she had stayed with him as the dust was settling. He couldn't help but feel suddenly exposed after years of living in the Depths, away from his family. Nate caught it quickly, as he always did.

"Seriously, Alec? You're going to play stoic now of all moments? We're really worried about you."

"We're?"

Nate rolled his eyes. His expression changed from worried to annoyed. "Yes, Alec, *we're*. Dad's worried about you too. I mean, he was going to notice a bunch of strangers in the shed eventually. After a couple of months, the head of the freaking Weather Bureau shows up at our door looking for you. Kinda hard to keep it under wraps after that. So, they told Dad everything. Everything you guys did. We only recently found out what it actually cost you."

Chen was surprised that Teresa came looking for him so quickly afterward. She had only seemed sentimental over Vandley, and after what she forced Chen into, he doubted she wanted to come looking for him any time soon. Hopefully, Morgan could keep delaying their request to meet for a little while longer. Nate could see his mind working and brought Chen out of his thoughts.

"And before you ask, yes, Alec, Dad wants to know how you are doing. He's just knee-deep with the bloc about how they're going to handle the next cycle now that we have no idea if or when it's coming. You know how he is."

"Yea, I do. The bloc comes first. Didn't you guys build a good reserve last season?"

"We did, and the spare parts have us off to a good start this season too."

"It's already started?"

"Yea. This growing season started a couple months ago. It was a welcome change until we found out why. People are on edge,

Chen, in a way I haven't seen since we were kids. It's a new world out there, and we're all afraid the good times won't last."

Chen did some quick calculations. The timeline of this new growing season was about a week or two after he had released the weather balloons. He hadn't known that his actions would have such an immediate effect. He guessed that was part of the point. Not knowing. Chen let the silence hang in the air for a few minutes, since neither knew what to say.

"How's Dad dealing with all this?"

"As well as anyone. He hasn't talked about it much, but you know what that means. He's nervous. After what Hightower told us what you did, he was almost in a state of shock. Then the work had to start again, and he's been burying himself deep in it with everyone else. And there's something he wanted me to tell you."

Chen felt his brother's firm grip on his shoulder.

"He wants you *home*, Chen."

"Dad? For what? This upcoming cycle? I don't know when it's coming more than anyone else does."

Nate got up from his chair and walked to the far side of the room. Chen could see his shoulders move up and down as he took some heavy breaths before turning around with a look of frustration on his face. "Alec, *come on*. You act like Dad's only got one motive for anything! Why can't he want you home to help *and* because you're his son?"

"Because that's *him*, Nate. He's always put the bloc first. That's why I left! I wanted the choice."

"Look, Alec. I'm not saying you don't deserve a choice. Everyone does. I mean given what your friend Hightower has been saying on the news, isn't that what this is all about?"

Nate crossed back toward Chen's bed and put a hand on the rail. Usually, this conversation riled him up as much as Chen was. Instead, Nate was calm.

"Just give Dad more credit than you did before you left. Before you make your choice, make sure you're doing it for the right reasons. If you've got everything you need down there, then I'm happy for you. And Dad is too, even if he doesn't show it."

"Fair enough."

They spent the rest of the afternoon catching up on what they hadn't had time to talk about at Last Chance. How Nate had explained to their father the presence of Morgan, Piotr, Wayne, and Hightower all in their shed. Margie remarrying after the death of her husband. Someone was vying for their father's seat on bloc leadership. Chen's mystery meeting with the new guard coming up. He didn't let Nate know how much he dreaded it, but it was obvious. They talked until sunset and Nate got called back by their father. Urgent business setting up for next cycle. Whenever that would be.

Chen thought about what Nate had said. How he wasn't giving their father enough credit. He'd always thought that of his father but never considered himself guilty of the same. But Nate was right. This was his chance to make his first honest choice. One free of outside control and influence. Before all this, it would've been impossible for him to consider going back. Now? He'd gotten a chance to see the other side of things, and it felt familiar in many ways. A life of illusory choices.

Chen turned to look out the hospital window. He was on a high floor at the edge of the on-High city, giving him a view all the way to the horizon. He could see the lights of farming equipment graze through newly uncovered fields. Even in the fading light, he could tell they were planting seeds for the growing season. They'd probably work through the night for weeks, trying to get as much work done as quickly as possible. What little nonarable land began showing signs of life as deadwood began developing immature leaves. He tried to think about what he was leaving behind in the Depths if he went back home. Nothing came to mind immediately.

He was probably just tired. Physical therapy took a toll. It was good seeing Nate, but the visit came with its own frustrations.

Chen brought the covers up and tried to get some sleep. It'd probably be clear in the morning.

25

Chen walked out of the hospital for the first time several weeks later. He had gained back about Fifteen pounds eating the best, nonrecycled calories he'd had in years. Better than he could ever afford. A nurse had insisted he get wheeled out to the shuttle stop, but he refused. He wanted to put his physical therapy to good use. Morgan forced him to compromise on a set of crutches that he quickly abandoned at the entrance.

It was the first time he got to go outside unburdened in the new growing season. Chen stood in the open space, letting the sun hit his face and the temperate air enter his lungs. His body felt a rush of energy enter from his chest and run down to his toes. It was a familiar feeling at the end of every cycle. The whole Depths seemed to light up. The surface was accessible again. At the start of each growing season, on High would allow a daily quota of Depths dwellers onto the surface with special dispensation. It was a rare moment of kinship that only nature could provide.

This time was different. He watched as people rushed from the shuttle to the hospital and back. He could feel the tension in their steps like Morgan had mentioned. The usual joy was muted. He was stepping out into a world he had helped create but didn't recognize.

Chen's thoughts were interrupted when he saw a well-built man in a suit making eye contact with him through a thick pair of sunglasses. Morgan had given him a heads-up but didn't know any details. Need-to-know basis, apparently. The man opened a door to a black car and motioned for him to get inside. There weren't any government markings he could make out, but given the man's demeanor, he worked for someone relatively high on the food chain. Chen crossed the street slowly, trying to enjoy the fresh air before sliding into the back seat. He felt the car rumble to life.

Chen opened the window as he watched buildings roll by. He had always loved looking at the surface at the end of each cycle. He remembered steering large pieces of machinery as the planting began. Small buds would be maturing about now, spurred on by the sudden shift in warmth and genetic engineering that made them speed through their lifecycle. The sun would be reflecting off tractors as they tilled any land broken by the Freeze and fertilizing the acres that had made it relatively unscathed. He'd often be sunburnt by the end of the first day, his skin not used to the influx of vitamin D after weeks of being in that shed. It was the only time he felt connected to the land he was chained to. Now, after his years in the Depths, the connection felt stronger than ever.

Several minutes passed before Chen saw a sign for the Weather Service entrance. They entered from the south and headed directly toward the main building on the north side. Neither spoke a word as they made their way up to the top floor of the building. The building looked much less intimidating in the light. It towered like a sentinel, quietly observing a lively sky. Scientists scuttled by him without acknowledgement. They'd certainly been informed of the events that took place on their own campus. Whether they knew Chen's role, much less likely so. Chen preferred it that way.

They got off the elevator where Chen had first met Teresa. A receptionist looked up and quickly pinged the phone in front of her. They were waved through. The door to her office remained the same, except entrances were open and inviting. A crowd sat in chairs around the waiting room. Some appeared to be press, others bureaucrats, waiting for their ten-minute visit into the sanctum. Some gave him knowing looks as he passed by. The man escorting him remained outside as he entered.

Teresa was sitting at her desk. The Weather Service logo loomed over her much like before, except now with a sense of comfort rather than foreboding. She offered half a smile as Chen came in and sat across from her. He did not return the favor. Anna sat in a back corner. She was wearing an official Weather Service uniform. She hardly acknowledged his entrance at all. Teresa spoke first.

"Chen, it's good to see you. I'm sorry I wasn't able to visit you in the hospital. I heard Morgan caught you up to what's been going on, and it has required my undivided attention."

Anna let out a light cough from behind Teresa.

"Excuse me. *Our* undivided attention."

"No, I get it. Sounds like shit really hit the fan for the Depths the night I got taken up. Morgan let me know I'm some kind of anonymous hero or something."

"Ha, something like that. I thought it better to keep your role in it anonymous. There's a lot of mixed feelings out there about what the loss of Persephone means for all of us, Chen. I thought it better to keep your name out of it unless you wanted otherwise."

Pragmatic as always. Chen appreciated the gesture, though he'd never admit it. He was just as likely to be held up as a populist icon than to be burned in effigy for what he did. Predictability was a hard thing to give up.

"What am I doing here, Teresa? Haven't I done enough for your 'cause'?"

Teresa leaned forward on her arms. Anna sat with her legs crossed next to her, inscrutable as always. "More than anyone will ever know."

Anna leaned forward and added more context. "And no one ever can. If everyone knew that this new order ushering in an age of uncertainty was initiated by a small team and a single man?

Let's just say it doesn't inspire confidence. And confidence is what we need most. The other cities are vying for payback, and the Depths needs to remain the center of scientific advancement to fight them off."

Of course. Teresa sounded more like a spin doctor than anything else. Chen turned toward Anna with anger in his eyes.

"And just who is *we*? What do I have to do with this? And after what both of you got me into, what incentive do I have to keep my *heroics* a dirty little secret?"

Teresa leaned back. Anna leaned forward and turned her head to Teresa, giving her a side glance. Chen could sense tension between them that they did not try to hide. Teresa broke the silence.

"You have a fair point, Chen. I am sensitive to the fact that you started this as an investigator and just followed the lead even as it evolved into so much more. While I can sit here and say the ends justify the means, I know that doesn't mean much. All I can do is try my best to make your sacrifice worthwhile. And to make sure you're taken care of."

"*Taken care of*? And what is the going price of my silence, exactly?"

Anna and Teresa looked at each other for another moment before Teresa continued. "We want to offer you a job."

"A *job*? After all you two have put me through, my big reward is gainful employment? And working for the two of you, no less. How is that supposed to work?"

Anna leaned forward and pursed her lips together into a thin smile like she was swallowing a bitter pill. There was some solace in that.

"Not just employment, Chen. We want you to head High Crimes. We need someone up here we can work with who's clearly capable and someone the Depths can trust. And who else other than someone from their neck of the woods? *Our* neck of the woods."

High Crimes? Him? After all he'd done to Polar Vortex's plans and what he suffered at the hands of on High?

"You want to work with me, Anna? Didn't I just flush years of Polar Vortex planning down the toilet in one swoop? And what would even make you think I'd work with *you* of all people?"

Anna leaned forward. Her smile grew, which only infuriated Chen. She had a way of finding the right emotion to counteract his own and drive him up the wall with it.

"I'll admit I was pretty...unhappy when I found out what all your little plans were. I took it a little personally for a while, even. But I'm not one to let grudges get in the way of the future. We're exercising our resources better than we could otherwise in this brave new world. The Depths need to maintain the balance, as it always has since the first Freeze. So, to answer your question, I think I've grown enough to be the bigger person to work with you."

Anna leaned back and let Chen digest the information. He couldn't tell if her phrasing was to direct Chen away from the offer or to make his acceptance more painful.

"And to sweeten the pot, you get to decide where High Crimes goes from here. Within reason, of course. We all know what it's like to live under their thumb. You more than most, Chen. If there's anything we've learned after this time, it's that you're capable. Capable and sympathetic. Having you head High Crimes would instill confidence that they're not just private security for the rich anymore. You have the chance to do real good here."

"Good for who, exactly?"

Teresa interjected before Anna could. "For whomever you think needs it, Chen. After everything you've done for the Depths, for us, we trust your judgment. The Depths need you, Chen, and we'll make sure they've got every reason to trust you."

"Oh, you both trust me now, do you? After both of you got everything you wanted from the fruits of my labor, the trust is suddenly there?"

Teresa tensed up at Chen's outburst. She hadn't been around in the shed to see this side of him.

"This wasn't just about us, Chen, it was about everyone! I'm sorry to have violated your trust, but it was for the greater good. And we were thinking after all this, you'd be the best man for the job to make sure that good doesn't go to waste. You know what struggle is like more than most. We think everyone could see the use in that."

"*Use?*"

Chen pinched the bridge of his nose and leaned back. The chair was plush, but his back still cried out in pain. It'd been weeks since Morgan rescued him, but he had a feeling that his body was never going to be the same again. That's all everything was, whether it was on High or in the Depths. Use. He let out a tense sigh and tried to get comfortable. He knew where he had to be. Where he was more than just his utility to the greater good.

"That's all I've been is of *use*. Use to Low Crimes, use to Polar, and then use to *you*. I think I've been useful enough."

Chen took a few deep breaths. He'd tried to present a good front, but this outburst took a lot of energy from him. And the gall of these two. The two who had already used him most.

"I'm going to have to decline, as generous as this all sounds. Wherever all this goes with the two of you at the helm, I don't want any part of it."

Teresa's eyes widened in surprise. Anna flashed a tight smile when she noticed the tension.

"But Chen, I thought, I just... I'm surprised! I thought you'd see the potential in this. In what we've started here. In where we're going."

"Respectfully, Teresa, all I see is another power play led by powerful players. I don't doubt your intentions are true, but aren't they always? It's the little guys like me that get caught up in the gears of the machine and ground up. Me, Wayne, Morgan, caught up in the ride. And I'm done."

Anna sat up straight and looked Chen in the eye. An honest look. He couldn't help but feel he was playing into her hand.

"You heard him, Teresa. He's done."

Teresa held her hand out to block Anna's eye line from Chen. She looked over at Anna with a chiding look like one might use on a petulant child. She didn't react.

"Chen, please. We really could use someone like you working with us. Working with me. Won't you reconsider? Neither of us want all this to go sideways after all you've been through."

"Frankly, Teresa, I don't care. I don't care how the cycles shake out, how the science works. Hell, I don't care if the Freeze takes a piss on your doorstep tomorrow and you slip and fall. I've done enough for you people. So if you'll excuse me, I believe this meeting is over."

Chen summoned up as much energy as he could and got up with a swiftness he knew he'd pay for the next morning. Teresa's mouth hung open as he left out the front door. Anna was chuckling under her breath. The man who had escorted him tried to offer him a ride, but he shook his head angrily. He held his limp back until he was clear of the office's view.

Chen made his way to the shuttle stop. He could hardly hear anything through the roaring in his ears. His body rocked back and forth as the shuttle rocketed itself through the surface stations. Chen hardly made note of the heavy machinery that peppered the landscape to each side. The planting was in full force because the last cycle had ended spiced with uncertainty. The shuttle rocked to a rough stop as he exited the tram and boarded the bus. The trip passed faster than he'd ever remembered.

Chen got off the bus and headed toward the old shed. This time of day, his bloc and his family were probably out sowing seeds like madmen. The shed was probably empty.

Chen gripped the handles of the shed and let himself inside. He sent a quick text to his brother as he calmly walked to the back of the shed to his old seat. The tools were in disarray. The machines were clumsily uncovered and in varying states of disrepair. Chen saw a project in progress on the workbench. Based on the handiwork, probably Nate's. It was messy. Tools were gathered around it in a desperate attempt to find the right size. The parts that he would've needed were nowhere to be seen. He felt a slight comfort in his chest as he picked up his old tools. Chen watched his fingers move over the part in front of him with growing familiarity.

The red numbers of the clock in the corner counted on without him noticing.

If you enjoyed The Almanac,
consider other works by NMN Wang!

Stay up to date with all his upcoming
projects and free short stories at:
www.nmnpublishing.com

Or let NMN Wang know what you thought
at **nmnwangbooks@gmail.com**